Reviews of *Hot Knife*

"If *Human Traffic* was the last great film of the Nineties, this is the last great novel" – Poz

"A fuckin' good read wi' loads a drugs 'n' rock 'n' roll, but no sex" – Nev

"I used to read books when I were in Armley nick" – Big Baz

"I'm tryin' to watch telly" – Carol/Vicky

"Two Es and an LSD" – Mercy

"Yeah, it were all right, were that' – Bea

"He missed all the best bits out, savin' 'em for the sequel" – Minstrel

"One for the beach in Ibiza" – Denny

"Wanna buy a really good book?" – Kelly

Acknowledgements

For their help, advice, support,
inspiration, friendship, love and stories,
thank you to Mick McCann, David
Grossman, Paul Hazelgrave, Andy
Horton, Damien and Dianne, Iain and Sue
Cummings, Janet Ellis, James Brown,
Richard Cretan, Rob Hodgeson, Kevin
Manton, Thiss, Wilkie, Nelly and Liz,
John and Joyce, Mum and Carl, Cousin
Eddie, Sean Carr, Adam Smith, Mick (R
Kid) Lake and Sue Weakley.

**Dedicated to the memory of
Cyrus Murphy.
We all miss you.**

Hot Knife

John Lake

**Love, bullets and revenge
in Leeds, Yorkshire, England**

Published by Armley Press 2008

Layout by Ian Dobson
Cover Design: John Wheelhouse & Mick McCann

Contact: <armleypress@hotmail.co.uk>
Armley Press, Hollywell House, Hollywell Lane,
Armley, Leeds, LS12 3HP
ISBN 978-0-9554699-1-6

Contents

1. Flying Boy

WHEN THEY finally caught up with that useless prick Eddie Whatsit's kid after he'd run off with a kilo of Big Baz's smack and sold it on to persons unknown, they decided that seventeen was old enough to be made an example of and to throw the little cunt under a bus.

Well that's what Baz'd decided anyway, and he didn't hear any objections coming from the gorilla that the Yardies'd sent down from Chapeltown to help him with the job.

Langston. That was the gorilla's name, or so he said. Baz'd seen him before, usually skulking in the background in his boss's, Delroy's, shadow acting like a celebrity bodyguard – but Baz'd clocked him. Yeah, he'd noticed him before. Never heard much from him though, except his name, which Baz'd only asked him tonight to look companionable, seeing as they were on a job together, the two of 'em. Never heard much of anything from Langston. Just did the work and kept his mouth shut. Probably the bottom of the food chain if he was the one who got sent out to work with the white guy. A dirty job but somebody had to do it, Baz bet the rest of Delroy's crew were thinking.

But a kilo of smack was a kilo of smack, and Baz explained it to himself like this: To the Yardies, on one level, helping him to sort it out was a protection of their assets – in this case him, the client. (He preferred to think of himself as one of their clients rather than one of their distributors; that way he could kid himself they were working for him, not him for them.) On another level, it was what they called Public Relations. Giving a warning to anyone else out there who might be toying with the idea of doing the same thing or something equally daft. Don't fuck with the Posse and don't fuck with our clients. Tonight, Langston was here on a PR job. Like all PR work, especially damage limitation, the best time to put the message across was right now, a-s-a-motherfucking-p.

But it was left up to Baz to decide where it would be delivered, and how.

One thing was for sure – he wasn't going to do it anywhere near his own doorstep. That meant getting Moz – that was the kid's name – away from Leeds 6. At first he'd thought about taking the little cunt somewhere out of town but after further cogitation he remembered a stretch of the Ring Road near the Gorge between Roundhay Park and Shadwell that'd be just perfect. There was any number of buses that must pass along there every hour, probably more in the evening. Baz never travelled anywhere by bus any more, he left that to life's losers, but if he knew anything about it, he knew the Ring Road was a major route into, out of and around the city, so there had to be an average of one every five or ten minutes. However often they were, once the kid got the message of what they were gonna do to him, it'd be plenty to ratchet up the tension level for the little cunt. Waiting for a bus'd never been such fun as this was gonna be.

Location was always a key factor in these matters, and this place had it for Baz on several counts. One was that it was a quiet, non-residential stretch with woodland on either side of the road for him and Langston to disappear into straight afterwards. It was a dark stretch, sparsely lit, and where there was lighting, the trees near the lamps threw dappled shadow everywhere. The driver might catch them in his headlights, but only momentarily because there was a curve to the road where it passed through the woods so the beam of the lights would be constantly changing direction. And in any case, Baz was planning on appearing out of nowhere and going straight back there. The poor fucking driver probably wouldn't believe what he was seeing anyway.

Second point was the lengthy gap between bus stops. The stop before there was a decent way back, and the curve was broad enough for a bus to take it at some speed – especially as it'd be travelling slightly downhill at that point and not having to stop to pick up for ages. A double decker going at thirty-five, maybe forty, downhill. He didn't want Moz holding on to the illusion that the brakes might save him. No chance, mate.

'Running Boy' was what the pigs called Moz on account of he'd never give in, even when he was cornered; on the handful of occasions that they'd come looking for him, he'd always made a break for it and kept on running till they physically pinned him right down. It'd been like that tonight when him and Langston'd found him sniffing glue in the empty play park. Fucking Running Boy. Tonight, they were going to turn him into Flying Boy.

They rolled the car along slowly in first to a spot just outside the woods on the downhill, eastbound side of the Ring Road, finding a space in among the trees. Baz'd been going to bring his Beemer, but maybe it was a good job he hadn't after all. He would have done it in that, no problem, provided he knew they weren't going to get any blood on it – shove the kid in the boot but put a blanket down first, sort of thing. But you could never guarantee these things. Besides, the Yardies were more than happy to throw in a car with Langston for this kind of job. Some crappy, old, Vauxhall sedan with false plates, a little less traceable and a little less conspicuous than Baz's BMW. The boot on it was a fair bit smaller than his, of course, but they'd still got the kid to fit in it. Baz opened it up, smelling the wave of Evo-Stick coming off him. That was good. Anybody smelling that would immediately assume it was an accident. The kid'd already done half their job for 'em.

'Yer still trippin', yer little cunt?' he said as they bundled the kid, hands and feet gaffer-taped together, out of the back end of the car. Moz didn't answer. His mouth was bunged up with a ball of rag strapped in with the same silver gaffer tape, the kind roadies use on stage. Only his eyes answered in the thin light dribbling from the interior of the car. 'Well I hope you're havin' a nice trip.' When they slammed the boot shut and picked him up and started carrying him into the trees still bound and gagged, Moz was even then only able to emit muffled shrieks that barely carried above the murmur of distant traffic.

They were surprised when the main road came out of the trees before them: it was dark and empty. The traffic noise was from farther off somewhere. They'd timed it well. Everybody still in the pubs for another hour. Little other traffic on the roads. Now all they needed to do was wait for a bus.

They hung back in the fringe of the woods while they got the kid ready. First they put the kid on the ground on his back with his hands stretched up above his head. That bit was hard enough; the kid wouldn't stop wriggling, even when Big Baz stuck the boot into his ribs. But the next bit was going to be even harder.

Baz was seventeen stone, spread over a burly six-foot-two-inch frame, and Langston was a more squat but equally hefty cunt, and the kid was nowt but maybe eight or nine stones of grease and spit. It was going to take all their strength, nevertheless, for this next part. That's what it was like when you were dealing with someone who thought they were about to die. They fought against it with everything. More than everything.

'You ready?' Baz said to Langston. Fucking silly, black cunt only nodded. In the woods. In the dark. At night. *Black* cunt. *Nodding.* Just lucky Baz was able to see the whites of his eyes and his teeth gritting behind the pulled-back lips. 'Hands first. Your end.'

He could see that Langston was having trouble keeping the kid's hands in one place so he could cut through the gaffer tape. The boot hadn't worked much. Maybe it was time to use psychology.

'Oi. Moz. Moz, mate.' The kid was still squealing to not much effect through the gag. In the meagre illumination from residual street light, he could see where the kid's face was puffed up and traced with tear lines. 'Listen to me, will yer? Just listen.' He waited till the kid calmed down enough to understand. 'Listen. It's gonna be a lot easier for yer if ya co-operate. If you help us we might be able to help you. You understand what I'm saying?' He waited for the kid to nod. While he was waiting, a bus went past. They watched it, a blur of light through the trees. They could make out that it was virtually empty. 'Well?'

The kid nodded.

'Good. Now all we want yer to do is relax. We're gonna fuckin' untie yer, yer silly cunt. Don't you wanna be untied?'

Again the kid nodded. Baz couldn't see the look in his eyes clearly but he could imagine what they were saying, giving you that desperate signal that they really wanted to trust you, hoping you'd be moved by the implication that you were somebody they *could* trust, and trust was a form of respect. Baz didn't need to see it because he knew it was a lie. What won that respect every time was not trust but violence. It'd always been like that and it always would be. He knew it. The Yardies knew it. And sometimes the rest of the world needed reminding of it.

'Right, untie his hands first.' Langston got the rope off. Moz didn't struggle, just rubbed at his chafed wrists while Langston kept a grip on his skinny forearms. This kid sure never worked out.

Baz got the rope off the kid's ankles and the sudden rush of freedom in all four limbs was too much of a temptation to him. Before he could quite kick off again though, Baz lunged forward and grabbed the kid's balls through the crotch of his jeans.

10

'Don't even fuckin' think about it.'

As a classic cliché, it was wasted on the kid. He had other things on his mind. He was blinded by tears and his voice was strangled in his throat. His only instinct was immediate compliance. Baz released the pressure of his grasp on the kid's balls and transferred the hand back to the free ankle.

'Moz. I need to have a talk with yer. Now don't start freakin' out again or it'll just get worse, all right? I'm gonna take that gag off yer and yer gonna have to answer some questions, all right?'

Again, the nod. He'd got the kid's full attention and co-operation now. Let's see how it went once they'd freed his tongue. While he pushed a knee down on the kid's shins, his fingers found an end of the gaffer tape in the dark and yanked it away from the kid's face, then pulled the rag out of the kid's mouth and stuffed it in the pocket of his fleece. The kid didn't make a sound other than a little panting while he got his breath back properly.

'Right. So far so good. Now what've yer done with it?'

'Baz, I swear—'

That was not what Baz wanted to hear. While one hand pinioned the kid's hips, the other shot out and gripped his face, its span covering all of it, like the embryonic creature in the *Alien* movies.

'I don't wanna hear any more *lies*. All right?' He was holding the kid's head rigid, stopping it from nodding. 'All right?'

'Yush,' the kid managed to croak against the acrid scent of Baz's enormous, dirt-lined palm.

'Good. So let's start again. For the last time.' He removed his hand from the kid's face. 'What've yer done with that key a smack?'

'I sold it. I told yer before, Baz, I sold it.'

'Yeah, yer sold it, right. And who the fuck'd be stupid enough to buy a kilo a fuckin' smack off you? Who the fuck'd be stupid enough not to know that you hadn't nicked it? Eh? Tell me that.'

'Students. Honest, Baz, it were a bunch a students.'

That stumped him. For a minute it stumped him so much that he actually laughed. Students. Course. That's who'd be stupid enough. Fucking students. But it was too easy as well. Fucking students. Anybody could say that and think they might get away with it.

'What students? Who are they? Where do they live?'

11

'I don't know, Baz. I mean I don't know where they live. You know what it's like, you meet some'dy round at some'dy's gaff, you see 'em round there a few times, you get to know 'em without actually knowin' 'em, you know what I mean?' The kid seemed to've got all his crying out of the way for now. His voice was tense, racing along, but it was trying hard to stay even, to put fear behind it, to cleave to a world of adult reason, a fictional world where this couldn't really be happening to him. 'I honestly don't know where they live. I can tell you their names though.'

'Go on.'

'One of 'em's called Michael. White guy, goatee and long, bushy hair as though he's tryin' to dread it up. White Rasta wannabe.'

'Michael who?'

'Whaddaya mean Michael who?'

'Whaddaya think I fuckin' mean? His surname. What's his fuckin' surname? Michael what?'

'I dunno,' said the kid, and Baz could tell from the way he said it that it'd probably never even occurred to the kid that the guy had a surname, as long as he had money and wanted drugs.

'Who else then? You said he were one of 'em. Who were t'others?'

'There were one other. Simon, he were called. Tall geezer. Likes to wear flash gear. Him an' Michael always hang around together. Always get into t'same shit together an' that. That's how come they took an interest in a key a smack when they heard one were goin'.'

'An' how did they hear that?' said Baz. 'Eh?' he added, digging a stubby finger into the kid's ribs. The kid's body jerked away from the stab of its own accord. 'Eh?' Dig. Jerk. The kid didn't say anything. Baz could tell that he'd started to freak the kid out again just when he'd got him easy to handle, but for a second or two he couldn't help himself. After all he'd done for Moz, just because he was Eddie Whatsit's kid and Eddie and him went way back to smoking scag together in Armley the first time they'd put him inside. Poor old Eddie, he used to think. A born loser. All this time later and he was still inside – again. Never did get his act together. Always too out of it to be bothered to make sure he didn't get caught. So Baz thought he'd help his kid out at least. Put a few little odd jobs his way now and again. At least help the kid earn a little walking-around money. Then, the first chance he gets, the little cunt, he rips off a key that Baz has fucking *paid* him to run an errand with, and he's flogging it to a bunch of fucking students who've got no idea what they're getting themselves involved in. Silly little fucker, what did he think was going to happen to him after that?

'So what did you get for it?' Baz said at last. 'Cos I hope it were worth it.'

'Two grand,' the kid mumbled.

'You what?'

'Two grand.' The voice smaller still.

'D'you know how much it were worth to me? Five grand. And that's just the mark-up.' He fought with his rage. 'Do you know how much it cost me? Eh? *Do* yer? Twenty grand. Do you know what that is all told? Yeah, go on, do the fuckin' sums. You can do them sums, can't yer? Eh? Twenty-five fuckin' grand, innit? Twenny-five fuckin' grand down the fuckin' swanny. This fuckin' whatsisname an' whatsisname—'

'Michael an' Simon.'

'Fuckin' Michael an' fuckin' Simon musta seen you comin'. They must be laughin' their heads off now. They must be happy as pigs in shit. Unless they're as fuckin' daft as you. An' let's face it, they can't be that clever, can they, or else they wouldn't have their fuckin' hands on my smack, would they?' Now that the cost of Moz's little adventure was established, he felt it was no longer personal. From here on, it was business. 'What they gonna do with it then? These students. What they gonna do with my smack?'

'I dunno. Sell it prob'ly. To their mates. I reckon that's what they'll do. Use what they want an' sell t'rest to their mates in bits and pieces.'

'Great. So when it runs out what they gonna do? When them an' all their mates want more an' they haven't got any more. What they gonna do then? They gonna come to me?'

'I can tell 'em, Baz. I can tell 'em that when it's all run out they can come an' see you. That way, it'd be business, wunnit? I'da got you some more customers, see what I mean?'

'Meanwhile, you owe me twenty-five grand,' Baz reminded him before he got carried away with his dreams. 'So where's this two grand?'

13

There was a long pause filled with the sound of the kid weeping and snivelling.

'Fuck, Baz, it's gone. It's all gone. Spent.'

'On what?' When the kid didn't say anything Baz said, 'Don't bother answerin' that.'

Baz and Langston looked up together at the faint whine of a bus coming over the top of the hill.

'Pick him up.'

Langston nimbly adjusted his hold on the kid as the wrestling and the screaming all kicked in at once. Fuck. The kid may not work out but he had some power in him when he needed it. With immensely hard work, they got him down to the edge of the road, just as the bus was appearing round the bend through the woods. *No*, the kid was screaming, and *Help Help Help*. What a fucking racket. Mind, your big white boy there was making just as much himself, yelling at the kid for no good reason other than he was loving it. *Scared are ya? Sorry now are ya?* Shit like that. For fuck's sake. He still didn't even know from the ugly, white son of a bitch what they were definitely gonna do. Were they just here to put the shits up the poor, little, white kid or were they really gonna go through with it? No one'd told him explicitly and specifically that the kid was gonna die. Fuck. He guessed he'd just have to play it by ear, like you always had to when somebody put one of these white motherfuckers in charge.

'Right,' said Big Baz, 'just like it's his birthday an' we're about to give him the bumps. Here we go. One.'

Baz started a side-to-side rhythm going. The kid kicked and screamed, making it difficult, but Langston caught up with Baz's swinging motion and worked at it until momentum played its irresistible part. Soon they were swinging him in such wide arcs that it didn't matter how much the kid struggled, it barely interfered with the to and fro. The kid was going like a hammock in a hurricane. Baz restarted the count.

'One-ugh... two-ugh...'

The bus was upon them. What did he want him to do? Let go for real or not?

'... three.'

They both let go.

They heard the sickening thud. Not that it literally made them sick but, objectively, you could only call it a sickening thud. They didn't see it, too busy running already, running into the woods. They heard the thumps like spuds knocking on the inside of a barrel as the body went under, and then the screech of the bus coming to a stop, but ten, maybe twenty yards further on down the hill. By that time, they weren't even bothering to run any more, and had slowed to a stiff saunter through the trees back to the car.

Baz, lighting up a fag, was the first to speak.

'I'll tell yer what, give the little cunt his fair dues, he didn't shit himself. Pissed himself, like, did ya notice? But he didn't shit himself right to t'end, did he? I couldn't fuckin' smell owt anyway, could you? Yer can usually fuckin' smell it on 'em when they've done it. But I couldn't fuckin' smell owt off him. He definitely didn't shit himself.'

'Bet he did when he hit dat bus,' said Langston.

It was the most Big Baz'd ever heard him say in one go.

2. Cast Off

WHEN KELLY looked up at the kitchen clock, it had taken him nearly half an hour to cut the cast off his own leg. He'd had to work at it slowly and steadily with the secateurs, working up a right sweat putting his shoulder into it to get the short curved scissoring blades to chew down the length of the tough hardened plaster of Paris. When the casing finally fell away, all he wanted to do was get his fingernails at the itching thigh and calf that had been sealed up for a fortnight. He allowed himself half a minute's worth of indulgence at this, then stood up, testing the leg for movement, getting the blood circulating properly again, and wafting the flaps of his leather biker jacket to cool himself down and spread some of the reek.

It was time to get his arse in gear. Tonight was a big night, one that he trusted some careful thought had gone into, and he wasn't about to be the one to fuck it up.

The first thing he did was cook up a tablespoon solution of speed to bang into his arm. He'd got a kettle of water ready but he'd forgotten about a clean spoon. It took him almost five minutes scrabbling among the bedroom clutter to find one that wasn't already so caked in soot from the candle flame that it was unusable without washing it up first. No time for that shit. And anyway, that would mean going downstairs to the kitchen, where Bea's eldest, Paul, might be about (though the chance was pretty rare). At least he had some clean barrels immediately to hand. If he waited till he got round to Stan's, he'd be sure to find the others cooking up too; but they nearly always shared needles – usually old dirty ones, the stupid bastards. All registered addicts, but just too untogether to make it round to the chemist's for a free supply of new syringes every once in a while. At least he hadn't sunk to that level.

The feel of the speed started surging through his body straight away. It was an extra joy now that the cast was off, all his limbs unfettered once again. Better get moving while the flood of feelgood sensation lasted and he was on top of things. All he had to do now was make it round to Stan's without being seen by anyone who knew him. They all had their alibis in place: the leg was his. Tomorrow he'd put a replacement cast on and nobody would be any the wiser. But if he was seen without it now, that'd be it. Goodbye free mazoolah. However, that just wasn't going to happen, was it? No point worrying about that because it was all fucking theoretical.

He hadn't used the bike for more than a fortnight, but he'd made sure to leave it with a full tank and see that nobody else who came round here took a fancy to a joy ride on it in the meantime. Once he got the helmet on with the visor down, anyone who did happen to see him would be unlikely to recognise him or the bike at night, especially as he would be the last person they'd be expecting to see riding round the streets. Once he got round to Stan's place, he could park it up in the back yard behind Stan's shed where it wouldn't be spotted by anyone from the street. A revamped 60s Triumph with fifteen hundred quids' worth of work just done on it tended to stand out around here, and he wasn't just thinking about robbers. I mean, don't get him wrong, he hadn't put in two years of the odd spot of hard graft on Clint's bike, on behalf of Clint's memory, to get it nicked by some dodgy little backstreet scrote; but in a way – in fact, in a number of ways – the consequences of the bike being seen by someone who recognised it as his, by someone who knew him, could be even worse. A lot worse.

It felt weird leaving the house without his crutches for the first time in two weeks. Kick-starting the bike took a minute or so but gave his leg some well-needed exercise. Once he was on the road, he knew it would only be a matter of five minutes before he was heeling down the bike prop and swinging his leathered butt off the saddle in Stan's back yard.

In fact, that thought was probably going right through his mind when he never noticed Greg, someone he occasionally sold blow to and got stoned with at student parties, walking past and turning his head as he zoomed along the Otley Road.

When he reached Stan's, the others – Stan, Poz and Denny – were just cooking up around the kitchen stove.

'Y'awright, Kel,' Poz said, shuffling nervously in the middle of the kitchen floor space – right in everybody's way, and too wired stupid to notice it. Thank God Kelly knew he could drive like this. As long as he'd been been drinking nothing stronger than council pop.

'Yo, Kelly,' Denny greeted him understatedly, deepening his voice and barely tilting his head up to lock eyes with him from beneath his mousy mop of hair; a gesture going right back straight as an arrow of time to when they first went to comp together and Denny thought he was John Shaft, the cat was that cool to him – even though he was what both their mams called a darkie. There was something different about the gesture tonight. Something fractured, out of place. Denny wasn't a kid any more. And Kelly just hoped and prayed he knew that himself.

'You sure you're totally ready for this?' Stan asked him, evidently referring to the job at hand rather than the speed that was going round – and as if Kelly would be here otherwise.

He played it cool to start with. 'Course I am, ya soft get.'

'You havin' a dig then or what?'

'I've already had one before I came out.'

'We've got some clean needles, if that's what yer worried about, ya ponce.'

'Go on then,' said Kelly just to be diplomatic: because he could see that Stan was winding himself up to something and he thought let him keep on winding for a while longer; and to be resourceful – might as well top up on the old chemical courage in the meantime. 'Fuck it, cook us one up. I'll have another for t'road.'

This time he banged it into the other arm, just to even things up. He'd thought about shooting it into the thigh that he'd just uncaked from the pot, but the jeans he was wearing had buttons at the fly instead of a zip, and he couldn't be arsed going through all the bother of unfastening then refastening them. He was too on edge, too wired already, to start doing anything fiddly. He was glad he'd cut the cast off before having a dig and not after: he'd have probably cut half his fucking fingers off with those secateurs.

'So who told you about this garage again?' said Kelly, addressing Denny.

'What do you mean, who told us about it?' said Denny, dropping the blaxploitation posture.

'Well, somebody musta said summat about it. I mean, it were your idea, it were your suggestion in t'first place. You targeted it. So where did you hear about it?'

'Hear what?'

Coming straight on top of two gees of whizz, Kelly wasn't up for Denny's naive act. He knew enough to hold on to the knowledge that this night was important and he wasn't going to be the one to fuck it up. He felt impelled to press on though. 'Well, for fuck's sake, Denny, you must've 'ad a reason for pickin' that particular place.'

'Well, what if I did? Why should I tell you?'

'Cos we're yer mates – an' if yer don't, we'll kick shit out a yer.'

'Aw yeah, I'd like to see yer try,' he said, suddenly quietly, with a smile on his face from a fond childhood memory.

'Come on, Denny,' said Kelly, 'we're fuckin' gonna go through with it with ya – yer can at least let us in on why.'

'It were Eddie Whatsit, wannit?'

'What, is he out?'

'They let him out for his kid's funeral. I got chance to talk to him an' he reckoned this place is a pushover. Heard it from some'dy inside.'

'It's not fuckin' dodgy, is it?' said Kelly. 'We're not fuckin' poachin' some'dy else's job 'ere, are we?'

'Are we fuck, yer daft bastard. It's fuckin' kosher.'

'Kosher's a word I don't like. I'm a pork eater. So it fuckin' better be all right.'

'Yeah,' said Stan. 'In fact the whole thing'd better be kosher.' He turned to Kelly, looking at his leg. 'Does Bea know about it?'

'No, she's away wit' young 'uns. Went to a school play or summat, so they're all stoppin' over at her sister's.'

'Coincidence or what?' said Stan.

'Yeah – as it happens.'

'What about the pot leg? She must know about that.'

'Yeah. So?' Kelly kept the tone firm but jocular, laughing through it even. 'What's all this about? What's all this about, eh? I haven't got a real broken leg, you know, I'm not a fuckin' cripple yet, I can still fuckin' deck yer for gettin' lippy.'

Kelly was just joking in his own fashion but Poz, seeing it all turning nasty, motioned to intervene to keep it on a friendly footing.

'Eh lads, fuckin' calm down, will yer?' he said, stepping forward. He was about to launch into specifics, but when three surly faces turned to him expectantly, he lost his bottle and turned all philosophical. 'You're bound to be a bit wound up, aren't yer?' he said, bobbing and waving ineffectual signals of conciliation while his wired brain did somersaults. 'Know what I mean? We're all

19

bound to feel a bit psyched up, aren't we? Know what I mean, Denny?' He was reaching out to Denny for moral support but he was to find it distinctly lacking there.

'I just wanna get it over with,' said Denny, 'so if you poncy cunts are ready, let's stop fucking about an' get on with it.'

'He's not fuckin' wrong,' said Kelly, turning away from Stan and giving his leg another scratch. 'Sooner we get it over with the better.'

'All right,' Stan sullenly agreed, and went about getting his act together. 'You do know, whatever we get tonight, we're all gonna have to pay most of it back to Big Baz, the greedy fat cunt. One way or another, I bet we all owe him money, don't we?'

'I owe him three hundred quid,' Poz admitted cheerfully, happier now that the aggression was turned against someone who wasn't in the same room.

'Denny?'

He looked down, the Shaft look again – and the voice. 'Five hundred.'

There was an intake of breath through pursed lips from both Stan and Kelly.

'How much is he into you for? Kelly?'

How much indeed, Kelly wondered. For him, it was complicated, the financial arrangements, what with Bea and all. It ran deep. But at the surface level, Baz was carrying around Kelly's IOU for an immediate two hundred.

'Enough,' he said.

What they collectively owed Big Baz for drugs was a depressing subject. Secretly, Kelly knew none of them wanted to do this, but now was not the time for them to mull over it, and to spur on the others as well as himself, he said, 'Come on, ya miserable sods, or neither Big Baz nor us'll be gettin' nowt. East End Park, here we come.'

Denny's two arms sprang up in a wedge and he snapped through the action of the not yet loaded handgun in his tattooed fingers.

'Fuckin' A,' he said Americanly.

3. Chill

THE WAY THEY'D planned it was, they would do one run past the all-night petrol station just to see if it was empty of other vehicles, and if not, do a U-turn, then pull up on the other side of the road to keep watch till it was all clear.

That was how it was supposed to go, and that was the scenario that they'd each imagined over and over again in detail: pulling up opposite, watching and waiting for what few other cars were around to leave the station before they moved in, hanging back until the time was right. They'd ended up losing sight of the fact that that was just the reserve option. So it was something of a shock to their senses to see the forecourt totally empty as they passed it on the first sweep. Poz, being at the wheel, was the first to freak.

'Are we going straight for it or what?' he said, tensing to make a late turn into the forecourt.

'No,' said Kelly.

'What the—' said Stan.

'Pull up to the kerb like we thought we would do. We need to talk for a minute.'

Poz was making the U-turn to bring them back around. The road too was empty of other vehicles, and the nearest set of traffic lights to worry about was a good thirty yards away.

'We shoulda gone for it then,' said Stan. 'Now we'll be sittin' here talkin' us-selves out of it.'

Kelly looked not at Stan but at Denny, as though it was him that might need convincing, and said, 'That's bollocks. We need to have a quick check on exactly how we're gonna do this so no one can be accused of fucking it up unless they do somethin' different.'

The car stopped. They all looked at one another. Poz jiggled the steering wheel with what-do-I-do urgency.

'Why don't we stay parked here?' he suggested. 'Roads around here are quiet this time a night. You lot can run across an' do it then run back over here. That way, the car's not gonna show up on t'security video.'

'No,' said Kelly. 'We stick to the plan. Pull up on the left, like we said, right round the side near the air supply, an' they won't

21

even see the car. If owt ends up on camera, it'll only be the front side panel. They're not gonna see the make or the licence plate from that angle.'

'I hope you're dead fuckin' sure about that, Kel,' said Stan.

'Listen, I'm only going on what Denny said. He planned it, remember?'

'Like I said,' said Denny, 'it's kosher.'

'Right – then it's not gonna be a problem, is it? We nip out the car, we approach from the side, we'll be in their blind spot. Stan gets up on me shoulders, like we practised, and as soon as that lens is out of action Denny moves in. I'm telling yer, we stick to the way we planned it, it'll be a piece a piss.'

Denny was wondering who made Kelly leader, but at least he was talking positive, unlike Poz skriking like a bairn and Stan whingeing like a mardy cunt.

They all looked at one another again. OK. Let's do it.

There was no squeal of tyres and brakes like in the movies. Poz pulled it up on the designated spot as smooth as if he was taking his test. If there was one thing he was good at, it was driving when wired. But, even though they all seemed to have it under control at last, you could tell how strung out everyone was. Quiet, but not calm. It was a holding-your-breath quiet, a trapped-underwater quiet. And inside the pressure capsule of the vehicle's interior, four minds were all going through the same agony of desire: turkeying for one more dig of whizz before the big moment. But there was no more whizz. The time for that had passed. At least until they got back home safe. For now, there was only the job.

They unrolled their balaclava masks down over their faces. There was a brief and bizarre snapshot in time when they were just sitting there, the four of them, all balaclava'd up literally to the eyeballs, must've looked like the fucking IRA, and the lot of 'em staring straight ahead through the windscreen as if they'd been sitting in Morecambe bay on a grey rainy day, gazing at the flat cold sea; wishing they weren't there and wanting to be home. Then time's camera wound on, and the doors were open and Kelly, Stan and Denny were out of the car and moving into action.

Kelly was aware of Denny hanging back as he should be doing while he hoisted Stan up and felt boot soles bite deep into his shoulders and heard the hiss of the can as Stan squirted shaving foam all over the camera lens. That part went OK, just like they'd practised it; Christ, if it all fell through, him and Stan could get a job in a circus together, they were that slick. Once the camera was out, Stan gave the OK and jumped down off Kelly's shoulders with a double clump of boots on the station's concrete fringe. Then Denny stepped out of the shadows with the gun aimed right at the cashier's face through the glass.

It was some poor college-aged-looking kid in a baseball cap, probably doing the night shift out of desperation for pocket money. Before Denny had time to say his line, the kid took one look at the gun pointing in his direction and dropped out of sight below the level of the serving hatch window.

'*Fucking get up! Fucking get up* off that floor, yer little cunt. *Now.*' Denny was doing his nut, banging on the glass with the butt of the pistol. 'Aw *fuck.*' With no time to fuck around, Denny strode the length of the frontage of the building from the serving window to the door to the shop interior. When he'd confirmed it was locked, he didn't hesitate for a second but took aim and shot a bullet straight into the lock.

In that same second, Kelly wondered what the hell had happened to the kid he'd known in school, and a fraction of that same second later, his own memory banks reminded him that he did know what had happened because he'd been through most of it with him. But this....

The crack of the gun sounded to Kelly just like a dozen similar percussions you might hear any night of the week from the comfort of your own front room and not know or give a fuck whether it was a wheel bursting a plastic bottle or what as long as it didn't come pinging through your window. Except it was a hell of a lot louder. It was a fuck of a lot louder. It was so fucking loud that it set his ears ringing, and his ring piece twitching like a sewing machine. It was a fucking miracle that Denny shot the bullet clean through the lock and didn't shatter the whole glass door to smithereens. Within another second the mad bastard was inside, marching down the aisle pointing the gun at the kid cowering on the floor. Kelly and Stan couldn't see the kid from outside because he was still below their line of sight from the outside of the hatch, but they could see the anger in Denny's eyes through the holes in his balaclava, and both of them were thinking,

Oh no, oh sweet screaming Jesus, no. Kelly didn't know morally whether he should dash inside or not but he knew logically that there wasn't time. They didn't have the luxury to fuck around here all night. He pressed himself up against the glass, watching without the power to control or influence what he was seeing. Denny was saying nothing, maybe thinking himself back into his taciturn Shaft routine, to distance himself from what he was doing. Except which side was the black cat on now? Whichever, he marched directly up to the kid and laced right in. As soon as Denny began kicking him, the kid manoeuvred to get out of the way, wriggling across the floor until he was quickly in Kelly and Stan's sight line.The kid held his hands over his head and curled up into a foetal ball, but it wasn't much use. Denny's booted right foot was working like a treddle and every kick connected hard, bludgeoning the weak defences aside. He brought the butt of the gun down once on the side of the kid's face. Then he shifted his attention away from the victim to rip into the cash register.

'Pass it through,' Stan was saying, trying to nudge Kelly out of the way from the window so he could get his paws on the money. Denny was stuffing notes into his jacket pockets inside the place. 'Pass it through.' Stan was all but peeing himself.

'Shut the fuck up and wait,' Denny was saying. His voice was barely audible through the glass. The kid hadn't switched on the microphone that gave sound from inside that all-night-petrol-station-counter tinniness. They saw Denny glance down at the kid. Denny could see that the kid wasn't moving any more, and started to work more methodically, using the Morrison's plastic carrier bag he'd brought for the money, clearing out each compartment of the till, then lifting up the tray for the float underneath and pouring the coins into the bag too. When the till was empty, he commenced casting his eyes over the floor, ignoring the kid, concentrating further back towards the private staff area.

'Come on,' said Stan. 'What the fuck are you doing?'

'There's a safe. It's in the floor somewhere.'

'Denny,' said Kelly, 'leave it. You said nothing about any safe. An' I'm tellin' yer, it'll be empty anyway. The money goes in the safe at the end a the night when they cash up and change shifts. You've got all of it, man. Come on, let's fuckin' go.'

24

A car swished past on the main road. Poz, from the driver's seat, window wound down, called out nervously. 'Let's get a fuckin' *move on*, for fuck's sake. What's he fuckin' doin'?'

'He's fuckin' about, that's what,' Stan said back tetchily.

'All right, I'm fuckin' comin,' said Denny. 'All right? I'm fuckin' comin'.'

Denny looked down at the kid on the ground one more time. For a second, Kelly thought he was going to plant one last kick for good measure.

'Leave it.'

Denny turned and hurriedly retraced his steps out of the shop. Within another seven seconds they were slamming the car doors shut and tear-arsing out of the forecourt.

'Slow down, Poz,' said Kelly. 'Take it easy.'

Poz eased off the accelerator, looked properly at the road and the mirror, even needlessly checked his lights were on, and tried to get his wits under control. *Breathe*, he thought, *breathe*. Stupid thing was, he couldn't stop breathing – big head-expanding gulps.

'What the fuck happened in there? You didn't fuckin' shoot him, did yer?'

'Nobody shot anyone. Just concentrate on the road, Poz,' said Kelly. 'Take it easy. Just chill. We'll tell you all about it. Just drive an' chill.'

4. Teresa Corchran

THEY WERE at Stan's kitchen again, filing in through the back door as the overhead strip lighting flickered back on. Kelly had tried to imagine being in an SAS team finally getting back to base from a vital mission involving national security and terrified hostages, and wondered if it would have been as stressful as that. But it had also been a success. Albeit a qualified one.

'Don't give me any a that crap, Denny,' Kelly was saying, in a shout suppressed to a whisper in case the neighbours or anyone in the street were ear-wigging while the back door was still open. 'We agreed beforehand that there'd be no shots fired.'

'Aw, will ya give it a rest, for fuck's sake?' Denny said, failing miserably to understand the thing with suppressing the volume level.

'Keep it down will ya?' said Stan, who'd shut the door but was thinking about thin walls and nosy neighbours and prison.

'That's fuckin' serious stuff is that now if we get fuckin' caught,' said Kelly.

'Look,' said Denny. 'If yer flashin' a live gun around, it's armed robbery anyway. So if yer gonna flash it around, yer might as well be ready to use it. An' let's face it, if I hadn'ta used it tonight, we might all be standin' wi' nowt but us dicks in us 'ands instead of a shitload a money. And besides, nobody got hurt.'

'Bollocks, nobody got hurt. I bet that poor kid in the petrol station dun't think nobody got hurt.'

'He'll live, for fuck's sake. All I did were give 'im a batterin'.'

'A batterin'? Ya kicked ten shades out of 'im.'

Poz was pacing up and down the limited dimensions of the kitchen, occupying even more of the floor space than before, shaking and wondering how he'd managed to drive, while the rest of them clung violently to the sink, shelf and cupboard-door edges at the fringe. Poz was still fretting about the car. Did the camera capture anything? Any detail that might give them away? Shouldn't they have got rid of it already instead of standing round this tiny little too-bright frigging kitchen bitching about rubbish?

'We need to get rid of the car – now!'

For the second time that night in Stan's kitchen, all heads turned in Poz's direction.

'Poz,' said Denny quietly. It wasn't Shaft this time. It was all pure Denny. 'If you don't shut up about that car I'm gonna make sure your dead body's in it when we burn it.'

That did the trick.

'Right,' said Denny, taking back charge now that they'd reached the debriefing stage. 'I've got plans for the car. OK Poz?'

Poz, wisely, said nothing.

'I know just the place we can get rid of it. We clean it down first, vac it, scrub any likely places for prints an' that.'

'Who's got a vac?' said Stan. 'I an't.'

'Jesus— It doesn't fuckin' matter,' said Denny, 'I'll drive it round to my gaff an' do it there. But Poz, you're comin' with me. We do it together. All right? You're doin' all the drivin' so yer'd better get yer 'ead round that.'

Poz nodded.

'Now listen.' He pointed a finger at Poz, then arced it round to include the others. 'There's no rush. It's better we dump that car right in the middle a the night, and we don't wanna be drivin' it round Leeds now for t'next few hours till we've all calmed down properly. Nobody's seen it, as far as we can tell, and as long as we drive carefully, we take it through t' residential backstreets as far as we can along the Otley Road, then get it the fuck out into the countryside. Like I said, I know a place. It's a long way out an' we'll have to get a bus back in the morning, so we'd better do another gee an' whatever else we need to do to be ready for that. In the meantime, I say we divvy up this money, don't you? Oh, an' let's not forget we have to put a hundred aside for Jason for sortin' the car out in the first place.'

Stan teemed out the cash on his kitchen work surface, sweeping soggy tea bags, blackened dessert spoons and used needles aside. Poz ceased his pacing to and fro and suddenly got over his recent death threat, showing a perky interest.

'And what about the gun?' said Kelly, drawing at least Denny's attention away from the cash.

'What about it?'

'How you gonna get rid of that?'

'Kel, it's all planned. It's all up 'ere.' He tapped his temple, a gesture that looked less like Shaft and more like Tommy Cooper – either a sad case or a mad genius. 'It's all thought through. You and Stan just make sure your alibis are in place. Once we're gone, you two can scrap about that to yer hearts' content; but let Poz an' me sort out the rest.'

Poz looked like he didn't know which to do first – fawn humbly in gratitude for Denny's declaration of confidence or shit his pants in anticipation of the long night ahead. Most likely in the woods. In the dark. With Denny. And a loaded gun.

'Fuckinell,' moaned Stan, counting the money out on to the work top, the different colours of the piles of notes made vivid under the strip light. 'You do know we're gonna have to pay most of this to Big Baz, the greedy fat cunt.'

'Oh, shut up, Stan,we've heard it already,' said Denny.

Stan went on counting without saying another word.

Kelly knew he wasn't himself a bad person. Denny shouldn't have used violence: he had the gun, the threat was there, that was enough. Not that Kelly hadn't used violence himself on several occasions more than he cared to remember. But not like that. Not ruthlessly; not without damn good cause or downright unavoidability. Not like Denny tonight. It was at times like these – times when you'd done stuff you're not proud of but that had to be done out of desperation – that his mind took him back to an incident in infants' school – what? – thirty, thirty-odd years ago. A little girl in her first year of school – he was a year or two above – he could still remember her name to this day: Teresa Corchran. His mam knew her mam, they lived in neighbouring streets on the same estate, and he could vaguely remember how, when she first started, they'd charged him with looking out for her, flattering his child's pride with a mantle of responsibility. He never really thought properly about what that might entail though – at that age, how could he? Especially when Teresa turned out to be a loner, taking herself solemnly off to remote corners of the playground every playtime and dinner hour to scribble her own solitary games in the dirt and gravel. It was easy to forget about her. Until one lunchtime he found her crying against the mottled red-brick wall of the school building, and she confessed to him, when he asked, what had been happening. Another boy – an older child, possibly Kelly's age – had been bullying her in the breaks for the last few days, morning and afternoon, seeking her out on her own, then looming over her, growling and snarling at her and and clawing his dirty fingernails towards her face, terrorising her to make her cry because he thought it was funny and exhilarating to have that power over a smaller girlchild. It was then that Kelly understood this thing their mothers had been talking about, this responsibility, this looking out for someone. Before, it had sounded good and made him feel grown up without really meaning much, but now that the duty was being called in, he knew exactly what to do. It never occurred to him to tell a teacher; this was something he should sort out. Teresa played her part beautifully; all she had to do was be herself and trust him and be brave. That same afternoon, when it reached the two o'clock playtime, he ran outside quickly and hid himself near the quiet corner of the yard that Teresa liked to inhabit. Sure enough, after five minutes, the boy in question got bored with his play mates and came prowling in search of his helpless little prey mate instead. Kelly recognised him immediately, a smaller boy than himself from his own class who he didn't have much to do with. Funny – he couldn't remember his name any more; he wondered if he ever knew it at all. Kelly bided his time, waited patiently until the boy went into his monster routine, not because he wanted to witness Teresa's distress but because he wanted the boy to know exactly what he was to be punished for. When he stepped out of hiding, the boy dropped the act with a clunk and his face fell. For a second, he tried to come over all innocent before Kelly grabbed him with both fists by his jumper and started spinning him round. The boy was hanging on to Kelly's arms and stumbling to keep his feet on the ground, his face a mask of surprise and scared indignation – an expression that mewled, *What have I done wrong?* 'Think it's funny, do yer?' said Kelly. 'Think it's funny to frighten little girls?' With a shove, he sent the boy skittering over the gravel in a welter of grazes. 'Now leave her alone in future, or I'll come lookin' for ya. Understand?' There wasn't any more trouble after that. Kelly couldn't recall what happened to the boy. They probably went through another year in the same class, then the boy went off to a different junior school. He couldn't remember them going through junior school together. Teresa stayed on, still solitary, remote from the other children, later to be seen lost in books in the school library. Kelly never let his responsibility to look out for her slip his mind, but little else changed; he rarely thought about her or spent time with her – not until years later when she was a teenager still living on the estate and he ended up developing a crush on her. But she was a high flyer at the grammar school by then, and he was at the comp, and that wasn't another story.

Kelly watched the others poring over the money from the robbery. His first robbery. He needed that money – yes, to pay Baz back, but for other things as well. There were other creditors at his door, and whatever was left for him, he would let Bea invest in her business. She was able to make money, enough to keep a family household together. Everything he touched turned to shit, or more precisely, to beer and drugs. If he could just let Bea turn the cash into speed then sell it off himself in bits and pieces without the urge to dip into it, that would be a start. He could make enough to reinvest and work towards attaining some kind of solvency. It would still mean at the end of the day that it all ended up in Big Baz's wallet; but it would also mean he'd never have to do something like this again. Then maybe Teresa Corchran would stop reappearing in his mind like some internal pop-up character reference.

'Two and half grand, thereabouts,' said Stan.

'There was a safe,' said Denny emphatically. 'I know there was a safe in that floor somewhere.'

Kelly couldn't be bothered to argue. He knew he wasn't a bad man.

5. Cast On

'I CAN'T BELIEVE I'm doin' this,' said Bea, tossing back a lock of hair that was dangling dangerously close to the tip of her fag. 'I mean it's fuckin' silly innit? You've only got to take one look' – she pointed to his leg with the pen – 'and yer can see it's all t'same handwriting.' She screwed her face up, as much against the smoke as frustration. 'Besides, I can't think of owt else to write. It's like when they pass round a birthday card for some'dy at work an' everybody else 'as written what you were gonna put an' you can't think of owt else.'

'Since when were you last at fuckin' work?' said Kelly.

'Oi. This morning, yer cheeky cunt. More than you, thank you very much.'

'That's not the kind a work you're talkin' about though, is it – doin' yer community service?' He shifted on the kitchen chair, getting sore, getting restless. 'Get kids in here, let them have a go. Where's Nita? Where's Damien?'

'He's out in t'street playin' football, where do you think he is?'

'Get him in here, an' get his fuckin' mates in an' all.'

'Aw yeah, let the 'ole street know. Use yer fuckin' loaf, Kelly. I thought it were supposed to be a big fuckin' secret. That's what you've told me. Anyway, we don't want that lot coming traipsing through the house when we've got it quiet. It's you who's always goin' on about what a fuckin' madhouse it is an' yer can't fuckin' hack it any more. I'll tell ya, yer might as well make most of it while it lasts cos it's gonna get busy round here after this afternoon.'

'Why? What's happening this afty?'

'I'm gettin' that fifty grammes in.' She gave him a pre-emptive look. 'I fuckin' *told* yer, yer dozy bastard. It's up to you if you don't listen.'

'Who yer gettin' it off?'

'Who d'you think? Fuckin' Father Christmas?'

'Fuckinell Bea, not Baz. Is he comin' round with it himself?'

'Well he will be, I suppose. He usually brings it himself, I don't see why today should be any different.'

'What time's he comin'?'

'I told you – this afternoon.'

'Can't you be more specific?'

'No I can't. Why? You're not avoiding him, are you?'

'I owe him some money.'

'Huh. Well who doesn't? Get to the front a the queue by all means. Anyway, what do you owe him money for?'

'For some gear.'

'What gear? You never told me owt about any gear. Where've you got money for gear from? On second thoughts, don't tell me, I don't wanna know.' She added in a mischievous undertone, 'You never fuckin' give me owt though.' She knew that would wind him up.

'That's a fuckin' lie. I pay me way. What about that pair a shoes Casey needed for school that time?'

'Kelly. That were about six fuckin' months ago. She needs another pair by now.'

'It's not even like they're my kids. I mean, don't get me wrong, I love 'em to bits an' all, but I'm not fuckin' obliged to help out, I can always keep me hand in me pocket if you don't appreciate it.'

'Yes Kelly, I do appreciate it. Yes Kelly, we all think the sun shines out yer fuckin' arse. Is that better, love?'

They were interrupted by a figure in the kitchen doorway, a scarecrow shape in a leather jacket, worn-through jeans and a ripped STATIONS OF THE CRASS T-shirt, and his hair sticking out all over the place like Sid Vicious.

'You got any barrels, Kelly?'

'What are you fucking like, Nev?' said Bea. 'Don't you ever think of getting some of your own instead a fuckin' scroungin' everybody else's?'

Nev was taken aback for a moment, then the penny dropped. The grin across his face that put that dimple just under his borstal teardrop tattoo said it all: she wasn't fooling him.

'Aah, you're only jokin'. Eh, you'd better be, cos the fuckin' business I put your way'd pay for all them barrels anyway.'

'Nev – I get 'em for nowt, ya silly cunt. Help yourself. They're in the top drawer of the unit there. In fact, I don't know why I'm fuckin' telling you. I fuckin' know you know where we keep 'em. I must be turning into as silly a cunt as you are.'

'She's lovely, in't she Nev?' said Kelly. 'What you doing now?'

'What d'you think I'm doing? I'm gonna do a gee in, aren't I?'

'A gee a whizz?'

'Kelly...' Nev stood over him, swaying to make his point. 'Do I look like I'm on whizz? Do I sound like I'm on whizz? Am I dancin'? Am I babblin' like you, yer whizzin' cunt?'

'No, but yer talkin' shite.'

'D'you want a bit a brown? I'll be a goody an' split my share with yer.'

'Aw,' said Bea, 'in't he a sweetie?'

'No, you're all right,' said Kelly. 'But before you go, fuckin' write summat on this pot, will yer?'

'What do you want me to write?' said Nev, crouching down with a creak of leather and knee joints.

'I don't know. Use what's left a yer fuckin' imagination.'

Nev selected a red fibre-tip and carefully printed one word, ANARCHY, in block capitals before going back and inscribing a circle round the first A.

'Put summat else,' said Kelly.

'What's wrong with that?'

'Nowt, but put summat else as well. I'm trying to fill the fuckin' thing.'

Nev got a black pen, wrote MoTöRHEAD in an arc, and drew a crude ace of spades underneath it; he shaded in the black with his tongue out like a kid at its colouring book.

'Who's in t'front room?' Kelly said. The sound of Boyzone had just started wafting through. 'Whoever it is, I wish they'd turn that shit off. It's doin' my 'ead in.'

'It's our Nita with some of her mates. I think they're watchin' a video or summat.'

'Why aren't they all at fuckin' school?'

'They've got a day off, haven't they? Cos a that little lass that got murdered. It's been in all t'papers an' on *Calendar*, you musta seen it.'

'Yeah, I did, it were fuckin' awful. Whoever did that, the cunt wants stringin' up.'

'Too fuckin' right,' said Nev, pausing over the leg. 'If that were one a my kids he'd done that to, I'd go after the cunt personally with a fucking big gun an' make sure I shot the cunt in his fuckin' knackers first.'

'Oh I know...' said Bea, 'and even that's too good for him.'

'Get 'em in here,' said Kelly.

'Get who in here?'

'Nita an' her mates. They've got fucking hands, an't they? They can write, can't they?'

'Oh, I'll see what I can do,' she said, leaving the kitchen.

'What's that?' said Kelly, trying to tilt his head upside down to understand the cartoon figure Nev was working on.

'It's Ned Kelly, innit? You're called Kelly, so it's Ned Kelly. Look, he's got a bucket on his head an' everything.' As Nev added the finishing touches, Kelly made out a pistol with the words BANG! BANG! shooting out of it. 'Right, I've done my bit,' he said, tottering to his feet to go back upstairs where he'd been getting ready to shoot up the heroin with a couple of mates that he'd left smoking a joint while they waited for the needles. He turned at the kitchen door and waved the bag of brown powder and the needles in the air. 'Hey. Gee up, Neddy. D'ya gerrit? Gee. Ned Kelly. Gee up, Neddy.'

A moment later, Bea trooped a quartet of 12- and 13-year-old girls dutifully into the kitchen.

'It's comin' on,' said Kelly, scrutinising the pot on his stretched-out leg after the girls had left their multi-coloured mark and gone running back to Boyzone, 'but it's still not full enough. First one had more on it than this.'

'Aw, for God's sake, Kelly, does it really matter? Who's gonna notice yer stupid pot anyway?'

'Get Damien an' them in here. Go on love, do it for us, will yer? They'll be in an' out again in five minutes if they all get round it.'

'You know, I'm starting to get worried about you, wanting a load a young lads crouchin' round yer crotch area.'

'Go on, Bea.'

'Oh, all right, I'll go shout 'em in. They won't thank you for it.'

'They will, they'll love it. They'll be writin' all t'names a t'silly pop groups an' that.'

'What decade are you living in?' said Bea. 'They're into DJs now, not pop groups.'

And so The Day After wound on towards The Afternoon Of Big Baz.

6. Lifeline

KELLY KNEW that Bea had kids from literally the moment he met her.

'I'm only 'ere cos I've got a babysitter,' she said, holding the broken Smirnoff bottle by the neck.

She was standing next to him at the cooker in the kitchen of a large flat in one of those converted Victorian mansions on Hyde Park Road. Somewhere in another room, Cameo was pumping out of the speakers: he recognised it because it was that Eighties hit they'd had, the one with the video of the toothpaste tube and the stiletto heel that they used to play on Music Box. Student music; it was a student party. It was party season. Just hang out at the Royal Park any weekend, but almost as likely on a midweek night, and you were bound to get wind of one, or somebody else would. The students? They never minded. It was a party, for fuck's sake. Anyone was invited to a party. That was its very definition. Otherwise it wouldn't be a party, would it?

All Kelly was there in that kitchen for was a hot knife. He'd just breezed straight up the hill from the pub with three mates and they'd successfully charmed their way past the grinning sweatshirted lager louts who'd answered the door to them, despite them carrying nothing in the way of offerings other than a plastic Morrison's carrier bag containing a broken bottle and two knives. Kelly's one thought, when they entered the labyrinth of the building and commenced worming their way up staircases and along corridors to the kitchen, sniffing it out instinctively, was to get a fucking hottie down his neck. He'd been in the pub long enough. There was only so much that drink could achieve. He'd look for beer later. First things first. Now was hot knife time. It was a party, for fuck's sake. Where were the drugs? In the end, he knew it would be up to him to get his gear out, as per fucking usual. In fact, where was everyone else? Clint was there of course – Clint must've been there, he was always up for a hottie. But the other two had disappeared all of a sudden. Probably gone straight off in search of ale – looked like there was none left here in the kitchen. Fucking poofs. Which meant they found themselves in the company of the self-selected one or two hanging around unabashedly in the otherwise empty unused kitchen rubbernecking the newcomers at the prospect of someone getting some drugs out. Always good people to know in a way, because they're the only ones likely to have any drugs on 'em themselves.

When Kelly got his dope out of his pocket and started placing rabbit-pellet-sized blobs of the stuff on the edge of the cooker top, the sharp-featured woman with the bright button eyes and mousy bangs gathered back in a scarlet scruncher moved forward with interest.

'Are you doin' what I think you're doin'?' she said.

'Fancy a hot knife, love?'

He had to be sociable, and she looked keen; he didn't want a fucking queue forming, though. He lit one of the front rings on the cooker with a Clipper from his jacket pocket then got the two knives out of the Morrison's bag. They were cast-metal table knives and their blades had been blackened by fire again and again. He positioned them with their blade tips resting in the ring of fire, right at the points of the bright blue inner flames at the core of the heat. Then he unwrapped the bottle from the plastic bag and handed it to the woman. It was a Blue Label Smirnoff bottle with its base knocked out cleanly to make it into a kind of tube or inverted funnel. Its inner surface was a deep chocolate brown, smoke-filled and oil-spattered repeatedly over time, creating this sticky uniform film of residue.

'I'm only 'ere cos I've got a babysitter.'

'Are you here with yer husband then?'

'God, no. Fuckinell. Husband? I don't want one a them, thank you. No, I've brung 'em up on me own so far, I must be doin' summat right. I'm Bea, by the way.'

'You what?'

'Bea. That's me name.'

'Oh, right. I'm Kelly.'

And did he introduce Clint at that point? Looking back, he couldn't remember. He must have done, surely. Clint was definitely there – he must have been: they went everywhere together in those days.

'You know, I think I've seen you somewhere before,' Bea was saying. 'Do you know Greg and Mercy and that crowd?'

'Live on one at' Brudenells.'

36

'Yeah, that's them. I'm sure I musta seen you round there one time.'

'I see 'em every now and again. An't been round there for a while though.'

'I reckon it coulda been another party.'

'They had one last year, or was it year before?'

'That'lla been it.'

'You ready?'

Bea moved the bottle up to her lips.

'Take it steady – I an't done one a these in years. Just give us a small 'un.'

The ends of the knives were glowing orange hot now. As Kelly lifted them away from the heater, they rang against the prongs of the cooker, *kerching kerching*. Before the blade tips had begun to dull and cool back to their fire-darkened black, he dipped one of them to the edge of the cooker to hook up the smallest of the cannabis pellets. The tacky moisture of the substance meeting the surface of the hot metal made it stick. Then Kelly lifted and brought the blades of the two knives together, pushing them up inside the broken end of the Smirnoff bottle, the smoking dope sandwiched neatly between them.

Bea sucked expertly for someone who hadn't done one in years, imbibing the smoke in short rapid bursts of intake. Minimum waste; a long profound exhalation of smoke that billowed and filled the kitchen, playing like oil on water in a shaft of lamplight from across the room. The way she dealt with it so coolly. No coughing, no fussing, no crowing. Just calmly handed him back the bottle and continued with the conversation while he put the knives back in for Clint.

Kelly kept coming back in his mind to that memory. Like the memory of Teresa Corchran, their first meeting, his and Bea's, was a rock, something good in his life that he needed to hold on to. Why? Because he still remembered vividly the connection they'd made that night. All the people they later found they had in common... it was a wonder they hadn't known each other before. But that wasn't what mattered really. It wasn't even what they found in common with each other – Kelly couldn't remember her doing another hot knife in all the time he'd been with her since that night. The important thing, the significant thing, was that that connection was still there. It wasn't just still there, it was getting stronger all the time. The memory of that first meeting was a rock, but Bea, in the here and now, was his lifeline.

7. The Afternoon Of Big Baz

'WHOEVER THEY ARE, I bet I know the fuckin' bastards that
did it.'

Big Baz was in Bea's kitchen. Like Kelly had watched Poz doing
in Stan's kitchen just the night before, but in a very different frame
of mind altogether – though not, as it turned out, entirely
unconnected – Baz was pacing what little room was available
around the obstacle course of the dining table, the kitchen chairs
ranged against the back wall facing the work area, the clothes-
horse draped with drying undergarments in front of the gas fire,
the ironing board that Bea was working at, and Damien's mountain
bike leant against the only free bit of wall space.

He couldn't sit down. He was too wound up. With Big Baz, that
wasn't very hard. Everything wound Big Baz up. But this was
personal. He didn't like it that way but this time it was very much
so. It was family. They kept banging on about it on *EastEnders*, so
it must mean something, mustn't it? Anyway, who else was going
to do anything about it? Who else had the fucking bottle to go out
and do something about it? His noticeable overbite – which
nobody ever mentioned in front of him, and which everybody
knew had been put to vicious use on various occasions in the past
– was folded away behind tense lips, busy chewing away at a bit of
loose skin, the habit of a speed dealer used to taking a little too
much out of his own stock for percy.

'D'you think they might be from round here, then?' said Bea,
squirting a spray of water on to one of Damien's school shirts.

'They could be – but then they could be from anywhere except
East End Park, couldn't they? That's the one place I bet they're not
from, cos they wouldn't shit on their own doorstep, would they?
Not unless they were fuckin' stupid.'

'Well what makes yer think you might know 'em then?' asked
Kelly with his new bogus pot propped up on a beer crate. He'd put
away all the pens from earlier, and Bea had cleared up all the
plaster of Paris mess down in the basement cellar from last night
(after returning from Stan's, Kelly had been up till five in the
morning putting it all carefully back on strip by strip, just the way
he'd learnt to do it the first time round; he'd even taken a toilet
bucket down there with him so he wouldn't have to disturb it too

39

much while it was setting) and together they'd chucked it all in a neighbour's skip down the alley round the back.

'Cos it doesn't matter where they're from, whether it's round here or Belle Isle or fuckin' Gipton or fuckin' Chapeltown, I bet I fuckin know' em is what I'm sayin'.'

'I know what you're sayin' but—'

Suddenly Baz was there towering crimson-faced over Kelly like an all-in wrestler with the finger pointing. 'Drop it *now* Kelly, just fuckin' *drop* it, cos I'm *tellin'* yer, I'll fuckin' break yer other leg in a minute.'

'Fine,' said Kelly, 'consider it dropped.'

'I've fuckin' twatted a fuckin' copper today already an' I'm fuckin' on one an' up for it, all right? Yer know what I'm sayin'? Yer know what I'm fuckin' sayin' to ya?'

'I know exactly what yer sayin', Baz.'

They'd heard the twatted copper routine before and realised it was just one of Baz's euphemisms, a way of letting you know he was in a bad mood rather than the gospel truth. Still, it was best not to rile him any further when he was like this.

'Eh, calm down, Baz, will yer?' Bea said. 'You're gonna give yourself a fuckin' heart attack.' Bea felt she had a right at least to say that much to him. It was her house, after all.

'I need a fuckin' fag. Has anyone got a fuckin' fag?'

'Here,' said Bea, getting out her Rothmans, 'have one a these.'

Baz lit it up and smoked aggressively. No one had ever seen him smoke any other way.

'Is he badly hurt, then?' asked Kelly.

'It doesn't matter whether he's badly hurt or not, does it? He's me fuckin' sister's boy, he's me fuckin' nephew, in't he? Somebody's got to look out for him.'

The words reverberated so loudly in Kelly's mind – Teresa Corchran again – that it was a wonder no one else heard them. 'Well is he in hospital or what?'

'Not any more. He went to Casualty and they kept him in the rest a the night then they let him out this morning. His face is in a right fuckin' state though, an he's got a couple a broken ribs.'

'I didn't even know you had a sister,' said Kelly.

'Why would yer? She never comes round this end. Only time I see her is maybe at Christmas if we both go round to see t'old lady. Fact, last time I saw her apart from today were two Christmases ago, when she were pregnant wit' youngest. Had a right fuckin' belly on her, she did. I told her to get fuckin' shirt off an' show us the Dunlop sign on her back before they floated her over Elland Road.'

'She must fuckin' love you then,' said Bea.

'Well nob'dy else is gonna look out for her,' said Baz. 'All t'fuckin' blokes who've give her kids've all fucked off, the cunts.'

'Aye, well some blokes are like that, aren't they?' said Bea philosophically. 'There's plenty round here like that. You've only got to step out in the street to find rats like that round here.'

'What were he doin' workin' in an all-night petrol station though?' said Kelly. 'That's askin' for trouble.'

'Silly little sod were tryin' to get some cash together, weren't he?' said Baz. 'If I'da fuckin' seen a bit more of him, I'da fuckin' told him it were a mug's game. He'da bin better off goin' out thievin', like everybody else. Sis wouldn't have him doin' that though, would she? Wouldn't want him growin' up like his big bad Uncle Baz.'

'Growin' up?' said Kelly. 'Why? How old is he? In't he grown up already?'

'Seventeen,' said Baz, and in a dark corner of his mind, a picture of Moz reared up, trussed up like a Christmas turkey in the boot of a car. 'I wouldn't fuckin' know whether that's supposed to be grown up these days or not,' he went on disingenuously. 'They're fuckin' out thievin' once they learn to walk these days. Fuckin' whatsisname, Ryan whatsit...'

'Who? Ryan Giggs?'

'No, ya daft cunt, fuckin Ryan whatsisname...'

'Oh – Sullivan,' said Bea, 'Ryan Sullivan? Lives up near t'allotments?'

'Sullivan, that's it. His youngest got pulled in by t'filth other day – 'bout two weeks ago. Breakin' an' enterin'. He's only fuckin' eleven, so they can't touch him for it, like. But fuck's sake, fuckin' eleven. Mind you, they were doin' me for GBH when I were thirteen, so I've got no fuckin' room to talk.'

It was a rare thing to hear Baz putting himself down, but neither of them remarked upon it.

'Didn't his eldest get put away for twockin' last Easter?'

'That's right. He's out now. They kept him in for fourteen months then had to chuck a load of 'em out to make room for some more. He were one of 'em. I think they commuted part of his sentence to community service.'

'Fuckinell,' said Bea, 'don't talk to me about community service. Them old biddies are fuckin' drivin' me mad at that home where I'm doin' mine.'

'Yeah, it's a cunt, innit?' said Baz.

'But aren't coppers doin' owt about it?' said Kelly.

''Bout what,' said Baz, 'fuckin' old people's homes?' and chuckled at his own joke.

'Your sister's lad.'

'What? Yer think I should fuckin' sit back an' wait for them to do summat about it? Course they'll be doin' summat about it, it's fuckin' armed robbery, innit? Silly cunts aren't gonna be sittin' at home swillin' tea, are they? They'll be out lookin' for 'em – but I wanna fuckin' get hold of 'em first so I can wring their fuckin' necks.'

'Course you do,' said Kelly, 'and good luck to you.'

'An' I've got me spies out. If anybody hears owt, I'll find out about it. You two an' all. If you hear owt, Bea, let us know. Ring us on t'mobile. You an' all, Kelly. Ask around if need be.'

'Course I will, Baz.'

'Right. You havin' this bag a whizz off us then, Bea, cos I'm gonna have to shoot off in a minute?'

'Yeah,' said Bea, putting the iron to one side and reaching into the leather waist pouch that she carried her cash around in, out of the way of temptation to Kelly and the kids, along with everyone else who trooped in and out of the house all day long. 'What is it, five hundred?'

'Yeah. It's pure gear, as per usual. Uncut.'

Bea felt like saying, *Yeah, course it is, Baz*, but even she wouldn't dare be sarky with Baz. It wasn't all cops and robbers with Baz: anybody who knew him knew that he'd be happy to give anybody a twatting, man, woman or child, if he felt they'd earned it.

After he'd counted Bea's money, he looked at Kelly with that manic grin of his spread across his face, and Kelly knew what was coming next. 'Got that two hundred, Kel?'

Two hundred? Bea thought, but kept her mouth shut.

Kelly pulled himself upright on to his crutches, an old-fashioned wooden pair someone had robbed from a clinic for him. He reached into his back pocket and pulled out a crumpled-flat wad of notes. 'There's two hundred there, Baz. I had it put to one side for yer.' Shit, why did he have to add that? Everybody knew he could never put money aside in a million years.

Baz uncrumpled the money, counted it and seemed satisfied though.

'Nice one. Right, I'm gonna shoot off. Got stuff to do. Unless anyone's havin' a dig. Wouldn't mind a dig for the road.'

Bea, back at the ironing, said, 'You're on yer feet, Hopalong Kelly. Get works out a t'drawer, will ya?'

Fuckinell, thought Kelly, I'm trying to get rid of him. But Bea wasn't to know that. How could she? What he'd told Stan and the others last night was virtually the truth. Bea knew there was some subterfuge going on, what with the false pot and that, but she didn't know it had anything to do with the petrol station robbery, or that he'd been involved in that in any way whatsoever. And she certainly didn't know that it had anything to do with Baz. For fuck's sake, he hadn't even known that himself until just now. Baz's fucking nephew, of all people. Denny, you flaming knob. You had the gun. You didn't have to even lay a finger on him. And now look.

While he got the works out of the drawer, the other two rolled their sleeves up ready to pop their veins for the needle. Oh well, if they were both having a dig, he might as well join them.

And so, for Kelly, The Afternoon Of Big Baz continued to wind on.

43

8. Sun And Snakebites

POZ, NATURALLY, was the first one to break silence and get in contact.

Not that he shouldn't have done particularly. Immediately after the robbery, they'd talked about leaving it a week or so before getting in touch with one another again, but then Kelly had persuaded them to reconsider: any irregularity of behaviour might provide a clue for tongues to start wagging about. If they were noticed not to contact one another, that would only draw attention from people around them. Kelly had told them straight that it would be OK not to call on him because he'd be taking it easy with his leg, putting on his recuperation act at home – and secretly he hoped that none of them would: he needed some time and space to come down from the enormous buzz of the event, to deal with the knowledge of what they'd done, in his own fashion. But they all knew really just how easy he'd be taking it – *not*. Kelly was a speed freak, and speed freaks didn't sit around for two or three *days* – never mind the two or three *weeks* that it would take to convince anyone they were recovering from a broken leg – doing sweet diddly squat. Besides, even a genuinely broken leg didn't mean you were a cripple. Life went on: the quest for the next fag – the next beer – the quest for the next dig – went on.

That was why Poz got in touch. Looking for someone to lay him on a dig.

Kelly met him in the Royal Park for the lunchtime sesh the day after The Afternoon Of Big Baz. Kelly stood the round of snakebites at the bar after Poz swore blind that he didn't have a penny. Poz picked up both pints and Kelly swayed behind him on his crutches out to the beer garden.

It was another sunny spring day, the kind that brings a sneak preview of things to come before the skies lock down again and you face the long miserable hiatus before the British summer begins. The students were out in force, all vests and pantaloons and immature blokes clowning around nice-looking girls, catching rays and shooting the breeze. They found an empty table and Kelly propped his crutches against its edge and they watched mothers and fathers chatting and drinking with one eye on their pints and the other on their kids. A pair of Rottweilers padded about up on

44

the pub roof before lying down, their muzzles perched over the roof edge, presiding over the scene below, dozing in the heat. Geoff's dogs, the landlord's. Kelly had seen one of them get hold of a cat once. Nasty.

At the final count round at Stan's that night, they'd come out of it with the best part of six hundred and fifty quid apiece. Kelly remembered Poz saying that he'd owed Big Baz three hundred quid. So if Poz was skint, that meant he'd spent three hundred and fifty, right?

'You've seen Baz then?' Kelly said.

'Baz? What, Big Baz? Man, he's the last person I wanna see right now.'

'Wait a minute, don't tell me – Poz, you haven't, have you?'

'Haven't what?'

'You haven't spent that money you owe Baz?'

'What money?'

'The other night. Before the— you know what. You said you owed Baz three 'undred quid.'

'Oh fuck,' said Poz, 'tough, he'll have to wait for that.'

'You mean you haven't paid im 'back yet?'

'I haven't paid 'im back yet cos I've spent it.'

Poz looked puzzled when Kelly started chuckling quietly to himself.

'What's funny about that?'

The dopey bastard hadn't even heard about Baz and his nephew. Kelly broke him the bad news.

'Fuckinell, Kel, that's no joke. Baz is a nutter. So what were he sayin' about it?'

'What d'yer think? He were doing his nut, weren't he? Completely. Threatened to kill whoever'd done it, break their fuckin' backs, all sorts.'

'An' what did you say?'

'I fuckin' chivvied him on, didn't I? You know what Baz is like when he's on one. If you're not with him, you're against him. He fuckin' nearly took a pop at me cos he din't think I were agreein' with him fast enough.'

'Fuckinell, Kel, what we gonna do? He's a fuckin' animal, he's gonna fuckin' kill us.'

45

'No he isn't, cos he isn't gonna find out, is he? Cos we're not gonna do anything, are we?'

'Well we're gonna do *some*thin', aren't we?'

'No we're not, Poz; that's what I'm sayin', innit? We're gonna do absofuckinlutely nothin' except behave as normal. Geddit?'

'Have you spoken to Stan or Denny about it?'

'No, I haven't been in touch with 'em. An' to be honest, I'd rather keep it that way fut' time being.'

'Well you're gonna have to talk to 'em, aren't yer? Denny'll wanna talk to you about it. You know what Denny's like. He's done it once – he'll have a taste for it now. He'll want us all to do another one. I'll fuckin' put money on it.'

'Have you been talking to him?' Kelly said suspiciously.

'No, course I haven't. But anyway, what if I have? But I haven't, all right? But you know what Denny's like, I'm just tellin' yer. He thinks he in't scared a Baz.'

'Poz, man, what yer sayin'?'

'I'm sayin' that Denny doesn't know what Baz is like. He thinks he does, but he doesn't. Now I've known Denny for a long time. Maybe even longer than you, off an' on. An' if I know one thing about the way his mind works, it's that he wouldn't think twice about lettin' Baz know it were him who did it just to fuckin' spite the fat cunt.'

'Yeah, but Denny doesn't know, does he? I mean he doesn't know that it were Baz's sister's kid that he paggered. If you haven't been in touch with him an' I haven't been in touch with him, who else coulda told him?'

'Unless Baz has been to see him, like he came to see you an' Bea. After all, Denny owes him money as well.'

'Fuck. I'd better give him a ring an' fuckin' sort it out with him,' said Kelly. Then he thought some more about it. 'Hang on, what am I saying? Not even Denny'd be fuckin' suicidal enough to take on Big Baz on his own.'

'No, nob'dy would,' said Poz innocently. 'At least not unless they had a gun.'

'Well you were with him. The other night. You got rid a the car, yeah?'

'Yeah. Tipped it in an old quarry somewhere fuckin' miles out.'

'And did Denny get rid a the gun?'

Poz shook his head. 'I didn't see him.'
That was when Kelly freaked.
That was when they both freaked.

9. Cluckin'

'IT'S A SITTER. It's a fuckin' *sitter*, I'm tellin' ya,' Denny was saying to Kelly and Poz. 'Stan fuckin' agrees wi' me, don't yer, Stan?'

'Sort of.'

'Aw, will yer listen to him, the fuckin' nonce?'

Kelly couldn't believe they were all back in Stan's kitchen just two days after the robbery.

'Denny. Denny. Have you heard a word I've fuckin' said?'

'Yeah. I heard. So what?'

'Yer right,' said Kelly, resorting to wrong-footing tactics. 'Yer exactly right. So what? It doesn't mean fuck all. As long as we play it cool. Just fuckin' take it easy for a while, that's all I'm sayin'.'

'So *what* if it were Big fuckin' Baz's fuckin' kid sister's sprog, or whoever the fuck's it is?'

'Have you seen him?'

'Course I fuckin' saw 'im, I kicked shit out of him, din't I?'

'Have you seen Baz?'

'No.'

'I thought you owed him five hundred quid.'

'All in good time.'

'Oh, fucking great,' said Kelly. 'So I'm the only one who's paid the greedy fat cunt his money back. Have you paid him? Stan?'

Stan hung his head.

'I thought the whole point of the fucking robbery was to clear all us fuckin' debts.'

'Look. I don't see what the big deal is,' said Denny. 'Baz knows how much I owe 'im – if he'd wanted it, he'da come round for it. And even if he 'adda done and I'd paid 'im back, he'd still've been none the wiser that it was us who had owt to do wi' that robbery.'

'All right. Fine. But what I'm sayin' is, let's lay low for a bit, let things cool off. I mean what's the point of going out on another one straight away? I'll tell yer what the fucking point is – because you lot've fuckin' spent all the fuckin' loot already an' now yer back to square one, still owin' fuckin' Baz a grand between yer.'

'This job's four grand minimum.'

48

'Fuckin' forget the job for a minute. It's too soon. It's just too soon. What about the pigs? Same gang doin' another one straight away? I mean, the kid saw three of us. All right, he couldn't identify us, but if another one happens straight away, I don't care how far away it is from the last one, the pigs are gonna turn it into— Fuck, I were gonna say, into the Ned Kelly gang all over again. We don't wanna be too hasty. That's all I'm sayin'. Just leave it for a while. At least till I get this fuckin' pot leg off, cos I'm not goin' through removin' and replacin' this fuckin' thing again, an' I'm tellin' *you*. I mean, come on, Denny. Is that too much to ask?' He turned to Stan. 'Is it, Stan?'

Stan knew Kelly was being reasonable, but he trusted Denny. Not so much trusted him as instinctively followed him. He'd known Denny a long time; not as long Kelly for sure, but he saw something of himself in Denny that he no longer observed in Kelly. Denny hadn't let himself be drawn into taking life too seriously. All this relationship shit that Kelly was into with Bea, playing happy families with other blokes' kids – it had skewed his vision, made him go soft. Kelly might be happy scrabbling round for pocket money selling bits of dope and speed to fucking students, like his missus's lapdog. But Denny and him wanted something better. Something bigger. As for Poz – well, Poz was basically spineless, but so much so that Stan was certain he could be led into anything as long as there was the promise of some drugs to put into his system at the end of it. But despite all that, Stan did recognise that Kelly was being reasonable. It *was* sensible to keep their heads down for a bit. And now Denny and he were both trying to win his backing. Maybe it was best if he just kept his mouth shut.

'Is it too much to ask?' Kelly persisted.

'Maybe not,' Stan caught himself murmuring. Shit, why did he have to say that?

'Is that all you can fuckin' say?' said Denny.

'Well, all I'm sayin' is, we could put this on hold, couldn't we? Do it when t'fuckin' heat's died down a bit. Leave it a couple a weeks or summat.'

Denny fixed a stare on the kitchen floor linoleum and let out a long philosophical sigh.

'Stan. Lads.' Denny wasn't so stupid as to not see as much as Kelly did that this one needed reasoning out. He forced his voice to become reasonable now. 'When I say it's a fuckin' sitter, what I mean is, it's a fuckin' sitter now. Do you see what I'm sayin'? *A'* – he poked a finger up for the first point in his argument – 'it's the right time of the month, if you'll pardon the expression. We're talkin' big fuckin' wads. Maybe four, five grand.'

'You said—'

'I meant, four, maybe five grand. Four minimum. Maybe more than five even. Secondly,' – he held up two fingers – 'we're ready now. We're psyched up for it. Can't yer feel that? Cos I can. We've done one, it were a piece a fuckin' piss, an' we should strike again while the iron's in the fuckin' fire. D'you know what I'm sayin'? I fuckin' know *you* do, Kelly, so don't tell me any otherwise. You're skint as the rest of us. Stan might think yer livin' in the lap a Bea's luxury but I know yer not.'

Kelly looked down at his pot leg for a minute while the others watched him doing it.

'Denny. We're talkin' about a fuckin' Post Office robbery. We're talkin' about a fuckin' Post Office robbery. Have you heard yerself? Yeah, yer right, we have just done it once, but I for one thought that were gonna be a one-off to pay us fuckin' debts off. An' now you're talkin' about doin' a fuckin' Post Office robbery out in t' middle a fuckin' nowhere.'

'I'm tellin' yer, Kel, it's a—'

'Hold on. Hold yer fuckin' horses for a minute there, fuckin' Tonto. You are right when you happen to point out that we've just fuckin' done one job, but to be quite fuckin' honest, I still need some more time to fuckin' chill after that one before I fuckin' go takin' an even bigger more stupid one on. An' have you asked fuckin' Stan an' Poz how they feel about it?'

'Well like I said,' said Stan, 'it's a fuckin' sound idea, don't get me wrong, Denny, but... maybe we ought to give it a week or two. Kelly's right, us fuckin' nerves're still on edge—'

'All right, all right,' said Denny, throwing his hands up, 'I've heard enough, yer fuckin' woman. Yer can stop yer cluckin'.'

Stan went all crestfallen. Meanwhile, Poz spoke up, bringing the conversation from specifics back to general angst, as usual.

50

'Lads, I'd say we need to talk about Big Baz. Stan's right, we can think about this Post Office thing later. More to the point is that Baz is gonna find out one way or another eventually that it were us who fuckin' paggered his sister's kid, an' he's not gonna let it go. Basically, once he does, we're all fuckin' goners.'

'Hang on, hang on,' said Denny. 'How's he gonna find out? Nob'dy else knows about it 'cept for us four in this room. Do they?' He looked back pointedly at Poz. 'I haven't said a fuckin' dickie bird to anyone.'

'Well don't look at me,' said Stan. 'Only person I've talked to about it is you lot.'

'Well I've said nowt either,' said Kelly, 'an' I suggest we fuckin' keep it that way.'

'Anyway, why are we worryin' about Baz?' said Denny. 'He's not fuckin' God is he? He's not fuckin' invincible. When it boils down to it, he's just some big ugly cunt who looks like he's breakin' teeth in for a Blackpool donkey.'

'That particular donkey can give you a nasty fuckin' bite,' said Kelly. 'An' don't forget his connections either. There is a reason why he can afford to drive round in a new BMW, you know. You musta seen some a t'dodgy characters he hangs around with. He fuckin' plays with the big boys, does Baz. Guys with fuckin' big farms back in Jamaica, you know what I mean? An' big guns tucked into their fuckin' big quilted jackets. They've got a lot to protect, he must be a good fuckin' customer a theirs, must Baz, an' if we go fuckin' with their business associates then we'd be slidin' us-selves into a fuckin' big tub a deep fuckin' shit.'

'Jamaica?' said Denny. 'What yer givin' it? He can't fuckin' stand darkies, can't Baz.'

'It's one thing not bein' able to stand 'em an' it's another thing not wantin' to do business with 'em if they've got what you happen to want. That's what I'm sayin'. He might look like a fuckin' Neanderthal, but he's not stupid, is Baz. Not when it comes down to doin' business an' influencin' the right people. Take it from me. I've seen what he's like.'

'I still say he's not too fuckin' big to be taken on if need be,' said Denny. 'An' if I ever meet *any* cunt who is, I'll suck all yer fuckin' knobs for yer.'

'Denny,' said Kelly, 'you don't take Baz *on*, you have to take him *down*, cos any other way, you're gonna lose. And you won't mind if I don't hold you to that promise, by the way? Now where's the gun?'

'You what?'

'The gun from the robbery? Did you get rid of it?'

Denny looked at Poz, who tried to look nonchalant.

'No. But it's safe.'

'Where?'

'Does it matter? Is that really somethin' you want to get yourself concerned with?'

'Have you got it here with you?'

'What? Do you think I'm stupid? Carryin' a fuckin' gun around? What is it, do you think I'm gonna take a pop at Baz with it? Is that what yer worried about? Kelly. I'm not fuckin' stupid. I'm not takin' any chances a goin' down for murder, not even for Baz. I've still never been to Ibiza, I'm not ready to be locked up yet.'

'Point is,' said Poz, 'what are we actually gonna do about it?'

'Well what do you suggest?' Kelly asked Poz.

'I dunno, do I? All I fuckin' hope is that he doesn't fuckin' find out, an' that things fuckin' cool off for a bit.'

'Well, there you are,' Kelly declared. 'There's your fuckin' answer. As I've been sayin' all along. Hold yer horses. Hold yer fuckin' fire. Take it easy. Chill out. All we've gotta do is keep us traps shut an' act like nothing's happened, pretend it's none of our business. After a few weeks, Baz'll lose interest in it. It's only his fuckin' nephew, for Chrissake, to a sister he hardly ever keeps in touch with. An' it's not like we fuckin' killed him. He's gonna be fuckin' sound as a pound. So where's the big fuss? Where's the big fuckin' deal? Kid comes out of hospital – in fact, he's fuckin' out alfuckinready – he gets better, he fucks off to college or whatever. It's part of his fuckin' past, you know what I'm sayin'? Part of life's rich tapestry. It's summat he'll laugh about with his mates at a party. An' Baz – given time – is gonna fuckin' forget a-a-l-ll about it. Like I said, he's got a business to run— Hang on, let me finish what I'm sayin'. An' when it's all forgotten, then we can start thinkin' about... where is it?' he said, looking at Denny.

'Burton Leonard,' Denny said, who had tried to interrupt.

'Burton fuckin' Leonard,' said Kelly. 'Never fuckin' heard of it. Where do you come up with these weird ideas from?'

'But what about Baz?' said Poz.

'Poz,' said Kelly and Denny together, 'shut up.'

10. Two Es And An LSD

WHEN KELLY got home, Damien was outside playing football with his mates under the streetlights. He ignored Kelly when he said 'All right' but he didn't take it personally: the kid was in the middle of a tackle and he ignored everybody most of the time; even the mates he played football with, apart from 'Go on' and 'Shot', Kelly didn't think he'd ever heard them say a word to one another, even when they'd been scribbling and doodling on his leg. On the rare occasions that you did hear Damien open his mouth, it was invariably in that dreadful mock Mancunian accent. It was a phase he was going through.

The front door wasn't locked, but at least it wasn't ajar like it usually was in the daytime. As he struggled up the doorstep with his crutches, he could see the telly screen flickering through the lace curtains of the bay window and hear the cheesy posturings of manufactured pop music from the front room within. He shouldered the door open, nudged it shut behind him with his arse and craned his head round the front room door.

'What thiyell's that?' he said to Casey. None of her friends turned away from the screen to look at him. Neither did Casey.

'Take That,' she said to the telly. 'It's an old video.'

'It's a summat video. Where are their instruments?'

'What d'you mean?'

'Where are their guitars? Where's the drummer? Where's the band?'

'I dunno. Aw, look at Robbie there.'

The girls chittered themselves into a frenzy for a moment. Kelly waited.

'Is your mam in?'

'Yeah, she's upstairs.'

'Is anybody else in?'

'I dunno. Maybe Paul.'

'Well have you heard anybody else?'

'Kelly! We're tryin' to watch Take That, and you smell of smoke and beer. Why don't you just go upstairs and find out?'

'All right,' said Kelly defensively, 'calm down. Don't take it out on me just cos your group's rubbish.'

He went down the hallway and checked the kitchen. Empty.

He'd become quite proficient at getting up the stairs by hopping
on his good leg while holding on to his crutches with one hand and
the banister rail with the other. As he neared the top step, Nev
appeared on the landing.

'Y'all right there, Hopalong? D'ya want an 'and?'

'Don't you start with that 'Opalong shit. An' leave Ned Kelly out
of it an' all.'

'What you in a bad mood for?'

'I'm not.'

'Well don't take it out on me, ya cunt.'

In no more illumination than candle glow and the fallout from the
telly, the interior of the bedroom appeared at first only as a
burnished haze of smoke after the 60-watt brightness of the
landing light. Smoke that was musky with the scent of heroin. As
he and Nev moved inside and out of the door frame, the extra light
cast into the room revealed human figures slumping at the edge of
the mattress, with Bea cross-legged in the middle of it.

'Shut door,' said Bea. 'Keep smell in from t'kids.'

'I were just off for a piss,' said Nev.

'Well what ya comin' back in for if you an't been?'

'Yeah. Right.' Nev shut the door behind him as he went for his
momentarily blind-spotted piss, and the bedroom descended back
into murk while Kelly's eyes got used to the meagre light.

'Y'all right, Mercy?' he said to one of the near-dormant figures
as it resolved itself out of the flame-wobbly gloom, identified by
its long greasy-looking hair and pigeon-chested torso shape rising
and falling on the cusp of slumber.

'Y'all right,' replied a sleepy voice.

Kelly hadn't seen Mercy for ages. 'How d'you spell Leeds?' It
was an old joke that had become a ritual greeting between them.

'Two Es an' an LSD,' Mercy's voice droned back somnolently.

'That's fuckin' crap,' said another voice from across the room,
which Kelly recognised as Carol's – or was it Vicky's? He always
got them two mixed up. Throat gritted, over the years, by a
zeppelinful of smoke and a liner of booze and no doubt the odd
blow job or two, she sounded like Bonny Tyler after lighting the
first fag the morning after a full-on bender.'That's a fuckin' old
joke, is that.'

'Fuckinell,' said Kelly, 'didn't see ya there. Me eyes are just gettin' adjusted.' The presence of Mercy and Carol/Vicky explained the smell. Chasing the dragon – that's what they liked to do most. When they weren't injecting it. His gaze lit on the plastic drinking straws and tin foil laid out on the bed between Bea's loosely crossed legs. Then the paraphernalia de-energised in a corona of light as Nev came back into the room, and for a moment after he shut the door and settled himself in his favourite spot on the carpet like a household pet, murk redescended.

'Not been diggin' it then?' Kelly said, nodding towards the gear on the bed.

'Too fuckin' wasted to go downstairs an' get some barrels,' Mercy slurred, sucking like the Elephant Man to stop himself from dribbling on the mattress.

'An' I'm not goin' for 'em,' said Bea, 'I don't dig it, I only chase it. Where you been anyway?' She didn't say it accusingly, just conversationally, which to Kelly was always a bit suspicious. With Bea, there was always an angle to every remark, usually a sharp one. If she said something that sounded neutral, Postman Pat conversational, or polite (unless it was sarcasm) then he knew there must be a subtext. Most of the time, that's what he loved about her, her sharpness, her quick mind. But when she employed this levelness of tone that he could tell she was affecting now, he recognised it as a signal of innocence undeserved. Did she know he disapproved of her going near smack? Of course she knew, who was he kidding? But then again, who was he to tell her what or what not to do? He'd just committed an armed robbery, for Christ's sake, and now he was letting his fucking friends try to talk him into another one.

'Listen, Bea, can I have a word with you a minute downstairs?'

'I just told you I'm not goin' downstairs. I'm watchin' this.'

There was a movie on the screen, *Terminator 2*, but the volume was muted and there was music playing low from the battery-operated ghetto blaster next to Bea's side of the bed.

'Hey, Kelly,' said Nev. 'They say telly's a drug, right? Well, in that case – look, I'm on telly. D'you gerrit? I'm watchin' telly, an' telly's a drug, so I'm *on* telly.'

'Yeah, Nev, we're all on telly. Look, Bea, it'll just take a minute. It's important.'

56

'Aw, Kelly! I've just got flamin' settled.'

'That's a lie,' croaked Carol/Vicky through the smoke of a Regal bubbling from her lips. 'She's been on that mattress for a good hour an' half, at least. I'm surprised she an't 'ad to go for a piss.'

'Did ya know t'fuckin' 'andle's bust on t'cistern?' said Nev.

'Shut up,' said Kelly, 'we're fixin' it. Bea. It's important.'

'Oh, fuckinell. As long as we don't have to disturb Casey an' 'er mates. Where's our Damien? Is he still outside?'

'Still lakin' at football.'

'Come on, then, if it's that urgent.' She started to rise from the mattress.

'Hey, Kelly,' said Nev. 'D'you want us to come with yer?' Kelly just looked daggers at him. 'It's a joke. I'm jokin'.'

'Yeah.' Kelly nodded at the screen. 'Hey, an' look, Nev, you're on telly.'

They all laughed when the silly cunt looked.

The kitchen was still quiet and empty, thank Christ. Kelly sat himself down at the table and lifted his leg up on a chair. Bea stood waiting.

'Listen, love, I want ya to look after some money for me.'

Bea uncrossed her arms.

'How much money?'

'Well – I don't just want yer to look after it, I meant I want yer to do summat with it. So that I can get a little bit a return on it.'

'What, you want me to put it on an 'orse?'

'What I mean is, you're good at business. You keep this family together. You make sure everybody gets by. An' it's not just off yer fuckin' social, we all know that.'

'Well what ya sayin'?'

'I thought— I were just thinkin'. If you could invest it in some gear, an' mebbe I could help shift it for yer an' take my cut a the profits...'

'Well why don't ya just do it yerself? What am I, yer bleedin' skivvy?'

'That's what I'm sayin' though, innit? I'll fuckin' sell it. All you have to do is manage it for us. Buy it – I'll help you weigh it out an' that, obviously.'

'Oh no,' said Bea.

'What d'ya me—'

'How much we talkin'?'

Kelly paused to think. It was all getting a bit too rapidfire for his taste.

'Four hundred.'

'Kelly!' said Bea, suddenly whispering. 'Four hundred? Where'd that come from?'

'Come on, Bea. You said you wouldn't ask any questions.'

'No. You wanted me to ask no questions. There's a difference.'

'Yeah, well I still want you to. Look, I promise, one day I'll tell you all about it. But not today, all right? Not tonight. Look, it's four hundred quid. It's no big deal. You handed five hundred over to Baz yesterday.'

Bea thought for a moment. She paced up and down a bit. She scowled to herself. Finally, she turned the scowl on Kelly. The end of her pointing finger, from his perspective, was like a bullet between her eyebrows.

'You'd better not bring the fuckin' police round to this house.'

Her tone nailed him to the chair.

'Do you hear me?'

'I swear, Bea—'

'I've heard your swearin', an' it's not that kind. An' I still meant what I said when I said oh no.'

'Oh no, what?'

'I'm not havin' you sellin' it. If you want to put four hundred quid into my business, then, yeah, I'll give you your profit, for what it'll be worth. But I don't want you sellin' it. Cos you know what you're like, Kelly. You wouldn't sell it. Oh, you might sell some of it – maybe thirty, forty percent. But that's no use.'

'Hang on a minute. You sell it and you use it.'

'Yeah. But like you said, Kelly, I'm good at business. You're not. So that's the deal. Take it or leave it.'

'Yer right,' said Kelly. 'I'd just end up doin' it in meself. But will ya do me a favour?'

'Depends what it is.'

'Whatever I make on that four hundred, don't let me have it. Put it straight back into the business.'

'Are you serious about this?'

'Yeah – I am,' said Kelly. 'I've never been more serious in me life.'

58

Bea didn't say anything else, but as she turned to leave the kitchen, she was smiling.

11. Eddie Whatsit

THE FOLLOWING MORNING, Kelly got an early phone call from Denny. Ten-thirty, for fuck's sake: that was well out of order. The house was quiet, probably empty, the kids at school and Bea out doing her community service. Paul might be in upstairs, that was all. Kept himself to himself; wise young man. It was that quiet, Kelly was lucky to wake up at the sound of the phone ringing, even though they had an extension in the bedroom. He was used to sleeping fitfully through noise, but when it was this quiet, it was REM time. He was still groggy when he picked up the receiver and croaked 'Yo.'

'There's summat I need to tell ya. Found out last night.'

'What?'

'Can ya come round?'

'Fuckinell, Denny, it's a bit early, innit?'

'Just get yersen round 'ere, mate, it's important.'

'It's about that job,' said Denny, after Kelly had bussed it over to his place in Woodhouse.

'The Post Office job?'

'No. The last one. East End Park.'

'What about it?'

'You know I told yer it were Eddie Whatsit who told us about it?'

'What, is he out?'

'No. Listen; don't go doin' a fuckin' *EastEnders* on me.'

'What the fuck you on about?'

'Jumpin' the fuckin' gun. I'm tryin' to tell yer summat 'ere if yer'd only listen.'

'All right, all right. Go on then, I'm listenin'.'

'Eddie Whatsit tipped me off about the petrol station while he were out of Armley for his son's funeral.'

'Yeah. You told us.'

'Moz. That were Eddie's kid's name. Did ya know him?'

'Seen 'im around. Got hit by a bus, din't he? Sniffing glue. Least, that's what I heard.'

'Did ya know he were a runner for Baz?'

'I mighta done. To be honest, I don't really know. I din't know him that well.'

'Neither did I.'

'So what's he got to do with owt?'

'Yer not gettin' the picture, are ya?'

'No, I'm not, so yer'd better 'elp me out.'

'Don't yer think it's a bit of a coincidence that Eddie set us up to rob a petrol station where Big Baz's nephew happens to work?'

'Are you sayin' it's more than just a coincidence?'

Denny didn't say anything for a moment, apparently contemplating Kelly's question.

'I spoke to a mate a mine last night,' Denny said at last. 'He happened to mention something he'd heard about Eddie's kid and how he died. Apparently, there's a rumour going round that it were Baz who pushed him under that bus on purpose.'

Now it was Kelly's turn to remain silent while he took this in.

'That dun't make sense. Why would Baz want to push him under a bus if he was working for Baz in the first place?'

'Because Moz, from what I heard, had ripped off some drugs he were supposed to be deliverin' for Baz. Kilo a smack apparently. Silly little sod only went and sold it to a couple a students for pin money by all accounts.'

'By your mate's account, yer mean.'

'Same thing, innit?'

'Hang on,' said Kelly. 'So you're tellin' me that Baz is a killer? A murderer?'

'I'm just tellin' you what I've heard, that's all.' He paused to gauge Kelly's reaction. 'Think about it. Baz kills Eddie Whatsit's kid for gettin' cheeky with his commodity. Eddie gets wind of it in the nick and figures out a way to take some small measure a revenge at least on Baz's nephew by gettin' us to do over the place where he's workin'. Baz's nephew gets hospitalised in the process. It's not exactly an eye for an eye, but it's gettin' there, don't ya think?'

'This friend a yours,' said Kelly after a while, 'where did he get hold of all this?'

'He didn't say. Loose lips an' all that, presumably. To be honest, though, it dun't really matter where it came from. It still freaks me out.'

'I know Baz is a nutter, but I've never heard of him actually toppin' anybody. Yeah, sure, he'll put you in hospital as soon as look at ya, but murder? That seems a bit out a Baz's league to me.'

'I'm just tellin' you what I heard, that's all,' Denny repeated. Kelly let the information turn over in his mind for another moment.

'Nah. I honestly can't see Baz as a murderer.' Even as he was saying it, a picture formed in his mind of Baz pushing the kid under the bus, and it was all too plausible. If the kid had been glued up, it would be an easy thing for someone like Baz to do. He'd barely have to think about it: just a little shove then walk away like he had nothing to do with it. He was forced to make an effort to dismiss the thought from his inner vision. 'Nah. Like you said, coincidence or what? I reckon it's a case of coincidence.'

Denny said nothing else on the subject, but Kelly could see that he wasn't convinced.

Furthermore, Denny could see Kelly wasn't a hundred per cent convinced either.

12. Madhouse

BEA'S PLACE was a flaming madhouse. She knew it. OK, she might accuse Kelly of always moaning about it, like she had done just the other day when he'd been getting people to write on his second pot leg. (What *was* that all about? It had to be connected to the four hundred quid he'd given her. In a way, she wished he'd tell her, but in another way, she was glad he didn't.) But she knew it was a flaming madhouse too, and she would be the first to admit it. The place was a complete lunatic asylum. And not just some of the time but all of the time.

The thing was, she knew that was the way Kelly saw it, and half the time he couldn't take it, even though most of the people round there were his fucking friends. OK, be fair, most of them were people she knew as well, some of them since Adam was a lad (or did it just feel that long?), and certainly since a long time before she'd started seeing Kelly, some of them. And yeah, most of them were people she liked, kind of, people who were kind of friends of hers as much as they were friends of Kelly's, and in some cases more so. But face it too, she had been living in that house, bringing her kids up there, for nigh on sixteen years now – girl and woman, you might say – but the pitch of madness had only tuned up to its present levels over the past few years, i.e. since Kelly had come on the scene. Yes, it was a madhouse, but he encouraged it. He was a major reason it was like that. He'd moved in and his entourage – like Denny, Nev and Clint, God rest his soul – had followed. Furthermore, though it hadn't been his doing intentionally, his male presence in the house had usurped a lot of her male friends. Nowadays, it was her they came to see to buy drugs, but it was him that they sat and consumed them with. Problem was, Kelly knew all that, and she knew he knew it. Moreover, he totally acknowledged his own part in it. But it was just getting silly and he couldn't take it any more. It was driving him more and more out of the house, away from the constant bedlam of kids, cronies and customers. It was sending him into a secret other life that he rarely told her about and that forced him to wear a bogus pot leg as an alibi for who knew what?

To be fair, it wasn't all him. OK, a lot of the people who came round and hung out there all the time were mates of his, but it'd be just being rotten to put all the blame on him by claiming they weren't her mates as well. And let's face it, she was the one doing most of the business. She was the one peddling speed to keep it all together (...*and if they catch me again it won't just be community service next time either*). She was the one encouraging all the custom she could get in order to keep the cash rolling in. (Hey, but they all needed it – Kelly, the kids, the lot of 'em – she was the provider in this house, and she was the one with the business sense and the restraint not to let all that cash rolling in roll right out again in one big speedball, like most other users would have done.) Through Kelly's eyes, though, she was sure he saw her as the one putting out the welcome mat to all and sundry. If, in the process, some dodgy bastard like Nev decided to rip off half her CD collection to go and flog it to one of the local secondhand shops in order to buy a wrap of the brown stuff, or Big Baz decided to give some poor cunt a good twatting in her kitchen for being a bit too lippy, or someone fell over in a drunken stupor and pulled the gas fire off the wall, Kelly always played the It's-Your-House card, and left it up to her to lay down the riot act. Except it was a hard thing to do. It didn't matter how much she knew it was the right and proper thing to do (it *was* her house, the deeds in her name alone, the mortgage paid off in just one more year), she was essentially a softy and she invariably let them off. Oh, she made damn sure they got a good   bollocking – even Big Baz wasn't exempt if he stepped out of line and she judged it right. But she continued to let them back in, again and again, time after time. At the end of the day, she guessed, it wasn't just her house, it was her place of business. She had to keep playing the charming hostess: she needed the suppliers and she needed the buyers.

And to be fair on herself, it wasn't all her own fault either. She had four kids living in the house (... *and don't get me wrong, I fuckin' love my kids, I'd do anything for 'em*), and all but one of them had moved into their teenage phase over the past five years, and that had only served to intensify the madness of the madhouse they all lived in together. (OK, she knew that Paul was looking for work, and he wasn't around that much, or when he was, he kept himself locked away in his room, and he wanted to get his own place and strike out on his own.) So aside from everybody else – hers and Kelly's mates – they had all the kids' friends to contend with as well, and even though some of them were nice kids right enough, she knew she couldn't trust any of them not to do the same kind of things that Nev or Big Baz or anybody else might do. Robbing and fencing, getting off their heads and smashing the place up in the process: they were only kids, weren't they? Impressionable. Monkey see, monkey do and all that. They all had a life to live too, and a right to live it, and if they were living at least some of it here under her roof, it was bound to add to the general madness of the place. What were you going to do? Pull in the welcome mat, close the place up, barricade the ramparts, reject all visitors? It might be a flaming madhouse but it was still a house, not a flaming mausoleum.

But she understood when sometimes the madness got too much for Kelly and he had to get out. It was his way of dealing with it. If he didn't, she was convinced they wouldn't have stayed together. Not that it was all 24-seven sweetness and light – whose relationship ever was? But they'd have been at each other's throats a lot more often than they actually were, and it would have been going on from a much longer way back. In fact, if he hadn't got himself out and about doing his own thing, it would have been a fucking miracle if both of them were still living and breathing.

But Bea felt it too, the pressure of the madhouse, and she had to get away from it as well sometimes, for the sake of her sanity.

That was why she felt so cheered up the second afternoon of the half-term holiday when the sun was shining and Baz was round just dropping off a shipment and they got nattering and he suggested going down the Royal Park for a pint in the beer garden.

A couple of regulars popped round to score because they knew she was getting some in and they'd been gagging for it all morning, but they didn't hang around, took off again sharpish. She noticed that with a lot of the newer, younger studenty-type faces that occasionally drifted in and out but rarely dipped into the scene for more than a year or two: if Baz was around they rarely wanted to stick around as well. She didn't really know if they knew who Big Baz was – i.e. the main man who put it up their noses or into their arms for them – but either way, he was an intimidating bastard at the best of times, to even the best of his friends, and she couldn't blame them wanting to get the hell out of his way. Last thing you wanted when you were gasping for a dig was some six-foot-plus, 17-stone nutter getting in your face and on your case. And what had all that been about when Baz had asked them what they were called and if they knew anybody called Michael and Simon? She swore he was losing it.

Baz gave himself a dig (she made him do it upstairs in their bedroom, cooking the spoon over a little blue calor-gas camping stove that Kelly sometimes used for hot knives when the kitchen was crowded with neighbours' kids), and she snorted a line because she was thinking about giving up digging it, and then they were both ready for the offski.

She poked her head into the front room from the hallway.

'Casey, love.' Casey was with her mates, sat in a circle on the carpet round some game or something. Boyzone was on the telly as background music. No, it wasn't Boyzone, was it? It was Westlife. Oh God, she could even tell the difference herself now.

'Listen, I'm just off to the pub with Baz for an hour, all right? Listen, Paul's upstairs int' attic room. He's on his computer, but if you need him for owt, just give him a shout, all right? Our Damien's out in t'front yard an' all, OK?'

'Where's Nita?'

'I've no idea, she's off somewhere.'

'Is Kelly in?'

'No.'

'Is anybody else in?'

'No, just you lot an' Paul, an' Damien's out front. He's got this front door open, so if he buggers off somewhere, make sure it's shut, won't you, or keep an eye on it?'

'Which pub are you going to?'

'Royal Park. If anybody comes round, tell 'em I'm in t'Royally, all right, love?'

'All right, Mam.'

'See you later, girls. There's some pop in t'fridge if you want a drink.'

'Are ya takin' yer phone?' Baz asked her from the kitchen doorway. Her mobile was still on the dining table.

'I weren't gonna, but I suppose I'd better, hadn't I? Otherwise, they're only gonna ring here an' one a t'kids'll have to answer it. An' that'll be poor little Casey, if Damien's got owt to do with it.'

66

It was a gorgeous day and it was only a ten-minute walk to the pub, but Baz took the BMW anyway. There was a lot of pretentious shit that somebody like Baz would never give a fuck about, but he did like to travel in style. He flipped open the sun roof and stuck some music on. Sounded like what Damien called happy hardcore. Total adrenalin music. It was weird, some of the shit Baz was into. Damien, yes – he was fifteen (though happy hardcore was definitely out – God knew what was in now). But Baz? He was her age. Watching him banging his head to it behind the wheel, she wondered where he got the energy from. Then she remembered, of course: from putting a needle in his arm.

Of course, once they got down the pub, Bea realised that getting away from the madhouse was one thing but getting away from the lunatics that normally inhabited it was another. Nev's dodgy crowd was in – Football Terry (as distinguished from Welsh Terry) and his girlfiend, Carla, with the crop top and the tattoo of a spider's web around her navel, and Doofer with his mate with the dreads whose name she could never remember. They were all round one of the pool tables shooting pool. The sun was streaming in through the big window behind them and, caught in the rays, their cues glowed like *Star Wars* light-sabres.

'Seen owt a Nev?' they asked her while Baz was getting in two pints of Lowenbrau at the bar. On the jukebox, a woman's voice was whispering 'Till I come' over a backbeat and a twiddly guitar line.

'Only last night, when he was off his head.' They laughed at that, as if it were unusual for Nev to be off his head, as if he weren't permanently off his head. Maybe they realised that she meant pissed, not just on the brown stuff. Nev liked a drink as much as anybody else, but any cash he ever got hold of was earmarked to go in his veins before it would go down his neck. If he was pissed last night, it was because he'd had a windfall.

'He had a good day yesterday, didn't he?' said Carla, looking at Terry for confirmation.

'Apparently, Mercy convinced him to put a fiver on a gee-gee, an' it romped home.'

'What? Nev puttin' money on 'orse race instead of in his arm? That must be a bleedin' first.'

'You know what Mercy's like with the neddies, though. He knows how to pick 'em. If he gives you a tip like that, it must be because he owes you a favour.'

'Or money, more like,' said Bea. 'Still, I suppose it's one way a payin' back yer debts, innit?'

Lori, one of her neighbours, was outside in the beer garden, doing the same thing as her – getting away from the kids for a well-earned half-term afternoon off. She was with Todd, one of her husband's mates. He lived with his girlfriend, Trish, further up the hill near the allotments, but Bea was sure there was something going on between him and Lori. If there was, they certainly weren't doing much to keep it a secret. Lori's kids were just about the only people in the street who didn't speculate about it, and that included her husband. They wanted to be careful, because it could turn nasty. She paused for a quick friendly word with them then went and joined Baz at an empty table for a sit down and a drink. The hot sun and the whizz and all that talking had left her parched. When she put the pint glass down from the first swig, it was half empty. Baz's was nearly down to the bottom.

'How's Kelly's leg doin'?' Baz asked out of the blue.

'Oh, it's doin' all right.' She tried to think what to say next. Was that why Baz had brought her here? To talk about Kelly's leg? 'They say that pot should be comin' off in a few weeks.' Shit. Why did she have to go and mention the pot?

'What did he do to it again?'

'Didn't he tell yer? He were helpin' do summat to some roof tiles or summat an' he fell off a ladder.' She deliberately avoided stating who he was helping or what he was helping to do with the roof tiles.

'Prob'ly nickin' 'em, if they were worth owt,' said Baz, and added, 'Silly cunt.'

If it had been anybody else saying that she'd have been straight in: 'Eh that's *my* bloke you're callin' a silly cunt, if you don't mind.' But she knew that, with Baz, it didn't actually mean anything. That was just something he said about everyone, from his mother to his children, if he knew who and where they were. At least the finality of the comment created enough of a pause for her to change the subject.

'Have you heard any more about your nephew, that lad who got beat up? Is he all right?'

'Yeah, he's gettin' over it, I think. I popped round to see 'em last night. Still got a few lumps an' bruises, but he's actually a tough little cunt after all. I 'alf expected him to be sittin' around mopin', but he were gettin' ready for a night on' tiles. I think he's takin' advantage of all t'sympathy he's gettin' while it lasts.'

'Aw, that's nice,' said Bea, and took a sip of Lowenbrau – just a smallish one this time: she didn't want Baz playing catch-up or stay-ahead when he had to drive. The big lump probably wouldn't even feel it anyway if he had a crash, but there were sometimes other people who got hurt as well - *and* he was the best supplier she had. Baz might be a nutter but he had a reputation for reliability: if he told you he was going to deliver fifty grammes on Tuesday afternoon, you knew you could start taking orders Tuesday morning that would be honoured by teatime, before the kids got in from school. Not like some of the other dodgy bastards she'd be forced to try and do business with if he wasn't around. He always went on about how pure stuff was, which she took with a pinch of salt as a dealer's sales blather, but he'd never sold her duff gear and he'd never tried to rip her off, or even asked for money up front. COD every time, which was the way she liked to keep it. She couldn't be doing arsing around with stupid twats full of promises which took long stress-filled days to come to fruition, *if* they hadn't done a runner with a bundle of your cash, or drugs, or both. No, he may be a nutter but he was all right, was Baz. Either deep down or on the surface – she wasn't really sure which, but one way or the other – he was all right. At least, with her.

'I'd still love to get me hands on whoever did it, though,' said Baz.

'Have you not heard owt, then?' said Bea.

'Not a fuckin' dickie bird. No cunt seems to know owt about it. Stuart reckons he heard one of 'em call one a t'others Danny.'

'Who's Stuart?' said Bea.

'Me sister's lad. One thing's for sure – some'dy did it, an' I'll find out who, eventually. I don't let things like that go, me. You know what I'm like – I don't have to spell it out to you.'

That was true; she did know what he was like. Oh, Baz could be as full of claptrap as the next bloke when it came to puffing his chest out and putting on a macho act for all to admire. Like all blokes, he loved to talk big, and like all blokes, the lion's share of it was just blather. All that crap the other day about twatting a copper. If Baz had twatted a copper, he wouldn't be sitting here having a drink with her right now, he'd be locked up in Weetwood, of that she had no doubt. But it was the stuff he didn't talk about that mattered, the stuff that he didn't have to spell out, as he himself put it. Bea had known Baz for a long time and, if there was one thing above all that she had learnt about him over the years, it was precisely that, unlike most blokes, he wasn't just all talk.

Baz swigged down the last of his pint and said, 'You ready for another?'

'Aye, go on, I'll have another Lowie.'

It was her round and she gave him the money for it. While she was waiting for him to return from the bar, her phone went. It was Kelly.

'Where are yer?' she said.

'I'm round at Denny's,' he said.

'What yer doin' round there?' It was an innocent question.

'We're just sortin' out a bit a business. Anyway, never mind about that. Where are you?'

'I'm sat outside Royally, havin' a pint with Baz.'

'Is he there now?'

'No, he's gone to t'bar. Why, what's up?'

'Nowt. What's he been sayin' to yer?'

'He hasn't been sayin' owt to me. Why? What's got you so paranoid all of a sudden?'

'Who's paranoid?' said Baz. He was standing over her with the two lagers in his enormous fists.

Bea held up a hand, signalling him to hang on.

'No,' she said into the phone. 'Why?' Pause. 'All right.' Longer pause. 'Yeah, all right.' Another short pause. Then the tetchy voice: 'Yeah, yeah, I *said* all right, didn't I?' Conversational voice back now: 'Well, if you get back before me, put some tea on for our Casey an' Damien, will yer?' Pause. 'Well use yer flamin' imagination. There's some fish fingers in t'freezer an' there's beans in t'cupboard. Yeah.' Short pause. 'Use them crinkle-cut chips, then, cos they need usin' up.' Pause. 'In t'freezer, where

70

d'yer think?' Pause. 'Yeah, well I won't be long. I'll prob'ly be home before you, anyway. All right. See you when I see you then.' She pressed the OFF button.

'What were all that about?' said Baz.

'Aw, just Kelly goin' on about nowt nor summat. He'll have been hot-knifin' it all afternoon.' She picked up her pint. 'Cheers, Baz.'

For the first time, Bea was starting to get the feeling that there was something not right going on. It was itching at the back of her mind as she took the first mouthful from the new pint, and over the next five minutes, while they pretended to talk about nothing, it began to worm its way to the front. Kelly had been weird on the phone about her being here with Baz, and she knew it wasn't jealousy but something else that he wouldn't or couldn't explain over the phone. What was more, Baz too seemed a bit funny all of a sudden. Not subtle or cryptic, he wasn't that clever, and not devious either: Baz wasn't too strong in that department either, which was why he resorted to using his fists instead. But the way he'd pounced on that word *paranoid*: she'd seen a certain look in his eyes. And now, as they burbled on to one another over their beers in the warm afternoon sunshine, she felt more and more conscious of trying not to show that she was worried about something, and the more she tried not to show it, the more she felt that the signals from her must be as evident to Baz as his and Kelly's had been to her.

But how to put it? More to the point how to put it to Baz? In the gaps between their stretches of talk she looked for an opening but could not find a way to broach it, whatever *it* was. *Is there something here I'm missing here?* What would be his answer to that one, other than phoney mystification. *Such as? I don't know – is there? What the fuck are you on about?* That would get her nowhere: it certainly wouldn't produce anything resembling a straight answer. So it had to be a straight question. But what? She couldn't put her finger on it herself. There was something weird going on with Kelly, that was for sure, but what did it have to do with Baz? *Is there something going on with you and Kelly?* Oh yeah, she could imagine Baz's reaction to that one. *You callin' me a poof, yer dirty fuckin' whooer?* No. The best thing was to leave it till she saw Kelly and then ask him about it before she went putting her foot in it for somebody, possibly including herself.

'My round,' said Baz.

'I'm gonna have to get home soon,' Bea said, but Baz wouldn't hear of it yet.

'I thought Kelly were puttin' t'kids' tea on.'

'Well, he might or he might not. Knowin' him, he'll still be gettin' off his head somewhere.'

'How's he manage to get around on that broken leg, anyway?' said Baz.

'He's not a complete invalid, he can still get on an' off a buses, you know. Anyway, are you goin' to t'bar or are you gonna stand there askin' me daft questions all day? Go on, I'll have another pint. But don't forget, you're drivin'.'

'I might just drive it as far as yours an' leave it parked there till later.'

'Aye, as long as you don't mind it used as a goal post.'

'I want to see Kelly about summat anyway. Is he home yet, d'yer think?'

'I don't know, do I?'

'Give him a ring while I go to t'bar. Give him a ring an' see if he's home yet.'

'What do you want to see him about? If it's that urgent, why don't *you* ring him?'

'It's not,' said Baz. 'Go on though, give him a ring.'

'What's wrong with your phone?'

'Nowt, but I'm off to t'bar, aren't I?'

'Oh, well bloody get goin' then. Pint a Lowie. An' get us a bag a crisps, salt an' vinegar.'

Bea didn't know what the fuck was going on but she didn't like it any more. Why the hell had she said she'd come to the pub with him? And what was all this cloak-and-dagger stuff from Kelly about Denny? Sorting out what business? She wouldn't normally ask about Kelly's business, if he wanted her to know he'd tell her, but if this was all something to do with Kelly's bogus broken leg and that four hundred quid, she'd bloody kill him when she got hold of him. At least she didn't know anything about what was behind all that. That was one thing to be thankful for. Still, it might be a good idea to warn Kelly that Baz was asking awkward questions about him. And if Baz was asking awkward questions about somebody, it could easily mean it was the prelude to a warpath. Not only that, now Baz was talking about coming back to hers and leaving his car there. She might never get rid of him.

When she rang home it was Casey who answered and told her he wasn't back. Damn. Why didn't he get a flaming mobile? If only to use till they took it off him for non-payment. Or there must be somebody who'd flog him a dodgy one cheap. She probably had Denny's number at home somewhere, but she was pretty sure she hadn't got it in the phone's memory. She was scrolling through it to check when a voice interrupted her.

'Hiya.'

She looked up.

'All right, Greg, how ya doin'? I an't seen you for ages.' He'd had his hair cut short and smart since she'd last seen him, which must have been months, possibly a year, ago. 'How's it going then?

'Sound, sound. How about you?'

'Yeah, I'm fine.'

'Nice one.'

'Haven't seen you around for a while,' she said.

'Oh, I've been about,' he said. 'Off an' on. Not for much longer though, maybe.'

'Why, where yer goin'?'

'Got a job lined up down south. Well, not definite yet. I've had a preliminary interview an' I'm off down again tomorrow to hopefully sort out the formalities.'

'Fuckinell, sounds serious. What sort a job is it then?'

'Workin' on a building site.'

'Yer jokin'!'

'I know. Mad, innit? Fuckin' two interviews, more or less. For a job heftin' fuckin' hods a bricks up an' down ladders all day.'

'Except, why would you be humpin' hods a bricks down a ladder? I hope you din't say that in the interview.'

They both had a laugh.

'What you want to go down there for anyway?' she asked.

'I don't really, but it's a job, know what I mean? I'm sick a bein' fuckin' skint all the time. Yer can't do anything. You know what I mean? I fancy gettin' a bit a cash together then go off travellin' towards back end a t'summer. Go abroad or something.'

'Have you done it before?'

73

'Workin' on a buildin' site? No.'

'That's gonna be bloody 'ard work, innit? Can you not find owt up here?'

'I dunno. It's not like I've got stacks a qualifications or anything, know what I mean?'

'God, tell me about it. Only regular work I've had recently's been me flamin' community service, an' they don't pay you owt for that.'

Greg took a sip of his pint. It was a while since they'd last seen each other and they'd got to that embarrassing part where neither knew what to say next.

'Sit down,' said Bea suddenly, looking at the sky. 'Do you know Baz?'

'Eh?'

'All right,' said Baz, who was hulking behind Greg, waiting to put the two fresh pints on the table.

'All right,' said Greg. 'I'm off in a minute,' he said. 'I just popped in for a pint cos I'd been to t'bookies. Had a bit of a win earlier.'

'That wasn't through Mercy, was it?'

'Eh?'

'Mercy. Did he give you a tip? I heard he gave Nev a tip an' it romped home for him.'

'Oh right. No.'

'Yer sittin' down mate or what?' said Baz, getting impatient holding the drinks and standing behind this geezer's arse like a complete 'nana.

'Oh, yeah, sorry,' said Greg, 'I'll get out your way.' He moved over so that Baz could get past him with the drinks. 'I were just wonderin' if Kelly's about. I were hoping to score a bit of blow off him if he's got any. I haven't seen him around for weeks, except once, but he were on the bike.'

'Who?' said Baz. 'Kelly? On t'bike?'

Greg shot a glance at Bea that said *Who's this again?*

'Ye-eah,' he said tentatively. He was still talking to Bea. 'He didn't see me, otherwise I'da flagged him down. It was dark an' everything.'

'Kelly?' said Baz. 'On t'bike? When? What day?'

'Can't remember exactly. Few nights ago.'

74

Bea said nothing. She knew she should say something, that now would be an appropriate time, but she didn't know what.

'Where were he?' said Baz.

Greg was starting to look puzzled now.

'Er... I can't remember exactly.'

'Well what can yer fuckin' remember?' Baz cut in viciously.

'I dunno. It was somewhere up on Otley Road. Yeah, that were it. I were walkin' along Otley Road. Maybe it wasn't him. Maybe it was just somebody who looked like him. It were dark, weren't it? Coulda been some'dy with a crash helmet on who looked like Kelly.'

'A few days ago,' said Baz, 'or a week ago?'

'I dunno. Sorry. Like I said it, were dark. Maybe it were somebody else who just looked like him. I take it he's not around then.'

'I don't know where he is at the moment,' said Bea, finding a voice at last. 'But I'll tell him yer lookin' for him if you like.'

'No,' said Greg. 'No, it's all right. There's no urgency. I'll see him when I see him.' He swallowed the rest of his drink and put the glass down on their table. It was so near the edge, it nearly fell off, but he managed an awkard catch before it would have tipped right off and smashed. He put it down gently this time. 'Look, I'd better make a move, right? I'll see you later, Bea.' He nodded cautiously at Baz. 'See you.'

Baz looked at Bea as if to say *What the fuck is going on?*

Bea smiled.

'He's a nice lad, is Greg, but sometimes I think he's got a few marbles missin'. Did you get us some crisps?'

Baz chucked the bag across the table top and scowled down into his pint pot as he got guzzling on his third.

'Get this one down quick, then we'll get off,' he said. 'I'm gonna leave me car outside your gaff where you can keep an eye on it for us. Then I've got some business to sort out. All right?'

'Yeah, sure Baz,' Bea said. She was hardly about to disagree with him.

13. The Undertaker

POZ WAS WASTED. His brains felt like cotton wool spilling out of his ears. And the music, you see – the music is not going in through his ears at all. How could it, man, with all that cotton wool spilling out of them? The music is... what? Seeping in through his pores. And vibing into his bones. And hot-wiring his mind.

Who was it? What was it? He had no idea. Oh yeah, something off *Dance Nation Six*. Something trancey and swirly and hold your hands up in the air and wave them around in front of the DJ box. Except he couldn't hold his hands up in the air. It was all he could manage not to let himself go completely horizontal, but he didn't want to show himself up in front of Carol and her mate – what was her name? Vicky. Couldn't remember the kid's name though. Wasn't even sure whose it was, Vicky's or Carol's. The kid was about six or seven maybe and it was playing with a dismantled air rifle on the coffee table. Where Poz was, sprawled out on the rug, he was in constant danger of being clobbered with a hefty piece of rifle barrel every time the kid started swinging it about, but he was too wasted to move out of the way, and there was nowhere to move to.

'Liam, will yer stop swinging it around. I've fuckin' *told* you about a thousand times now.' The kid kept on swinging.

'Are you havin' another one, Poz?' said Carol. She was arranging lines of powder on a square of silver foil. They'd chased the last dragon about fifteen minutes ago... or was it fifteen hours? Who knew? Who cared?

'Yuh.'

'Y'll have to sit up, then.'

Where did she summon the energy from to get another hit together? Where was he going to get the energy from to sit up for it? He managed to prop himself in a relatively upright sitting position against the arm of a chair and took the foil and the straw and the lighter. As he exhaled the smoke, there was a knock on the door.

'Who the fuck's that?' he said, instinctively fumbling to conceal the paraphernalia. It was weird, because just when he was coming up again and he knew it was going to be *really fucking good* this time, the voice he heard, when Carol opened the door, sent an arctic chill through his bowels and, suddenly, with all the force of concrete hitting concrete, he knew it was going to be really fucking bad.

'All right, Carol love.'

'All right, Baz. Come in.'

'All right, Baz.'

'All right, Poz. All right, Vicky love.'

'All right, Baz.'

Liam looked up and said, 'All right, Baz.'

'Eh, you,' said Vicky. 'You play with yer gun.'

'What you watchin'?' said Baz, looking at the TV – on with the volume killed.

'WWF. It's on cable.'

'Oh right. Who's that one I like? The Undertaker. That's it. Big scary fucker.'

Poz focused on the pantomime wrestling. He didn't want to look at Baz. Big mistake.

'What's up with you then?' said Baz, giving Poz a friendly kick against the legs.

'I'm fuckin' stoned, man. Wrecked off me tits.'

'You're fuckin' stoned? Where'd *you* get money to get fuckin' stoned from?'

'I 'an't got fuck all, me. It's your gear, innit, Carol?'

'Actually, it in't till she's fuckin' paid me for it, is it Carol?'

Carol pulled a wad of notes out of her purse.

'There you are, chuck. You havin' a tin a beer? Smells like you've had a few already.'

'Been down t'Royally with Bea, 'an't I?' said Baz, moving round the coffee table to sit on the settee at the opposite end to Vicky.

'D'you wanna beer, Poz?' said Carol as she ducked into the kitchen.

'No, I'm all right. I'm floatin'.'

Actually, Poz's thoughts were whizzing more than floating, or at least they were trying to. But all that cotton wool was getting in the way... slowing them down. All he was getting was a picture of the words *I Do Not Fucking Need This*, an orange neon sign screaming into his eyes through the fog in his brain.

'Just heard a weird one down t'pub,' said Baz. 'Some geezer talkin' to Bea. Reckons he saw Kelly on his Triumph last week.'

Carol came out of the kitchen with a tin of Tennent's Super-T and handed it to Baz, who cracked it open and started slurping.

'I thought he had a broken leg,' said Carol.

'So did I,' said Baz. 'Now I'm beginnin' to wonder.'

'What did Bea say about it?' said Vicky.

'Said this geezer were a bit of a dopey cunt, din't she? You wouldn't know owt about it, would ya?' Baz said to Poz.

'About what?'

'What d'yer mean, about what, yer fuckin' little cunt?'

'I mean about *what?*' Poz was trying to shout him down. It was classic drugs reasoning. But Baz was more pissed than drugged up. And Baz was Baz.

'You must know if Kelly's really got a broken leg or not.'

'Why should I know?'

'I'll tell yer what,' said Baz, 'you tell me what you know or I'll come round this table an' kick yer fuckin' rib cage in.'

'Eh, Baz,' said Carol, 'what the fuck is goin' on? There's our Liam here, you know.'

'I know there is, an' that's why I'm tryin' to be fuckin' reasonable with the cunt.'

'All right, he 'an't got a broken leg,' said Poz. 'So what?'

'Liam. Go upstairs to your room for a bit, love.'

'But Mum...'

'Liam. Upstairs. Now.'

Poz watched his last chance walk out of the room with the kid. And there was fuck all he could do about it. *I Do Not Fucking Need This.*

'What is goin' on Baz?' said Carol.

'Why's he got a false pot on his leg?'

'I don't know,' said Poz.

'Why's he got a false pot on his leg? And I won't ask you again.'

'Fuckinell, Baz—'

That was it. In a split second Baz was over the table top with the barrel of the air rifle in his hand. In the commotion, the TV set went over on its back and went dead with a bang.

'BAZ!' It was Carol and Vicky crying out together as Baz hunched over and pummelled Poz's ribs with the length of metal pipe and they tried to pull him off him. His fist round the gun barrel was big and firm as a ham as he used his other hand to keep

Poz's arms pinioned across his own body. Silly stoned cunt just lay there and waited for it coming.

'*All right, all right,*' Poz was screaming, and in a second, it was all over. Baz laid off as suddenly as he'd kicked off, but the pain, to Poz, felt like the blows had gone on for hours.

Baz put the gun barrel back down on the coffee table, which remarkably had survived the ordeal. The agility with which he d gone over it was incredible for a man of his size, not to mention state of inebriation.

'Now calm down!' Carol was shouting. 'Just fuckin' calm down, all right? It's *my* house! It's *my fuckin'* house!'

'Sorry, Carol love, I'll get you a new one,' Baz was saying about the telly. 'I'll sort you out a new one today, all right, love?' He turned back to Poz, who was slumped against the armchair, holding his side. 'An' *you*, yer *bastard...*' He launched a kick at Poz's thigh. It set Carol and Vicky off pawing at him again, but he couldn't leave it without giving the cunt a dead-leg, could he? 'You'd better get up off that *fuckin'* floor an' tell us about this fuckin' broken leg.'

'Baz, I'm tellin yer, man—'

'Baz, let him fuckin' speak, will yer? He's tryin' to tell yer, if y'll let the poor sod talk.'

'Well he'd better fuckin' talk, an' quick.'

'All I fuckin' know is that Kelly put a pot on his leg cos he wanted an alibi for summat.'

'Alibi from who? From t'pigs?'

'I suppose so.'

'Whaddaya mean, *suppose*?'

'I *don't know*. I *truly* don't fuckin' know, Baz.'

'Bollocks.'

'I don't *know* what it was. But I think it mighta been summat he were doin' with Denny.'

'Denny. I *fuckin' thought* as much. It weren't *Danny*, it were fuckin' *Denny*. He's *always* had a fuckin' death wish, has that cunt. Well he's got it comin' to him now.'

'What's he done?' said Carol.

'I'll tell you what he's done,' said Baz. 'In fact, no. *He'll* tell you what they've done.'

'Who?'

'Fuckin' Denny an' Kelly, that's who. Innit,' he said, bending over Poz, 'yer snivellin' little cunt? It were them who did that fuckin' petrol station, wannit? It were them who kicked my fuckin' nephew's head in, wannit?'

'I don't know,' Poz was squeaking in a girlish falsetto.

'Fuckin' sit up,' said Baz, grabbing hold of his scrawny T-shirt.

'What, your Tracy's young 'un?' said Carol. 'No. Not Kelly. Kelly wouldn'ta done that.'

'They fuckin' did do it though, didn't they?'

'It weren't like that,' said Poz.

'You what?' Suddenly the scales were really lifted from Baz's eyes. 'You were fuckin' *there*, weren't yer? You were fuckin' *there* with 'em.'

'I were only t'driver, Baz, I swear. I couldn't even see owt from where I were. I didn't know owt about anybody gettin' hurt till after it were all over.'

Baz picked the rifle barrel up again, quick as a lion-tamer's whip hand, and lashed out. Poz got his guard up in time, but his forearms took a couple of hefty cracks before Carol and Vicky grabbed Baz and managed to bundle him back. After a minute's apologising and remostrating with the girls, the interrogation continued, with Poz nursing his folded arms.

'So he had a gun?'

'You what?' said Poz through angry tears, too concerned with his pains to worry about the risk of more violence ahead from continuing to piss Baz off.

'Who had the gun?' said Baz. 'No – don't bother answerin' that. It were Denny, wannit? Course it were fuckin' Denny.'

Poz didn't want to see Kelly blamed for something Denny had done, and there seemed little point in holding back the truth now. At least he'd kept any mention of Stan out of it so far.

'It's right what Carol sez, Baz. Honest. Kelly wouldn't do owt like that. Not to an innocent kid.'

'Who'd he get this gun off? Eh?'

'I don't know who he got it off. He's had it for ages, man. He bought it off a some dodgy geezer in t'Newlands. Before it got burnt down. That's all I know about it.'

'What sort is it?'

'I dunno,' said Poz. He was a bit calmer now, still whining and snivelling, but quieter, rubbing his arms, trying to be delicate with them. 'I don't know owt about guns.'

'Well fuckin' think,' Baz said through clenched teeth. 'How big is it? What's it look like?'

'I dunno, honest,' Poz repeated in an exasperated tone. 'It's a hand gun. It's not a fuckin' Uzi or owt flash. It's just a hand gun. That's all I know, honest to God, Baz.'

Baz reached out and scrunched up Poz's dribbling mouth between his fingers and thumb till his cheeks met in the middle and he looked like a cartoon guppy. He watched the panic rise back up into Poz's eyes. The strength in Baz's jumbo-sausage fingertips was tremendous, the flesh pressed so hard as to feel industrially stapled.

'You'd better not be pullin' my fuckin' pisser. Do you understand?'

'Yufffr,' said Poz.

Baz let him go. His face flushed with blood, leaving a white hand shadow.

'I'll get yer that telly before t'day's out, Carol.'

'Yeah, well you'd fuckin' better, Baz. In fact, yer'd better make it one a them fuckin' widescreens. Comin' in 'ere an' fuckin' kickin' off. It's *not on*. It's *my* fuckin' house. Respect where respect's due, yer know what I'm sayin'?'

'I do, love. An' yer know I wun't do it to you on purpose. Yer a good customer, I don't shit on me good customers. Do I? Well do I?'

'No, yer don't, that's not what I'm sayin'. Just that it's my 'ouse, an' I've got to protect it. That's all. I know yer upset about yer nephew an't that, but next time try an' take it somewhere else. All right?'

'I know, love. I'm sorry. Don't you worry, I'll sort that telly out later this afty.' Baz looked down at Poz. 'Might be better if you weren't 'ere by then.'

Funnily, Poz was thinking the same thing. It wasn't to be until much later in the day, however, his mind unclouding from the smoke and the terror of that afternoon, that it occurred to him that if Baz didn't come back after him to kill him later, then Denny would. But by then, he was in the hospital, feeling like he never wanted to leave.

14. James Woods

'NO. OH NO. You're jokin'. You're jokin'! You're *jokin'!* You are *fuckin' jokin!'*

'Wha'?' Denny muttered, half asleep.

'All right. Yeah. Yeah, thanks for callin', Carol love. Yeah ta-ra.' Kelly hung up the phone. 'That were Carol,' he said to Denny.

'Yeaghr,' said Denny. It was more of a snore than a word. Despite the illusion of the power of speech, Denny was out of it. He was all but pushing up zeds. And that wasn't going to make Kelly's job any easier.

'Denny,' said Kelly, 'basically, that were Carol on the phone. She were just tellin' me that Poz were round there gettin' off his tree when who should show up but Big Baz. An' basically gives him a really fuckin' hard time. An' when I say an 'ard time, I mean a really fuckin' hard time. I mean, basically, he beat all but the poor cunt's head in. Big style.'

'Yeahh,' Denny sighed with dreamy contentment.

Kelly looked at Denny and he could tell that Denny was out of it. He meant really fucking seriously out of it. Mostly pissed out of it more than any other kind of out of it. Well yeah, OK, that made sense: they'd been drinking all day, they'd had a fucking skin-full. They'd been sipping pints of lager and getting off their heads for the lunchtime sesh outside the Skyliner with a bunch of cricket fans who'd preferred to be sitting talking about the game at the pub than be round the corner inside the ground watching it. Kelly and Denny didn't mind – they couldn't give a toss about cricket, they were too busy drinking. But it was just drinking. Drinking was drinking – you know what I mean? It was just honest-to-goodness par-for-the-course drinking. That was all. Just a few drinks. And it wasn't like they'd been pub crawling or anything. Well OK, it was. They had actually moved on and snuck in a couple down the Dry Dock afterwards, surrounded by the student crowds opposite the Poly or whatever they called it these days. *God*, there were some fucking lovely women down there, students mostly, quite a few of 'em foreign looking with lovely deep tans and lovely flat stomachs and that. Thank God for them crop tops, though he never knew where to look when he saw little Casey and her mates in 'em. When they got back to Denny's, they found a couple of bedsides left over from the night before: tins of lager – warm, and flat as fuck, and only half full, but beer all the same. After they'd necked the best part of that, they'd both noticed that it had crept into late afternoon territory, and so Kelly managed it on his crutches to the Indian, which was the nearest place that sold ale, even if they did charge you over the odds. It was worth paying a quid or so extra just to avoid a longer trek that would realistically have been a taxi ride in his state. And there was no way he was forking out for a joe-baxi in the middle of the fucking day. Denny was already too out of it, and so the upshot was that he hobbled there on his todd *and* managed to sweet-talk Ganesh into serving him a four pack of Stella – who he didn't know why he needed fucking sweet-talking because it *was* in the middle of the fucking day, for Chrissakes, so what's the big fucking deal? So if Denny was crashed out fast asleep when he got back with the booze, then he – fucking Denny – deserved his just rewards: *i*-fucking-*e*, fuck all: all the more beer for the Kelly man. Except the Kelly man had got that fucking almighty awful phone call from Carol, and once it had entered his right eardrum there was no way on earth that he wasn't going to share it with Denny. It was just too fucking freaky. No matter how Denny felt from necking 'em back, Kelly felt just as equally obliged to disturb him in his innocent gentle slumber and let him know what the fuck he'd just found out was going on.

'Denny. Denny. *Denny*. Wake up, man.'

'What? *Whhaaattt*?'

'Denny. Wake up. That were Carol just on t'phone.'

'Who's Carol?' Kelly could tell Denny must be out of it: he hadn't even had the energy to insert a *fuckin'* between the words *Who's* and *Carol*.'

'Poz's mate, yer barmy cunt. Her with the fuckin' little kid, Liam.'

'Fuckinell,' Denny mumbled, 'Liam. Smart little nipper. Thought he were Vicky's.'

'Exactly,' said Kelly. 'Well listen to this. I've just had a fuckin' phone call from Carol, right? Fuckin' Baz's been round there while Poz were round there an' all, fuckin' boxed out of his tree. Chasin' t'fuckin dragon, like. Anyway, Baz turns up, right? Gives him a right planishin': turns out Poz sez summat or other. You know what he's like. Can't keep his trap shut if he's gettin' a kickin' in. I love him an' that, but—'

'Hang on,' mumbled Denny. 'What y'on about?' He was so gonzoid it was barely a question – more a truism sucked up from the soggy bilge of an old beer tin.

Kelly had seen this coming. Just as Poz had played it up, he'd played it down – but knowing. Knowing that somewhere along the line it would all go pear shaped, as they said. As they were fucking wont to put it. Yes he knew – he had fucking known all along that it would be Poz who fucked it up for them one way or another. That was why he'd stuck up for him, for Chrissake. He knew it'd be Poz. He knew it would be Poz all along. But the difference was, he'd never held it against him. Even though he'd known well in advance through sheer intuition (well no, actually, through sheer fucking knowing Poz) that Poz would be the one, if any of them, who cracked first.

Oh, fuck it. So it was Poz. So fucking what? Baz would have found out anyway. He'd said it himself plain enough the other afternoon – and what Baz said Baz did. He wasn't a talker. At least, not just a talker. He might like to jaw it off but he wasn't a bullshitter. If he said he was gonna find somebody, he'd find them – and now, when Kelly looked back on the past week, he wondered what he himself had been thinking of all this time. Of course Baz was gonna find out. OK, Baz was Bea's dealer and they'd known him for donkey's years, ever since he'd been a kid like the rest of them, burgling student flats on Chestnut Avenue. But once Baz got a bee in his bonnet about something – which he patently had with this nephew thing – he wasn't going to let go of it in a hurry. Basically, Poz – despite the fact that he'd blabbed under pressure from what Carol had just reported – Poz had been right all along. Right to worry about Big, fucking Big, Baz all the while that they'd been cacking on about some other shite.

But hang on. Hang on. *What* other shite? That was why he needed to revive Denny just now. Because Denny was totally off his sweet tiny bollocks and the shit-bomb had dropped just at the exact moment that nobody had wanted it to happen. Kelly didn't unwish all the beers and hotties that they'd just done in together that afternoon, no way José, but he suddenly wished Denny was awake and compos mentis, because the silly bastard had dropped off again.

'Denny. Yo, Denny.'

'Wha'? What time is it? Have we missed *The Simpsons*?'

'Never mind about that. Listen. I've got summat serious to say to you. Sit up.'

Denny, like a stone finding life, coming round from drunken REM.

'Denny. Listen.'

'What? What? What is it?'

'That phone call I just got from Carol,' said Kelly.

'Carol who?'

'Carol with the tits.'

'Oh, that Carol,' Denny grunted like a man with an oesophagus full of wind and puke – in fact it wasn't strictly a simile.

'Yeah, Carol.' Kelly was losing patience. He was gonna start hitting him in a minute, see what reaction that got. 'Will yer fuckin' listen?'

'What? What's up with her? She's all right, in't she?' Denny's head dropped on to his chest and his breathing went all deep and sullen again.

Right, that's it, Kelly thought. Actually, what he thought after that fell into two parts of the same thought. The first part was something along the lines of *I'm never going out afternoon drinking with a part-timer again*, while the second part was *Right, I'd better put some fucking coffee on and sober this cunt up so he can take in what I'm telling him*. As he jived clumsily on his pot leg into Denny's kitchen he wondered how and why he'd considered the two separate thoughts as one in the first place, worrying about it unnecessarily, until they finally merged into one anyway, then melted away with the steam spouting from the kettle, leaving him with the one original sense of urgency to tell Denny that Big Baz had been round to Carol's and twatted Poz and got hold of the knowledge that it was *them* who'd battered his dear baby nephew.

'Clint!' he shouted across the room.

Fuckinell, where did that come from?

'I mean, Denny!'

86

It was then that he saw the way. Lateral thinking! If only he'd thought of it! Except he had! Kelly dug his baked fingertips into the penknife pocket of his jeans – the first place any pig would search – and managed to scrape out his last blimp of blow. Some soapy shit that he'd scored off Mercy, but it'd got 'em stoned this afty all the same. It took a bit of fiddly concentration – it was hard as fucking iron and too small a piece to soften with a lighter without burning his finger ends – but he managed to get his teeth to what was left of it and bite it into two HKs. Little 'uns, but enough to make a difference. He leant across Denny's sprawled out legs – his jeans had the consistency of engine rags – put them on the edge of the hearth, lit the gas fire with a Clipper, and stuck the knives in. He *knew* that would do it. The *kerching kerching* brought Denny back from the land of nod.

'Denny, man. Sit up, will yer? Look, I'm pullin' you a hottie.'

'Nice one,' Denny said. It was only a burble but it was plain that he was coming round.

'I've got you a coffee together as well, man. Are yer still up for it?'

'I'd rather have one a them fuckin' bedsides, yer poof,' said Denny. That was when Kelly knew he was truly coming round. He found a can with a dribble still left in the bottom of it and handed it to him.

'Here.'

'Cheers. Nice one, Kel.'

Should he get it in quick now before Denny relost the plot or wait until after Denny had had his HK? Best to wait – the dope hit might bring him round a bit.

Denny put the bottle to his lips, sucking the smoke in short bursts to let it cool: *Tsst. Tssst. Tsssst.* He finished it off: *Tsssssssst.*

'Cheers. Nice one, Kel.'

'Denny, Baz is on to us.'

'What? About the petrol station?'

'What else?'

'Fuck. Is that what you were just on about?'

'Course it flamin' is, whadja think?'

'Well where is he now? Does he know where we are?'

'I fuckin' hope not. Fuck. But he knows where Bea is, doesn't he?'

'What's it got to do with Bea? I thought she didn't know owt.'

'She doesn't,' said Kelly, 'but Baz doesn't know that, does he?'

'Come on, Kelly man, he's not gonna do owt to Bea.'

Kelly looked Denny gravely in the eyes.

'You don't really know Baz at all, do yer? You've got no idea what he's capable of.'

'I've fuckin' known Baz for as long as you have. I mean, what do you think he's gonna do to her? Specially with the kids there.'

'That's what I'm sayin'. The kids, whoever... It doesn't matter to Baz who's there. He dun't care. That's what he's like, for a start.'

'All right, all right, I know what you're sayin'. But I'm just tryin' to be rational about it. If he goes round there, what's he actually gonna do?'

'Are you really this fuckin' naive, Denny, or are you just windin' me up here, or what? He'll fuckin' batter her. That's what Baz does. He batters people. He's already battered Poz this afternoon. He's probably fuckin' batterin' our lass as we sit here speakin' now.'

'Come on, Kelly, think about it. Baz operates on fear, and Bea in't scared a no-one, certainly not Baz. In that situation, he's just all fuckin' mouth. Besides, she's one of his best customers.'

'*What?*' Kelly couldn't believe what he was hearing. 'Listen, Denny, if that's your fuckin' take on what Baz is like then you're fuckin' welcome to him on your own. I'll just fuck off out of it – a very long way out of it. Surely I must have some fuckin' rich old auntie in Australia that's never met me.' Kelly paused to mime the dawning of realisation. 'Aah, I know what this is about, all this crap about how Baz is all talk an' everything. You're tryin' to convince yer*self*. It's since that conversation you had wi' that mate a yours.'

'What yer givin' it? Look, if you're worried, man, give her a ring.'

'I'm too fuckin' pissed, man. Me head's spinnin'. I can't think straight.'

'Do you want me to ring her?'

'No. No, you're right. I should get me act together an' ring her meself. An' that's exactly what I'm gonna do right now.' Kelly did not move. 'But what am I gonna say to her? She's gonna wanna know what's goin' on. I don't wanna set her off worryin'.'

'Just ring her up. Don't say owt, just ask her if she's all right an' tell her you'll be home soon. Then think about the rest later. At least it'll set your mind at rest for a bit till we can sort it out.'

'You're right, you're absoluckinfutely right,' Kelly spoonerised.

'Yer fuckin' pissed-up cunt. Go on, get on with it.' Denny jerked his thumb toward the phone.

It got picked up after five rings. It was Bea, she was in. 'Are you all right, love?' Kelly said, trying to sound natural. It was an impossible mission. Kelly had never in his life rung Bea up before just to ask her if she was all right.

'Yeah, I'm fine.' She didn't sound all right. 'Where are yer?'

'Why?'

'I wanted you to pick summat up on your way home. Which way you comin'?'

'I'm still round at Denny's. Why, what d'yer want?'

'Er, we need another litre a milk, we've run out.'

Kelly played along, wondering what was going on.

'Can't you send one a t'kids out to t'Co-op?'

'Yeah, all right Kel, it doesn't matter. I'll sort it out, it's not important. When you gettin' back, have you any idea?'

'Pretty soon, I reckon. I'll see you in a bit love, yeah? Listen. I'll sort meself out with summat to eat, OK?'

'All right, see you later, love.'

Kelly put the receiver down slowly.

'She all right?' said Denny.

'Yeah. I think so.'

'See. I told yer.'

'I dunno. She sounded a bit funny. Or is that me just bein' paranoid?'

'It's you. Believe me, it's you.'

'No. She din't sound natural. She were too reserved. No sarky comments. Nowt. Now that is not like Bea. You know what I'm sayin'?'

'No. What yer sayin'?'

'There's summat up, I can tell.'

'Well worry about that later. We need to think about this business with Baz right now. What did whatsername say?'

'Who? Carol?'

'Carol, that's it.'

'I told yer. Baz were round at hers givin' Poz a batterin' apparently an' he knows now that it were us who did it.'

'Well what state is Poz in? If he knew Poz were in on it but Poz is still breathin'—'

'The only reason Poz is still breathin',' said Kelly, 'is because he wasn't the one who battered the kid, was he? With all due respect, Denny, it's you that put him in hospital when there were no need for it.'

'Fuck off,' Denny roared. 'No need? He weren't exactly bein' co-operative, was he? You were there, you saw what happened.'

'All right, all right,' said Kelly, holding up his hands. 'What's done is done. There's nowt we can do about that now. What we need to decide is what we're gonna do about Baz.'

'Yeah. Well that's what I fuckin' said, innit? We're talkin us-selves round in circles here.'

'All right, Mr Data, then – suggestions.'

'Let me think a minute.' Denny sipped the warm dregs of lager. 'Let me just think a minute.' He tottered to his feet, went to the chest of drawers the TV was on and pulled open the top drawer. After rummaging around inside for a bit, he pulled out the hand gun that Kelly had thankfully not laid eyes on since the robbery, and didn't want to see now.

'Aw no. Aw no, Denny.'

'Hold yer horses, will yer? You haven't even heard what I'm gonna say yet.'

'I'm more worried about what you think yer gonna do, with that thing.'

Denny pushed the drawer shut and said, 'Taz's brother-in-law.'

'Eh?'

Denny sat down cross-legged, cradling the pistol in his lap.

'You remember Taz? *You* know. Tariq Aziz. Me an' Stan used to be at school with him.'

'Turkish lad? Played in t'rugby team or summat?'

'That's him. 'Cept he wasn't Turkish, was he?'

'How should I know? What the fuck you on about him for?'

'Cos he were fuckin' Iraqi, wan't he?'

'So?'

The telephone rang.

'Hold on,' said Denny, getting up to answer it. 'Hello? Yeah.' He held out the receiver. 'It's Bea for you.'

'Hello?' said Kelly, grabbing the hand set.

'I don't know what the *fuck* you've done,' said Bea, furious, 'but you'd better shift yer arse *now*. Baz's been round here after your blood. He were round here just now when you phoned up. I *had* to tell him where you were. He's on his way round there now.'

'*Fuck!* Are you all right?'

'Never mind about me. Just shift yer arse *now* if you value it at all. An you'd better tell Denny to do t'same by t'sounds of it.'

'Thanks, love. I'll be in touch. Are you sure you're all right?'

'Just *go!*'

'What?' said Denny when Kelly put the phone down.

'Baz is on his way round here now. We've got to get the fuck out of here.'

'Is that what Bea said?'

'Course it is. Would I make it up?'

'Did she sound scared?' asked Denny.

'Yeah. She did,' Kelly lied. He was already at the door, slotting his crutches into his armpits, and suddenly he'd never felt more sober. But Denny was fumbling at the top drawer. 'What yer doin'?'

Denny was scooping bullets into the palm of his hand, then into his pockets, and tucking the pistol under his waist band like he was James Woods.

'Got 'em,' he said. 'Let's go.'

15. Planning And Finance

'YO. HOW DO YOU spell Leeds?'

'Two Es an' an LSD.'

Mercy saw Kelly standing with Denny in the signing-on queue two positions down from the one he was in. It was a Wednesday morning.

'Y'all right, lads?' he called to them across the office.

'Just sign there please, Mr Killings,' the dole attendant said to Mercy, pushing the form across the desk. Mercy scrawled his proper name, *Stephen Killings*, and picked up his giro.

'How come you get it straight away?' asked Denny.

'NFA, aren't I? No fixed abode: instant payout.'

'Lucky bastard.'

'Yeah, I'm over t'moon about it,' said Mercy with just enough shade of scarcasm for it to go over Denny's head. 'What you up to?'

'I'm hanging around with you,' said Kelly, 'till you've cashed that giro an' paid us that tenner you owe us.'

'What tenner?'

'Exactly. It's that bloody long back you've forgotten.'

'Oh right, that tenner.'

Kelly wouldn't be getting his giro for another two days, but bumping into Mercy on his giro day when he owed him a tenner was totally sweet. And it gave him an idea. He could think of at least three other people who had debts he could try calling in today, maybe more. Sign of humiliating desperation or what? But it was better than nothing. And it was even better than that: they were all people who Baz didn't know particularly well, so they were unlikely to encounter him on their travels.

Denny and him had decided to stick together. Partly it was a matter of safety in numbers, but it also halved the number of places Baz could find either of them, because if he caught up with one, it could only be bad news for the other.

Kelly had stayed well away from home since they'd escaped in the nick of time from Denny's place. That had been thanks to Bea's call. All Kelly could think of was what Baz might have done to her in the interval between those two phone conversations between Bea and himself. She'd sounded OK the second time, angry but not in tears or pain. Maybe what Denny said was right: maybe she really wasn't scared of Big Baz. But that was irrelevant. Because he also kept wondering if Baz had tried to bother her again since. But why should he? Bea had told him where they were at the time. What else could she know beyond that? Unless Baz got it into his head that Bea had been in the know about the robbery and his nephew's injuries all along. Then he'd be capable of anything, and there'd be little reasoning with him once he got that notion in his fat head. Kelly hoped and trusted that she had the good sense to take the kids to her sister's and lie low there for a day or two. That night, no matter how off his head he got, he found himself slouching towards prayer, begging that she was safe.

They'd tried to contact Stan but no sign. Maybe Poz had warned him already. That's what Kelly was hoping. In that case, at least Poz would have done the right thing, and he needed to build up a lot of brownie points in Denny's books round about now.

After he'd escorted Mercy to the Post Office and collected his tenner, Kelly told Denny he had some house calls to make, and Denny said he'd tag along. First stop, Minstrel's, then. He owed him a tenner too, from about three weeks ago. Kelly would have asked for it back sooner if he'd happened to see him, but he hadn't, and it hadn't seemed worth going out of his way. Now it did. He figured out a route that would avoid going past the White Horse; it was one of Minstrel's hangouts when he wasn't at home, but if they stuck their heads in there, the smell of ale would charm that tenner Mercy had just given him out of his pocket and down their necks.

Luckily then, Minstrel was in when they knocked on his door.

'Y'awright, Kelly? Come on in. Awright, Denny?'

'Awright, Minstrel. How's it goin'?'

Minstrel was dressed in a long-sleeved T-shirt and tracksuit bottoms and a pair of well-worn carpet slippers, so it didn't look like he was about to go anywhere.

'Not bad, not bad at all. I'm just makin' a brew, d'you fancy one?'

'Yeah, why not?'

'What is it, tea?' said Denny.

'Whatever you like – tea, coffee...'

'Go for t'coffee,' said Denny.

'Yeah, me too,' said Kelly. 'Two sugars.'

'None for me, thanks,' said Denny.

'Take a pew.'

As soon as he'd gone through to the kitchen, Denny was up off the sofa and rooting through stuff on the mantelpiece.

'What the fuck yer doin', Denny?' said Kelly.

'Just havin' a look, aren't I?' He slipped a 20p piece and a broken cigarette into his pocket.

'Fuckin' sit down, will yer? What yer like, you?'

'All right, keep yer fuckin' shirt on.'

'What's the plan anyway?'

'What yer fuckin' askin' me for? Yer never fuckin' like any a my plans. Burton Leonard were a plan, but yer didn't fuckin' like it, did ya?'

'Yeah, well it's startin' to look a bit rosier now, I admit, all right? What about Stan an' Poz though?'

'*Poz?* Yer can fuckin' forget Poz, man. He's out of it. Out the picture, all right?'

'Well what about Stan?'

'Well, we can't get in touch with him, can we? We don't know where the fuck he is. Like you said, if he's got any sense he'll keep his head down, hopefully for a fuckin' long time.'

'But we're gonna have to find somebody to do it with us, aren't we?'

'Why?'

'It's more than a two-man job, innit?'

'Why? Look, all we have to worry about—' He broke off as they heard Minstrel returning from the kitchen with three mugs on a tray.

'There you go, lads.'

Minstrel's sitting room was kept in its usual gloom with the curtains drawn against the attentions of the street. He had a game up on the Play Station – every few seconds, a warrior's mugshot would loom to the front of the screen with a printed rundown of his or her fighting specs – and it was only the light from the TV colours that flickered upon the dark Appalachian array of amps, cabs, guitars, keyboards, drums and flight-cases that shored up the boundaries of the room. That was partly why everybody called him

Minstrel. His music. That, and his tendency to tell incredible stories. Thing is, usually they turned out to be true.

Minstrel lowered the Tetley's beer tray to the floor. Across the amount of space left in the middle of all the surrounding gear, it wasn't difficult to reach forward and help yourself, though Kelly had to have his passed to him: there was barely room for him to have the pot leg stretched out. How much longer did he have to put up with it? It was out in the open with Baz now anyway. Yeah, sure. But it wasn't with the cops. Baz wouldn't grass them up, he'd never have anything to do with a copper that wasn't confrontational. But there was no guarantee that they wouldn't come snooping round on some hearsay or another still. And besides, the alibi might yet have to see him through this Post Office job.

'How's the leg doin' then?' said Minstrel.

'Not bad,' said Kelly, adding with genuine feeling, 'but it's so fuckin' *itchy* all the time.'

'Bad one.'

'Aw, fuckin' tell me about it. Can't wait to get fuckin' thing off for good.'

'It's funny, I were talkin' to Greg the other day and he reckoned he'd seen you out an' about on Clint's bike. He didn't even know you'd broken it.'

Kelly tried not to look at Denny. He could feel the way Denny was looking at him.

'Mighta been Poz. I let him go out on it one night.'

'I said to him it'd be some'dy else.' He nodded at the leg. 'Got plenty a fuckin' writin' an' shit on it now, 'an't yer? Where's that thing I drew on it, that alien head?'

'Oh, it's round t'back, innit?' said Kelly, remembering that it was the *other* cast that Minstrel, unbeknown to himself, was talking about. ''S prob'ly been drawn over with summat else by now anyway. I got a Ned Kelly, look,' he said, grasping at the straws of embarrassment and pointing it out. 'Nev. He thought it were funny.' He looked around for an excuse to change the subject. 'What's that yer playin'?' he said, pointing at the TV. All Kelly knew about Play Stations was that Damien had one – a dodgy one that Kelly had swapped off Welsh Terry for him once for a half ounce of blow.

'*Lethal Warrior Three*. Yer basic blood an' guts. Nowt special.' The game vanished as Minstrel zapped it over to the TV with the remote. He muted the chatter of Richard and Judy then reached behind Kelly's head to fiddle and flick a couple of switches on an amp.

A snare beat cracked like lightning and recracked in an endlessly diminishing echo, a spidery rhythm guitar skittered over their heads across the ceiling, then a thunderous roll and a kick brought the bass in. The Appalachians shuddered under the impact of an earthquake, and for a sickening moment, Kelly's and Denny's internal organs spasmed to the punishing sound of one hundred and fifty kilowatts of dub. Minstrel brought it right down on the amp and thankfully the moment was past as the bass volume abated to a tolerable level.

Then he reached into a shadowy recess between two speaker cabinets and pulled out a glass bong about twelve inches in height, its tubular mouthpiece standing at an angle like the pointed barrel of a sawn-off shotgun. He filled it from a lump of sandy-coloured hash that he pulled from his pocket and unwrapped from cling-film, playing a Clipper flame underneath it then crumbling it off into the bong's pipe bowl.

'What is it?' said Kelly.

'Bit a slate. Got it off some dodgy fucker in t'Hayfield.'

'Fuckinell, you get around, don't yer? I haven't been up Hayfield's for donkey's. I though it'd be all weed or skunk in there.'

'It is normally. He wasn't one a t'regulars who I got it off.'

'I wouldn't even know any a t'regulars these days,' said Kelly.

'No, neither do I really. I don't go in that often. 'S dodgy as fuck, innit? I were just up there for one a t'Glowballistic nights up at West Indian Centre. Happened to pop in to t'Hayfield for one first with a couple a mates I know who live up there, so they're known faces, know what I mean? Guy I got this off were off his tits an' skint so he were tryin' to sell what little gear he had on him just so's he could get himself another pint.'

'Nice one.'

Minstrel sparked up the stacked bowl, took a deep draw on it and passed it to Kelly along with the Clipper. Kelly did the same and passed it to Denny. The room filled with the sweet scent of the burning dope and the rolling clouds of exhaled smoke.

'What you up to then?' Minstrel asked finally.

There was no point going through a long prelude, thought Kelly, he could be doing that all day. 'Out callin' in me debts, I'm afraid.'

'That bad?' said Minstrel.

'In't it always?'

'Who d'you owe? It's not that dodgy bastard that your lass buys off, is it?'

'Who, Big Baz?'

'That's the one, Big Baz. Yeah, I've seen him up at Hayfield's a time or two. Don't really know him. Don't really want to.'

'Baz?' said Denny. 'In t'Hayfield? In Chapeltown? I thought he fuckin' hated darkies.'

'I told you he were fuckin' connected an' you wouldn't believe me,' said Kelly.

Denny kept his mouth shut and the moment lengthened into a pause.

'Sounds heavy,' said Minstrel, 'an' probably something I don't wanna know about. Anyway, I'm afraid you've picked the wrong day if yer after that tenner I owe yer, cos I'm totally boracic. Don't get me giro for another two days.'

'It's only a fuckin' tenner,' said Kelly, 'can't yer get hold of it from somewhere? I know I'm puttin' t'fuckin pressure on a bit here, Minstrel, but I really could do with it today.'

'Why? What's up?' forgetting his intention not to pry.

'Nowt's up,' said Denny, 'he just wants his fuckin' tenner, dun't he?'

'Keep out of it, Denny, it's nowt to do wi' you. What about your lass,' remembering Minstrel's girlfriend, Ruth, 'd'yer think she'd lend it yer?'

'Gone to Wales to see t'parents.'

'There must be some'dy yer can borrow it off.'

'I'm not sayin' I won't try to get ya yer tenner,' said Minstrel, starting to scent the bones of a story, 'but what's all t'sudden desperation for? I'm just interested.'

'Minstrel, you're always interested. An' yer know I'm always a cagey bastard, so I don't know why you're wastin' yer time askin'.'

'Aw, go on.'

Kelly sipped his coffee.

'He's not gonna tell us, is he?' Minstrel said to Denny.

'Huh,' Denny laughed. 'Not if he's got any fuckin' sense, he won't.'

'Fair dos. Tell yer what,' he said, picking up the phone, 'I'll give Ben a ring. He only lives round t'corner. If he's in, he might be able to lend us it. Take us ten minutes to pop round. You'll have to come with us though,' he added as a quick afterthought, looking round at all the expensive music gear, not all of it his, and imagining leaving it in Denny's custody. He knew what Denny was like.

'Nice one,' said Kelly.

Bastard, thought Denny.

'I know the guy, right? I mean, not that well, but he's all right. He used to be in, like, Iraq's equivalent a t'Navy Seals.'

'Navy Seals? In fuckin' Iraq? It's all desert, innit?'

'All right, fuckin' equivalent a t'SAS or summat. Whatever. Basically, he's hard as fuckin' nails, is what I'm sayin'. Bites heads off whippets for breakfast, all that sort a stuff.'

'How do you know we can trust him?'

'He's a fuckin' Iraqi, in't he, for Chrissake? Probably livin' over here half illegally anyway. He's hardly gonna shop us to t'pigs, I don't think.'

'Half illegally? When he's married to Taz's sister? How d'you make that out? Anyway, I don't mean that, I mean how we gonna trust him to do the job? In fact, we don't even know what the fuckin' job is yet, do we? What exactly are we askin' him to do?'

'Fuckin' put frighteners on him. Scare him off.'

'I thought you were the one who weren't scared a Big Baz. An' I don't mean I want me fuckin' dick suckin', if that's what yer thinkin. So how's he gonna put frighteners on Big Baz, eh? Go on, tell us, cos I'm dyin' to fuckin' hear.'

'You haven't even fuckin' met the guy, have yer? You don't know what he's capable of.'

'I know what Baz is capable of, which is more than you fuckin' seem to, Denny, if yer don't mind me bein' completely honest.'

'This guy right? Hamed, right?'

'Hamed? As in the fuckin' joke?'

'Hamed, right?'

'An' this is Taz's brother-in-law?'

'Will yer fuckin' shut up an' listen?'

'All right, I'm listenin'.'

'He fought in t'Gulf War, right? For t'Iraqis.'

'Presumably. They lost, din't they?'

'Outside some little fuckin' village somewhere, in charge of his platoon or whatever. He's a captain, right? There in t'middle a fuckin'... Kuwait or wherever the fuck it wa', right? He hears from one of his patrols that there's a fuckin' wounded American, GI or marine or summat, bein' looked after by a local family in t'village. Right? So what does he do? He knows this village is bein' guarded by some bunch a fuckin' rebels from t'other side, right, so he sets up some sort a diversion for 'em. You know, sends a bunch a troops off to blow up a fuel dump or summat. While they're doin' that he fuckin' steams in to t'village with his crack team, slaughters the fuckin' family that's lookin' after this Yank, grabs hold of him an' takes him back to his camp in t'desert. Two days apparently he spent torturin' the poor cunt. Car battery bulldog-clipped to t'knackers, fuckin' all sorts. Finally gets it out of him though an' wins himself a fuckin' medal from fuckin' whatsisname? Old Saddam whatsit?'

'Gets what out of him?'

'I dunno do I? Fuckin' tank positions, whatever.'

'An' who told you all this?'

'Fuckin' Taz. Straight up.'

'Sounds like he's been readin' too many a them fuckin' Andy McNabb books.'

'It's fuckin' straight up. I'm tellin' yer.'

'But that still doesn't answer the question. What we expectin' him to do?'

'Put frighteners on him. Get him off us backs.'

'How?'

'I don't fuckin' know how, do I, all right?'

'We're gonna have to come up with a better plan than this, Denny.'

'I'm tellin' yer – the guy is fuckin' sound. All we have to do is meet his fuckin' price.' Denny lowered his voice, as if anyone passing by in the street gave a toss. 'After t'Gulf War, he worked as a mercenary for a couple a years.'

'Bollocks.'

'He fuckin' *did*. Fuckin' Africa, Cambodia.'

'Yer pullin' names out of a fuckin' hat.'

'Taz told us. He wan't fuckin' bullshittin'.'

'Denny, I haven't even fuckin' seen Taz for about twenty years.'

'Well I have, 'an't I? I fuckin' keep in touch with him. We're boxin' buddies from t'old youth club days.'

'Fuckin' boxin' buddies. If he's a fuckin' military hero back in Iraq, what's he doin' livin' on a council estate in Belle Isle?'

'Ask him yerself.'

'Later, Denny, later. I've got shit to sort out first.'

It was late afternoon by the time they'd made the last call and, apart from one tin of Special Brew apiece from the offie on the way round to Football Terry's, they'd managed to stay sober and keep their heads together, as well as not run into Big Baz. Minstrel had managed to scrounge that tenner off his mate and after a few more house calls Kelly had recouped seventy quid. As usual, Denny possessed fuck all.

'Seventy quid's not gonna go far, is it, if we still want this geezer to get Baz off us backs for us. How much is he likely to want?' said Kelly.

'Fuck knows. A lot more than that. I'll tell you what, though. If we had a set a wheels it'd get us to Burton Leonard an' back.'

Kelly sighed. He knew it would come back to this eventually. 'Well, that's not gonna happen today, is it? Post Offices'll be shuttin' in about an hour anyway.'

'No,' said Denny, 'but if it doesn't happen tomorrow, then we can forget about it for another fortnight. It's pension city round there every other Thursday.'

'Apart from a car, what else we gonna need?'

'This,' said Denny, patting his jacket pocket.

'Yeah, yeah,' said Kelly, turning away, 'apart from that.'

100

'Balaclavas we've got. We're gonna need a rucksack or summat. We're gonna have to dump the car sharpish afterwards an' make us way back by alternative means, so we'll need a bag for t'cash. Summat countrified, make it look like we've been out hikin for t'day or summat, know what I mean?'

'Better make it two of 'em then,' said Kelly. 'Fill one of 'em with picnic stuff.'

'Fuckinell, steady on. It's not a real day out, yer know.'

'Is there owt else we should take?'

'Few bits an' pieces, maybe.'   ·

'Like what?'

'This an' that,' said Denny.

'What I mean is, is seventy quid gonna cover it? Cos I don't see any cash comin' from anywhere else before tomorrow.'

'Question is,' said Denny, 'is *fifty* gonna cover it?'

'Why fifty?'

'Cos you're not tellin' me yer not gonna bang some of it in yer arm before today's out. An' yer not tellin' me yer gonna let me stand by an' watch without joinin' in.'

'Fuckinell,'   said   Kelly,   knowing   he   was   right.

16. Shurrukens

IT WAS NEARING dusk and the day had turned cold and grey with the threat of drizzle and they were in a field on the edge of Belle Isle with a lone shaggy brown horse tethered at one end staring inscrutably into the deepening twilight and the rumble of the dual carriageway not far distant, and Kelly was asking himself what the hell they were doing there.

Denny of course was trying to put a brave face on it, but you could tell that he was pissed off as well. It was chilly, it looked like it was gonna piss it down, the fucking field was muddy to start with, he looked like he needed a dig right about now and, to cap it all, he'd put a splinter the size of the Emley Moor Transmitter in the side of his hand from helping Hamed get the wooden board out of the back of the estate car. Kelly had wormed out of it with his pot leg routine, which must have pissed Denny off even more.

'That's right Denny, we put it here.'

It was actually five 4-foot-long sawn-off builder's planks held together in a row, like a raft, with three 2-inch-thick cross slats. God knows how Hamed had managed to get it into the car in the first place, but when they'd got there to his house, Hamed had been waiting for them outside in the garden and it had already been wedged into the back of the estate ('My wife's car – for shopping') at an angle filling the whole space diagonally, with the back seat down, and a couple of scaffolding poles slid in underneath it. To be driven down to the field, Denny had had to crawl into the triangular space beneath the board and make the short but uncomfortable journey sprawled flat out next to the cold ironmongery. Kelly's crutches lay on top of the other side of the board in the angle where it met the side of the car. As for Kelly, pushed for space by the woodwork behind his head even in the front passenger seat, Hamed had insisted:

'Me, I drive with your leg across my lap.' Slapping his jeans with two massive meaty hands. 'See? Good strong thighs. No problem.'

That had been a fucking weird one. He wondered if this was how they'd transported the wounded in Kuwait. Denny hadn't been quite so jealous of his pot leg right then he bet.

'Now you. Here. Broken Leg Man. Help Denny hold this up here while I go get the rods.'

Kelly and Denny held the board of planks standing upright and Hamed returned with the two scaffolding poles cradled in his arms like firewood. He positioned them as props round the back, shored up against the underside of the top cross-piece with their feet ends dug firmly into the grassy earth. Now the board was almost independently vertical, just leaning back at a slight angle, coming up to about Kelly's and Denny's breastbone height. Hamed took a step back and looked at the ensemble – the upright board with Kelly and Denny standing either side of it like two gate posts, wondering what the fuck was going on. He flapped his arms at them sea lion fashion. 'Move in, move in.' Like fools, they moved in to stand side by side in front of it. 'Good. Good. Stay there.'

As Hamed walked back to the car to fetch something else, Kelly said to Denny, 'What the *fuck's* he doin'?'

'Said he had to show us summat.'

'I know that, I weren't deaf, I were there remember? But what?'

'Summat he wants us to help him out with. If we do this for him, he'll do summat for us. That's how it works where he's from.'

'Denny, that's how it works everywhere, yer daft cunt.'

Hamed came striding back across the grass towards them. Against the fading light, with his crown of shaggy black hair, his barrel chest and his not inconsiderable height, he briefly but vividly reminded Kelly of the Jolly Green Giant. Somehow though, he had a feeling in his bones that he wasn't about to deliver them a jolly experience.

He was carrying something – they couldn't see what until he stopped about eight or ten yards in front of them. Even then, when it revealed itself, they weren't sure what it was. It looked like a belt of some kind, but it was too big. Unless it was a wrestler's championship belt. There were shiny metal bits embedded in it like a wrestler's belt might have. Badges, trophies, whatever they were. Those big linked stud things. Hamed wrapped his fingers round one of them and pulled it away from the belt.

'OK, boys. Don't move now.'

To be fair, it didn't happen in a flash. He did pause and take aim, but not for long. His forearm whipped forward and they heard a knock on the wood on Kelly's side – about waist height. When they looked down to where the sound had come from, there was a gleaming wheel of silver metal sticking out of the planking.

'What the fuck are you doin' man?' said Kelly. He couldn't believe that he was saying it, not shrieking it. He didn't know whether he was trying to hold it together or whether his voice was failing him. He said it again to test it, harder this time. 'What the *fuck*... do you think you are fuckin' doin'?'

'You like, huh?' said Hamed, grinning. 'Good trick. Don't move.'

He picked another throwing-star off the belt – fucking lethal-weapon sheath, holster, whatever! – and before they could have moved anyway another of the fuckers clunked into the wood on Denny's side, three inches away from his kneecap.

'Fuckinell, 'Amed,' said Denny, 'this in't funny, you know.'

'Not funny. Good training. Don't move.'

This time Kelly thought *Fuck this* and started swinging his crutches around to hoist himself away from the target. Suddenly his pot leg gave an involuntary jerk (for a second he thought to himself, Funny that's never happened before) and a star had appeared half way between the knee and the ankle, embedded in the plaster, right in the heart of Nev's Motörhead Ace of Spades logo.

'I told you not to move. Stay there. And no need to worry, OK? Trust me. I'm good at this. Good training. Don't move.'

'No!' Denny and Kelly said together, but they were already too late. The next star bit into the board about eight inches away from Kelly's head. Then the fifth and final one followed quickly, thudding into the wood with sickening solidity – vertical, and right smack dab in the meagre crack of space between Denny's thighs.

'OK. You can move now.'

Denny was frozen – and not by the weather. 'Are you sure?'

Kelly bent over and pulled the eight-pointed metal missile out of the plaster of his cast.

'Sure I'm sure,' said Hamed.

'That was not fuckin' funny,' said Kelly.

'Hey, lighten up, Broken Leg Man,' said Hamed, slipping back to the car. He pulled something out of the glove compartment and Kelly thought, Fuck, what next? 'Here,' handing them each a carton of 200 Dunhills, 'you good boys. Brave boys – although you never were in any danger. Good training.'

'So you keep telling us,' said Kelly. 'Where d'you get all this training?'

'In my country.'

'Iraq?'

'Of course Iraq. But that is all I can tell you. The rest is state secret. Military secret.'

'But you're not in the army now, are you? So what's the big secret?'

'Special trainers. Special training methods. If I tell you what, it's like... betrayal. It's like I am a traitor.'

'But you're in England now. What you doin' here if you're still loyal to Saddam Hussein?'

Hamed looked at Denny, who seemed to be just emerging out of the shock of almost having his genitals pinned to a length of builder's plank by a Chinese death-star. 'Your friend here, he asks a lot of questions.' He looked back at Kelly, his eyes fixed. 'I am here because of the love of a beautiful woman.'

'Taz's sister,' Denny explained unnecessarily, which was exactly what Kelly had been thinking already but with a question mark most firmly in place at the end of it. Taz's sister? A beautiful woman? She must have had plastic surgery then since school days. Still, he wasn't going to say it out loud to Hamed. The crazy bastard probably had a pair of nunchakus up his sleeve or a fucking samurai sword under his jacket.

'I thought them things were Chinese or Japanese or summat, anyway. Don't ninjas use 'em?'

'Heh-heh – that's me. That's what I am. I am a ninja. You think we don't have Middle Eastern ninjas? But these' – Hamed leant over and started plucking the stars out of the wood – 'these I get from a friend of mine in England. He calls them shurrukens. Runs a shop in Soho. You know Soho?'

'What – are these like... sex aids?' said Denny.

'I think he means a martial arts shop,' said Kelly.

'That's right – a martial arts shop. I go there for all my equipment. Old friend, you see.'

'In Soho? This friend a yours – he wan't that nail bomber, was he, by any chance?'

'Hey, no saying bad things about my friend. He's good friend. Seen much combat together. Saved each other's lives many times.'

'Where?' Kelly said.

Hamed leant in close to Kelly.

'You don't want to know.'

After they'd packed everything and one another back into the car and got back to Hamed's house Taz's sister was in the front room with her feet up on the sofa watching an enormous widescreen telly flanked by shelves of videotapes and DVDs. It was the first time Kelly had clapped eyes on her in what? Sixteen, seventeen years maybe? Actually, she had changed. She'd grown more womanly. Still not Kelly's type by a long chalk – but they had different standards of beauty in Arab countries, didn't they? Not that you could have told, by Hamed's manner towards her. It was pretty diffident, as was hers to him. A handful of words in English and grunts in Arabic was all that passed between them. She said a cheerful hello to Denny though before taking a moment to twig on to who Kelly was.

'Hiya, Kelly. God I haven't seen you in years. How yer keepin'? What've yer done to yer leg?'

'Yer not gonna believe it but I fell off a roof. An before you say owt, I wasn't robbin' tiles off it.' He realised that he didn't know her name. He didn't think he'd ever known it. To him she had always been Taz's Sister. 'Are you all right love, anyway?' Shit. Why did he have to call her love in front of Hamed? Now he'd be thinking they'd shagged each other at school or something.

'Come. We go upstairs. To my den.'

'Yeah, well keep it down up there,' Taz's sister told her husband. 'You know the kids are in bed.'

'The children,' said Hamed. 'Or the boys. You know I don't like it when you use that other word. Kids are baby goats.'

'Well the boys need their sleep, so please try to be quiet.'

'We will close the door. Then it is sound proof.'

'Yeah, that's what you say. So keep it down anyway.'

'See you later, Maha,' said Denny.

Maha. He should have been thinking, *That was it*, but he realised now that he'd never known her name, only that she was Taz's sister.

Teresa Corchran flashed through his mind.

Hamed had brought the shurruken belt inside and was carrying it with him upstairs now. 'Kids,' he said to Kelly and Denny with disdain as they climbed the staircase up to the attic room. 'She know I don't like that word. You know it's different for her. All her life she has lived here, in Leeds, so she talk different to me. That's OK. She can say what she likes. But not kids. Not that one word only. Boys. My children, they are boys.'

'Your English is good though,' said Denny diplomatically.

'Special training,' said Hamed. 'All part of special training. We had real English language teachers. With qualifications. But maybe I shouldn't tell you that.'

He unpadlocked a door and, switching on a light, admitted them into the attic. It was pretty roomy, occupying virtually the whole ground space area of the house beneath. There was an overhead bulb dangling naked on a flex from the crook of the inverted V of the ceiling, but as soon as they were inside Hamed switched on a couple of tall floor-standing anglepoise lamps at their socket sources before killing the too-bright overhead light. In the more subtle illumination, Kelly took stock of the layout of Hamed's den.

The first thing Kelly noticed at the near end of the room was the computer, its screen already aglow with a screensaver as if constantly left switched on in operational mode. And not just a computer. Kelly didn't know much about new technology but he could recognise a multimedia rig when he saw one, and he was looking at one now: CD-ROM, monitor as big as an aquarium, massive speakers, laserjet printer, the works. State of the art. It was becoming clear that Hamed was not short of a bob or two. That mercenary line Kelly'd been spun by Denny and by Hamed himself was becoming more and more believable when the payoffs like this lot and the TV and DVD downstairs were so evident. For a brief moment, Kelly's mind lost itself in calculating how much all this would be worth to burglars, and how come nobody had taken it, in Belle Isle of all fucking places? Looking around the rest of it soon told him how come. Next to the computer were two sets of magazines. One of them looked like a year's worth gathered together in a collector's slip-case embossed with the title *Combat & Militaria*. The other lot was stacked up flat next to that with the front cover of the topmost issue announcing itself as *Fighters Incorporating Kickboxing News*. And if this was the business end of the room, the far end was like some kind of workout zone for the SAS. That whole section of the floor had gymnasium mats put down on it. There was a punch bag hanging from the rafters and one of those post-mounted kung fu practice dummies with wooden limbs sticking out at various angles. Hamed took the shurruken belt and replaced it on hooks on the wall amid an impressive array of other deadly items, each one an offensive weapon carrying its own potential criminal charge. Kelly couldn't see a samurai sword, but there were all kinds of other blades, big and small, curved and straight, smooth and serrated. Then there was a fine collection of sticks: kendo poles, what looked like American police style nightsticks – asps, they called 'em here – and yes, the inevitable nunchakus, foot-long batons joined by about six inches of chain, given pride of place, draped on the wall in the same classic arrangement with which they were draped between the hands of Bruce Lee on the original *Enter the Dragon* poster.

The other main thing Kelly took in virtually straight away was Hamed's endeavours at soundproofing, which consisted of the old tried-and-tested but never quite 100% successful egg carton method. The problem was that however many egg trays you lined the walls with – and Hamed had done nearly the whole room – sound still escaped through the floor to the levels below, which is where presumably the kids' – sorry, boys' – bedroom was. But aside from that, Kelly wondered what sound Hamed was trying to prevent from escaping. There were the speakers connected to the PC, but surely they alone didn't warrant all this. Maybe he brought his mates up here to spar with him on the mats. Maybe he brought hapless enemies up here to use the place as a torture chamber. Or maybe he was actually trying to stop noise from getting in, creating himself a haven from the demands and distractions of the family down below.

'OK boys,' said Hamed, directing them to pull up a couple of folding wooden chairs while he installed himself in the high-backed leather-upholstered swivel seat at the PC console like an ensign at the helm of a sci-fi starship. 'Sit down and let's talk business.'

For the next ten minutes Kelly and Denny tried to explain the situation to Hamed and what they wanted him to do for them. It wasn't easy. First of all they didn't want to tell him anything about the robbery or the exact reason why Baz had got it in for them.

Leaving these things out, providing him with an edited version of events, was as difficult a job as deciding what to put in, two halves of the same problem – compounded by Hamed's unrelenting questions.

'So what he do to you?'

'Nothing. Yet. It's what he wants to do to us.'

'What he want to do to you?'

'Kill us, probably. Well maybe not kill us. But definitely break us legs.'

'But you already got broken leg, Broken Leg Man. Did he break your leg already?'

'No.'

'No, you fell off roof, I hear you tell my wife. You worried this man is going to break your other leg, huh?'

'Yeah, summat like that.'

'Why he want to do that?'

'Does it matter?'

'Maybe you fuck his wife, eh? Maybe you fuck this man's wife.'

'No – he wants to break both our legs. I mean all our legs. I mean all three of our legs. You know what I mean.'

'Maybe you both fuck his wife, heh?'

And so it went on. Eventually Hamed seemed to get the message that, for reasons that they did not want him to know, or which they did not deem relevant, a man known as Big Baz wanted to cause both of them considerable bodily harm of one sort or another and they wished to hire Hamed's services in helping them to find a way to prevent such an eventuality from occurring, and was he interested in taking on such a job or not?

'Tell me some more about Big Baz,' Hamed said, wrapping his fist around the mouse at rest on the mouse-mat. At once the screensaver vanished and he brought up a new Word document on the monitor. As he swivelled round away from them to face the screen, he withdrew a pack of Dunhill cigarettes from the breast pocket of his shirt, offered them round and placed the ashtray on the end of the desk where they could all get to it. Then he lit up and started typing, beginning with the word NAME followed by a colon.

'Name?' he said.

'Denny,' said Denny.

'Not yours,' said Kelly, 'Big Baz's.'

'Oh. Big Baz,' said Denny.

Hamed just gave him a look.

'Barry Croft,' said Kelly.

'Fuckinell, I didn't know that,' said Denny.

'Barry?' said Hamed. 'This is a name? Barry? It's not short for something?'

'Such as? Barrington, maybe? I don't know. Just Barry, I think – as far as I know.'

'OK. We stick with that. Bar-ry Croft,' he said, typing it in. 'Age?'

'Not sure. Mid thirties. Thirty-fivish.'

'Thir-ty-five ap-prox,' Hamed intoned slowly as he set it down.

'What you writin' all this down for anyway?' said Kelly. 'Is it really wise?'

'I make a dossier. This is the professional way. We build a profile of this man who is bothering you. Then we look at the profile. Then we study the profile. Then we know what to do about the problem. Understand?'

'And what if the police get hold of your computer. Aren't they gonna
wonder—?'

'Ah – police. So now we get to the meat. You want something illegal to happen to this man, this' – he peered at the screen – 'Barry Croft?'

'Well... yeah. I guess so. Maybe. If that's what it takes.'

'That's what we work out from the profile. What it takes. Something legal, something illegal. Who knows? Yet. But don't worry. I keep all my dossiers on disc, on CDW, you know?' (CD*W?* thought Kelly, but didn't say anything.) 'And no one is going to find that. No no no. No one ever finds that.' That made it sound to Kelly as if someone had already tried. What other information might be on that sinister Grail of Data? 'Now tell me all about Mr Barry Croft. I want to know everything about him, from what kind of car he drives to what he eats for breakfast.'

'I don't know how much I can tell you about him.'

'Just everything you know, that's all.'

'First though,' said Kelly, 'how much is this gonna cost us?'

'For the profile, nothing. After that, depends. Depends on what we decide we need to do, depends on what you want me to do. You want me to talk to him, cost little. You want me to hurt him, cost more. You want me to kill him, cost plenty.'

Fuckinell Denny, Kelly was thinking, exactly who have you got us involved with here?

17. Langston's Finger

WHEN BAZ got a call from Delroy, he had half an idea what it was about, but the Yardie didn't want to talk on the phone. He told Baz to get himself round to an address in Chapeltown straight away. Baz didn't like being told what to do and when to do it, especially by a darkie, but he was prepared to grin and bear it. It was business, and in business, you had to make your bed with whoever it took.

He recognised the terraced house when he pulled up outside as the venue of an old blues club he used to go to back in the early Eighties. That was fifteen years ago and they'd all been shut down long ago, but after he'd rung the bell and one of Delroy's gorillas had let him inside, he saw that little had changed about the place since. Internally, it still had the layout of your typical Victorian terrace, but the main reception room housed a well-stocked bar and a pool table, there was music playing in the background, and half a dozen of Delroy's boys were slouching about the place sipping Red Stripes or whisky and Cokes, generally treating it like a private drinking club.

'Through there,' said the gorilla who'd answered the door, thumbing him past the bar and down the hall towards the back of the house. He was directed into a small low-lit room muffled in ganja smoke. Through the fog, as he entered, he could make out Delroy sitting behind a desk, in the middle of taking a drag on a huge Camberwell carrot. The viscous smoke twined round his shoulder-length dreadlocks as he passed the joint over to a beefy-looking cunt jammed into an armchair against the wall, who wedged it straight between his overstuffed lips. It was Langston. Maybe he'd got it wrong about Langston being at the bottom of the Yardie food chain. Looked like he might have been promoted to Delroy's right-hand man. Baz gave him a peremptory nod but couldn't tell whether Langston nodded back or just stared him out. Neither of them spoke. Baz's gaze dropped to an object that the nigger was toying with in his fists and he made a point of not reacting when he saw the connected bones of a human finger. Langston was clicking them like rosary beads.

'Sit down,' said Delroy, indicating the chair facing him round the other side of the desk.

112

Baz sat down. Relax, he told himself. Don't let these bastards wind you up.

'I got sump'n fer you,' the Yardie boss said. He opened a drawer in his edge of the desk and reached in. Baz made himself not show a flinch. He might have to deal with these people, but he didn't trust them for one second. He wasn't going to be intimidated, though – not by Delroy, not by anyone.

Delroy pulled out a slip of paper and pushed it across the desk top towards Baz. Baz picked it up and unfolded it. It was an address in Leeds 6: Flat 3, 37 Kensington Terrace.

'Is this who I think it is?' he said to the Yardie.

'Michael an' Simon,' Delroy pronounced. 'Them boys took yo' stuff.'

Baz looked down at the address again, then back at Delroy. The Yardie stretched out a long beringed hand towards Langston, beckoning back the spliff. Then he leaned back in his chair in an easy manner, puffing on the smoke.

It seemed to Baz that there was no point in hanging around waiting for his turn. 'Is that it?' he said, standing up.

'That's it,' said Delroy, waving a hand to signal him away.

Baz lifted the note.

'Thanks for this.'

He glanced in Langston's direction as he turned to leave. Delroy's voice stopped him at the door.

'Make sure you take care your own business from now on, ya hear me?'

Baz thought about saying thanks again, then thought better of it. As he shut the door, he couldn't tell if the clicking behind him was the sneck or Langston's finger.

18. Kensington Terrace

'CHEERS FOR THIS, Terry,' said Kelly.

'Yeah, nice one,' said Denny.

'No problem. No problem at all. Sure you don't want a cup of tea while you're at it? I can put the kettle on, no problem.'

'Nah, yer all right,' said Kelly, 'I'll be sorted with this.'

'Yeah, me too,' Denny concurred.

'OK, well I'll leave you to get on with it then. I'm gonna nip into the other room and get a spliff together if anyone's interested.'

'Yeah,' said Denny, 'in a minute, definitely.'

'A thousand pounds,' Kelly said to Denny after Terry had gone. 'A thousand pounds. That is a hell of a lot of money,' he added ruminatively, as if Denny would somehow not know it already. 'And we still don't really know what he's gonna even do for us.'

'We know he's gonna put him out of action for a while,' Denny replied, 'and by the time he comes back, that should be the end of it. Anyway, the money's not a problem as long as we get us act together and do this Burton Leonard job tomorrer. Like I said before, we're lookin' at maybe four, five thousand quid. But that's as long as we get us act together. An' I mean early. We've got to get there and get it done early before all t'pensions get shelled out to t'local fuckin' fogeys.'

Denny eased the spike out of the engorged vein in his arm and loosened the belt from around the bicep. Kelly was just finishing rolling his sleeve down, having already done his share and got first use of the needle. They were in Welsh Terry's kitchen, which was up on the tenth floor of a block of flats in Little London. From up here, half the city was spread out in lights before them – you could see all the way to Seacroft and beyond from Terry's gaff. You didn't need to worry about net curtains or nosy neighbours because no other blocks as high as this one overlooked this side of the building. It even offered a good lookout over the car park way down below in the unlikely event that Big Baz's BMW should pull up. And Welsh Terry was cool about them using his kitchen to have a dig, even though he wasn't into it himself. It was a good port in a storm, sure enough. Only problem was, it wasn't where they needed to be right now.

'Where are we kippin' tonight?' Kelly said. 'Is there gonna be any joy at Jason's, d'yer reckon?'

'Well we stayed there last night,' said Denny, 'I don't see why he should object to us kippin' there again tonight.'

'And what about this car for tomorrer? Is he gonna be able to sort it for us?'

'What you askin' me for?' said Denny. 'He sorted it last time, didn't he? He didn't have a problem with it. I don't see why it's gonna be any different this time.'

'Don't yer think it's a bit short notice?'

'Short notice is what he specialises in, innit? Nob'dy wants a twocked motor for a dodgy job a week in advance do they? Short notice is the whole fuckin' point. Jason gets it for yer, yer do the job an' yer ditch it fast. It's not twocked for a fuckin' leisurely family outin'.'

'Well how much is he gonna charge us for it?'

'Kelly, yer fuckin' know how much he's gonna charge us. Same as he charged us last time. Same as he always charges everybody. A ton. That's what he fuckin' charges. That's what he does. Flat rate. That's all he's bothered about, innit? Makin' a ton a time. Now will yer stop frettin'. Yer startin' to remind me a Poz.'

'He must be fuckin' mad, only chargin' a ton a time. He could ask for a fuck of a lot more than that if he wanted.'

'Yeah, well he dun't, does he? Who knows? Maybe he just likes dealin' with round figures or somethin'. I don't know. But don't knock it, just be fuckin' grateful, all right?'

'How's it going boys, OK?' Welsh Terry came into the kitchen.

'Yeah, sound.'

'What shall I do with this?' said Denny, holding up the hypodermic. 'You're not gonna want it for owt, are yer?'

'Oh no, man,' said Terry, withering inside at the thought, 'sling it. There's a bin in the cupboard under the sink. Just throw it in there for now. Do you want a bit of this?' He held out a spliff to Denny who sucked on it rapidly half a dozen times before dragging the smoke down into his lungs and passing it over to Kelly. Kelly had just taken a couple of drags before Terry said to him, 'Here, give us a blowback, will you?' and he reversed the joint in his mouth and blew smoke between Terry's puckered lips, but he was damned if he was going to give it up yet before a few more tokes.

'Right,' said Kelly, after he'd passed it back to Terry, 'how we gonna get this cash sorted for Jason then?'

'I wouldn't worry too much about that. We can sort it out with him afterwards,' Denny said.

'Are you sure about that?'

'That's what he said. That's what we did last time.'

'Well what we doin' here then? Let's get us-selves round to his place.'

'Sure you boys wouldn't like a cup of·tea before you get off?'

'Nah, yer all right Terry. Got some business to sort out. Need to be makin' a move.'

'OK. Well mind how you go.'

'Thanks for t'use a yer cooker an' that.'

'No problem. Any time.'

From Terry's place to Jason's was probably no more than a mile and a half as the crow flies, but Kelly and Denny weren't crows, and now they were faced with the question of how best to get there. One option was to cross Otley Road and cut diagonally across the park. Problem with that was that although the park was likely to be dark and pretty deserted, there was a greater chance of running into Big Baz once they came out of it the other side, since that particular bit of the Hyde Park area was where Baz's mates – or clients, at least – tended to live. Maybe the safer option, they decided, was to skirt around the park, sticking to the Woodhouse side of Otley Road as far up as Hyde Park Corner, then weave their way through the streets down to the Picture House, and then beyond that down towards the bottom end of Cardigan Road and Jason's place in Burley just over the railway line.

'This *fuckin'* pot leg's really gettin' on me tits now,' said Kelly, swinging on the crutches.

'Fuckinell, Kelly man, you might as well get rid of it now. You're gonna have to get rid of it if we're doin' this job tomorrer anyway.'

'It's all right sayin' get rid of it, but it's fuckin' easier said than done. I can't just start cuttin' it off in t'street, can I? An' anyway, what am I gonna cut it off with?'

116

'Look, I've got a penknife in me pocket. Let's get somewhere out a sight so we can fuckin' try an' deal with it.'

They ducked down Kensington Terrace. There were a couple of ginnels down there that cut underneath the terrace of houses through to Brudenell Road on the other side. They'd be well hidden from anyone's view in one of those. The problem was that access to the tunnels was through the back gardens of the houses they ran beneath and either the property owners, or more likely the tenants, had got so pissed off with people using them as a public right of way that they had boarded up the ends.

As if that was going to stop somebody like Denny.

'Hang on,' he said, and grasped the edge of the board. Kelly stood leaning on his crutches looking up at the red-brick façade above them. No doubt the building was partitioned into flats and probably occupied by students, but each of the windows remained dark and free from activity, despite the racket Denny was making as the boards and nails cracked and tore away from their moorings.

'Can't see a fuckin' thing in here,' said Kelly once they were inside the tunnel.

'Hold on, I've got a lighter. Give us yer leg over here.' Denny had the flame in one hand and a knife in the other whose blade, in the feeble gloom, couldn't have been more than two or three inches long. Kelly felt Denny start working the blade at the top outside edge of the cast. 'Ow! Fuck!' What little light there was went out altogether, leaving them back in pitch blackness.

'What's happening?' said Kelly.

'Just hold on man. It's easier tryin' to do it without holdin' t'lighter. Just bear with us.'

'Fuck, watch me jeans. Don't fuckin' slash me jeans, I don't wanna be walkin' round lookin' like a fuckin' fashion victim.'

'Just fuckin' shut up an' let me get on with, it will yer?' Kelly felt more sawing and tussling going on, but when he heard another exasperated 'Fuck!' from Denny he knew it was useless. 'I'm not gettin' anywhere with this fuckin' thing. It's this knife, it's too small.'

'Leave it, Denny.'

'Just one more go.'

'Leave it, man. It's no good, I've done it before, remember? You need summat like a pair a pliers or gardenin' shears to cut through that bastard.'

'Fuck.'

'Let's get round to Jason's. We'll have to sort it out there.'

'What if he's not in?'

'Why, what time is it?'

'Fuck knoz.'

'It must be gettin' on. It were gettin' on when we left Terry's. If he'd been out, he must be back by now.'

'Happen so, if he's been in t'pub, but what if he's gone out somewhere else? What if he's still out somewhere?'

'Fuckinell, Denny, if he's out he's out, but I'm not hidin' here in a dark fuckin' hole all night long wonderin' about it.'

'All right, all right, keep yer shirt on. They've fuckin' boarded it up at this end an' all, an' I'm fucked if I'm off back all t'way round t'block.'

'Well fuckin' kick it down then, but get on with it, I'm startin' to get claustrophobic in here.'

It took three or four good boots to shift it, Denny making enough noise to wake the dead. The yellow light from a street lamp fell on an unkempt patch of yard-like garden overgrown with chickweed, dandelions and tall spears of rosebay willow herb. And two of the local residents, just coming home through the gateway at the end of the garden. Two young blokes, studenty looking, back from the pub by the looks of it – a short white Rasta and a tall smooth-casuals dude who looked like he'd just danced out of a Gap commercial.

'Oh come on, man,' Mr Smooth started to protest at the sight of Denny and Kelly emerging from the dark recess of their property, 'that is not a public footpath.'

'Give it a rest, pal,' said Denny, approaching them.

'We're trying to keep out glue sniffers,' the dread head chipped in. 'There's hundreds of the little buggers round here.'

'Well that's not our problem, is it?' Denny said, pausing for Kelly to catch up behind him.

'I hope you haven't been pissing in there,' the tall guy said. 'That's why we boarded it up, because it fucking stinks from people like you pissing in it.'

That was probably the drink talking but it was enough for Denny. He wasn't going to give that one the benefit of the doubt. In a second he'd lashed out and put the guy on the floor with something that was only half a punch and half a shove, but which took the guy by surprise all the same.

'Oi, oi,' said his mate.

'Fuckin' back off,' said Denny, pointing, 'unless you want some an' all.'

The guy put his hands up and backed out of the way while Kelly swung past, following Denny out of the garden and on to the street.

'Wankers,' the Rasta said at their departing backs for the benefit of his mate, who was cranking himself back up on his feet. 'Come on, let's get inside. We'll put the board back tomorrow.'

'I fucking hate prats like that,' his mate grumbled as they unlocked their way into the hall, switched on the light and climbed the stairs to their flat.

'Yeah. What you gonna do, though – punch a guy on crutches? Even if he does look like a lowlife.'

'I don't care. The fucking cunts would have deserved it.'

'Just chill out,' said the Rasta, inserting his Yale key in the lock. 'That's certainly what I'm going to do just as soon as we step through this door.'

He switched on the light and opened the door wide. When his flatmate closed it behind him, a big grinning giant was waiting there for them.

'Hello, boys.'

'*Jesus!*' they said together, all but jumping into each other's clutches.

The hulking figure didn't move and it didn't disappear. It wasn't an apparition, it was real, standing right there in front of Simon's Cindy Crawford poster, her beachside smile beaming through breeze-tousled strands of wet hair at them over the giant's shoulder, and it was still grinning. Then it spoke again in its rough taproom-brawl intonation, trying to feign the politeness of formal introductions.

'Now which one's Michael and which one's Simon?'

19. Pension Day

WHEN KELLY woke up he was in a great mood. He was in a fantastic mood. In fact, he was in the best fucking mood he could remember in a long time. Optimistic. Things were going to change. He was going to make them change. For the better.

Weird. Particularly as last night had been such a massive fucking downer once him and Denny finally made it back to Jason's place. Great, yeah, Jason was in when they got there *and* he'd got the car sorted for tomorrow. Today. But it was when Kelly phoned Bea that the downer part set in. He got her on her mobile. She was at her sister's. It was the first time they'd spoken since him and Denny had done a runner from Denny's gaff after Bea had warned them that Baz was on the warpath.

'So what's happenin'?' said Bea in her 'reasonable' voice which Kelly recognised immediately.

'Whaddaya mean?'

'I mean what's goin' on? All this business with Baz. What's it all about? I wanna know an' I wanna know now.'

'Oi, just hold yer horses, I were *phonin'* to ask about *you* – how *you* are. I were fuckin' worried about yer. Other day when Baz were round. He didn't touch yer, did he?'

'Oh, for fuck's sake, Kelly, what do you think? He wanted to know where you were and he were convinced that I knew an' I wan't tellin' him. What do you think he did?'

'What?'

In place of an answer there was nothing. Just dead silence on the line.

'I'm all right,' Bea said after a moment.

'Bea.' It was Kelly's sternest most serious voice. 'What did he do to yer?'

'Nowt, nowt. He just hit us about a bit, that's all. An' when I say that's all, I'm not sayin' it's all right for *you* to hit us about a bit, I'm just sayin' it's nowt serious, there's no lastin' damage done, he didn't put me in hospital. He gave us a black eye, that's all. I've had worse. And I could tell he wan't puttin' all his force into it. He still wants me as a customer.' Slight pause. Just a couple of heartbeats. 'To him, it were just business. Family business.' Then the quiet feminine touch, the martyr syndrome, half kidding: 'I'll live.'

'I'm glad.'

Now it was Kelly's turn to be silent.

'Well don't sound so pleased about it,' said Bea, deftly switching to sarcasm.

'I can't believe what I just heard,' said Kelly, finally. His voice carried disappointment down the line. 'Do you really believe that I'd be lookin' for an excuse to start hittin' yer?'

'What?'

'That's what you said a minute ago. Do you really believe that I'd ever hit yer? Have I ever hit you in the past? Eh? Or any a the kids even?'

'Kelly – I *know*. I know. I'm sorry, I didn't mean it to sound like that, it were a joke. It were just a joke.'

'In poor taste if you ask me.'

'I know. I'm sorry.'

'Well sorry's not good enough,' he said, putting on the voice he used to coax her to make up to him when they were alone in their room.

'Kelly. Come on love.' Here came the sexily persuasive come-on love voice. 'Come on. You know yer not gonna win. Kelly? Baby? Sweetheart?'

'Still not good enough.'

'Well tough. Now just accept the apology while it's still on fuckin' offer, will yer, yer daft soft cunt?'

That moment was a real relief to Kelly. It was the first sign that however hard Bea had been clouted by Baz, she was back to her old self. Which in turn hopefully suggested that it hadn't been that hard, like she'd just said. At least she was back to her old sense of humour. Humour in the face of life's misfortunes – that was why he had fallen in love with her in the first place. Soul mates. Whatever life threw at them, Kelly knew they'd tough it out together.

It turned out that Bea now knew most of what had gone on, from what Baz had said, and also from having talked by phone to Poz, who would live. She'd also spoke to Stan, who was suddenly staying with a mysterious relative in Cornwall, but keep it to herself from Baz or anyone who might be a mate of his. Hitched down, took him thirteen hours. Christ, the number of service stations he'd been dumped at along the way. Still, thirteen hours wasn't bad going. No, Bea said, she supposed not. She'd never hitched anywhere in her life, or travelled much further away from Leeds than the distance it is to get to Blackpool. Except that family holiday to Benidorm once in 1970...

While Bea was strolling down Memory Lane, Kelly was figuring out what else he should tell her. The upcoming Post Office job was the first thing on his mental agenda, but that had long been crossed off as a no-no: that one would not be revealed to Bea except under extreme and, so far, unimaginable circumstances. The petrol station robbery that was the cause of all this fucking nightmare? Ditto to Post Office robbery. The false pot leg? Well she already knew about that. That was no reason to feel guilty. So basically, what the fuck was there to feel guilty about at all?

Fuck. The beating. Bea had taken a smacking from Baz for something Kelly had done. How could he have forgotten about that so soon. Except that he was totally fucking out of his skull. That was it. Fuck.

'Babe,' he cut in. 'Listen. Are you OK? I mean are you hurt?'

'Course I'm not hurt, yer soppy bugger. I've got a bit of a black eye an' a bit of a swollen lip, that's all. He knew he wasn't gonna do any more than that.' She could hear/sense/imagine Kelly's lips opening in protest. They had to, didn't they? He liked to think of himself as a gentleman, and in many ways he was, and that was part of what had made her fancy him in the first place. But she cut him short. 'An' I'm not makin' excuses for him. I'm just sayin' he's an animal. He only understands one thing deep down. You know what I'm talkin' about, don't yer?'

'No.'

'Yes you do, Kelly. Don't try to pull one over on me, cos I know when you're bullshittin', I've flamin' lived with yer long enough, haven't I?'

'Bea love, truth be known, I'm fucked. I'm completely fucked out me skin. I've been fuckin' runnin' round chasin' people up for money all day an' silly shit like that an' then me an' Denny did in some whizz round at Terry's... No, Welsh Terry's. An' now we've just done a double round of massive hotties round at Jason's an' I've got a tin a Spesh in me hand. It's fuckin' brilliant but I'm fucked an' I 'an't got a clue what yer goin' on about. Fuckinell, I shouldn't be tellin' you all this information 'bout where I am an' that, should I?'

'Oh, I won't be seein' Baz an' he won't be seein' me in the near future. No, I'm gonna stop round here at our Cheryl's till it all flamin' dies down. Well, for another few days at least. I don't need that kind a flamin' aggro in me life. I've had enough of it in t'past, I can't be doin' with any more. I've got Casey round here with me, an' Damien's here but I think by tomorrer he'll be flittin' back an' forth. God knows where Nita is, but yer know what she's like, she'll be stayin' at one of her mates. I'm losin' customers while I'm here though, an' it's a long way to go to do me community service. Not that I've been from here yet.'

'Don't fuckin' miss it—'

'I haven't missed it.'

'Cos yer know what they're like, they'll be straight on to you.'

'Kelly I haven't missed it yet, it's not a problem.'

'Listen. You look after yourself. Keep out a Baz's way. An' if he phones you up, you haven't heard from me. OK?'

'What are you gonna do?'

'Don't worry about that. You leave it to me. I've got it all under control.'

'Well how? Yer not gonna do owt daft, are yer?'

'Bea, leave it. Just leave it. I'll see you in a few days.'

'Well where you gonna be? How do I get in touch with you?'

'It's not a good idea. Don't worry, I'll stay in touch with you. It's easier that way cos I'm gonna be movin' about a bit, most likely.'

'Well make sure you do stay in touch. All right?'

'I will, love. Promise.'

'Yeah, right.'

'Good to hear you've got yer sense a humour back.'

'I never lost it, yer cheeky cunt.'

'G'night love.'

Bastard! Baz had fucking had a go at Bea. The sooner they got the fucking money to pay Hamed the better as far as he was concerned now. Except that it took away the pleasure of doing it himself. But no matter how out of his skull Kelly was, it was at a deeper level beneath instinct, at the level of intelligence, that he re-admitted to himself what he already knew: that he'd never have a hope in hell of taking Baz. Or at least, like Poz had said the other day, not without a gun. And Kelly didn't want to go down that road.

Oddly, it was partly that same sense of fury towards Baz that had been such a downer, hearing about what he'd done to Bea last night, which this morning filled him with a clean sense of purpose and helped to put him in such an optimistic frame of mind. The thing was that he hadn't been furious at Baz before because all Baz had really been doing was trying to look out for his sister's kid. If anything, it should have been Denny that he was furious at for kicking the kid in in the first place, but the time for that was long past. But yesterday he hadn't known it, or at least not acknowledged it to himself, that he felt guilty: guilty of what they were getting Hamed to do to Baz. Now that Baz had taken his fists to Bea, it was time for Kelly to look out for *his* own. It had replaced guilt with a more domestic and ennobling instinct.

The other part that accounted for Kelly's feeling so good was waking up without that damn cast on his leg. It was as if a shackle had been removed: a sensation of freedom that was more than just physical, coursing through his mind as well as his body. Whatever happened today, however things turned out, it was going to be a good day, if only for that one reason alone. Anything else positive (hopefully around five thousand other positive things) that came their way would only be a bonus on top of that.

There was some minor wrangling over who was going to drive the car. Denny was capable of driving but had never bothered to take his test. Kelly, on the other hand, had passed his test many moons ago but was currently on a two-year ban for a lengthy string of minor offences and misdemeanours that they'd finally caught up with him for just before last Christmas. Still, he hadn't let it stop him from riding around on the bike, and besides, it was all academic anyway since they were going to be travelling in a stolen car which, despite having been resprayed and given bogus licence plates, was not going to fool any copper that happened to pull them over for very long. In the end Kelly agreed to drive. It'd give his newly uncased leg something to get to work on and enjoy doing anyway.

After a dig for the road (they'd managed miraculously to keep back some of what they'd scored yesterday for today's expedition) they took the A61 north out of Leeds past Harewood House with its famous bird gardens and on to Harrogate. They'd have liked to have driven round Harrogate instead of through it, since that would have offered even fewer chances of bumping into any nosy coppers, but it would have proved an unnecessarily long detour. Besides, it wasn't as if Harrogate was a sprawling metropolis full of riot squads barely keeping the inner-city cauldron from exploding. Even in the morning rush hour, it was a quiet spa town noted for the civic pride it took in its prize-winning municipal gardens, and the twenty minutes it took them to drive through didn't bring a single police car in sight. After that it was simply a matter of following the Ripon Road further north through the tiny castle town of Ripley until the turnoff east for Burton Leonard.

How Denny had come to target this particular place was still something of a mystery to Kelly. He bet this one wasn't down to Eddie Whatsit. He'd certainly give it one thing: it was pretty much the back of beyond. The few quiet residential streets in the vicinity of the Post Office didn't look like posing much of a threat by way of anyone being likely to give pursuit, and there couldn't be a police station within at least five miles.

'Right,' said Denny as they pulled up under some trees overlooking the quaint old cottage-like building, 'just one thing. After we come out, I drive.'

'No way,' said Kelly. 'You're not experienced enough to drive getaway, Denny. I'm not lettin' yer. Besides,' he added, as if he needed another reason, 'you're in charge a the gun. You keep yer mind on that an' I'll keep mine on the car. And no arguments.'

'All right,' said Denny, 'but listen. When we start drivin', you follow my directions. An' I don't want any arguments with *that*. I've fuckin' planned this proper an' we have to stick to it.'

'Listen,' said Kelly.

'What now?' said Denny.

Kelly dug something out of his hip pocket and held up the little paper wrap – that lovely little paper wrap.

'I managed to save us a last little line each.'

Denny laughed.

'I hope you've got a fuckin' note to snort it through, cos I'm totally fuckin' boracic.'

Kelly reached into his jacket and produced a sawn-off Burger King plastic drinking straw about four inches long.

'Never go anywhere without one a these.'

'Fuckin' beauty.'

They did the lines in and donned the full-face balaclavas.

'Just one more thing,' said Denny. 'No names. Got it?'

'Loud an' clear.'

'If you need to call me anything, call me... cunt.'

'OK, got it. Cunt.'

The road outside was vacant of cars and pedestrians. One old lady had gone in earlier when they'd first pulled up, but although they'd been distracted snorting the speed and hadn't noticed her come out, she must surely have buggered off by now.

'Sound. Let's do it.'

It was a world away from the all-night garage job. It was nine-thirty in the morning, there was a light mist, but potentially crisp sunshine was starting to cut through it. The day felt like it was going to be good. Despite the mist, maybe because of it, there was an unreal clarity to everything. It felt like nothing could go wrong. Kelly knew he shouldn't tempt fate by even thinking it, but then if you didn't go in with a positive attitude why go in at all? There was hardly anybody around. How the hell had Denny found this place? Kelly couldn't believe it was pension day. Back in Leeds 6 they'd have been queueing outside Brudenell Road Post Office from quarter to nine. Here there was nobody.

Except the little old lady who they thought must have come out and disappeared ages ago. *Oh fuck*, thought Kelly, *let's not have any macho fucking showing off Denny, please.*

'Hands up!' Denny pronounced grandly, brandishing the handgun. Crikey, what was this? It was the first time Kelly had heard Denny pronounce his aitches in his life.

'What on earth is going on?' said the little old lady. The words stamped an impression of her on Kelly's consciousness that required capital letters. Immediately she was Little Old Lady – like a character in a script for *The Bill*. Except they were in the North Yorkshire of *Emmerdale* country. Headfucker already. She had on one of those granny hats like a tea cosy stretched out of shape by having a football stuffed into it. Dye it red, yellow and green and she'd have passed for a white Rasta.

'Move away from the counter an' you won't get hurt,' said Denny, covering both her and the proprietor behind the counter with the gun.

'This is outrageous,' she started to protest.

'Maybe you should just do what they ask, Mrs Fiddis,' said the bloke. He must have been getting on too but he was younger than the woman. Different generations, you could tell. He was the smart one. She was the one itching to climb on her high horse.

'Listen to 'im lady. Do yourself a fuckin' favour, all right?'

'Oh,' she uttered. The gesture that went with it suggested that her indignity had moved to a plane beyond words. Still she didn't move.

'Are you deaf or what?' said Denny, grabbing one lapel of her coat and thrusting her to one side. 'Watch her, will yer?' Denny said to Kelly, and Kelly reached out to get hold of her as she stumbled. She looked down at the insolent hand folded round her thin arm then up at the face hidden behind the balaclava.

'How dare you? Get your hands off me!'

While all this fuss was going on behind him, Denny turned to the Postmaster, who was looking concernedly over Denny's shoulder at whatever the old lady was up to. 'Right. Money. All of it – in there.' Denny shoved a plastic Morrison's carrier bag over the counter. The guy was still gawping at the old woman. 'Come on,' said Denny. 'Today, if you don't fuckin' mind.'

The man started moving, his bald head craning into view and catching some of the light as he bent to the task of filling the bag. He kept looking up nervously and saying, 'Mrs Fiddis, please...'

'Let go of my arm,' the woman kept repeating in a stern and supremely unafraid tone of voice. Denny couldn't see what was going on with her but it sounded like Kelly had got his hands full.

'All of it, mind,' Deny reminded the Postmaster.

'There isn't much, I'm sorry,' the man said.

'It's pension day,' Denny shouted ,'don't fuckin' lie to me! I'm not stupid!'

An expression flickered across the Postmaster's face that said he begged to differ, but it soon reverted to simpering obeisance. 'OK, OK. Just give me a minute,' he said, opening a drawer with a key.

'I'll give you a fuckin' bullet if you don't hurry it up.'

'How dare you?' the woman was saying behind him. 'How dare you come here to our village and behave like this? Who are you? Who *are* you? You should be locked up for good, the pair of you. *I'll* see to it. *I'll* see that you're put away, the pair of you.'

Denny's body jerked as something crashed into the side of his gun arm. The old lady's handbag. The kind you'd see fading in some forgotten charity shop window. She'd smacked him one with it. This was turning into a bad sitcom sketch. '*Oi!*' Denny spun round on her, raised the gun and fired.

Kelly jumped out of his skin. He let go of the woman's arm like it had suddenly turned into a snake. It remained elevated in the mid-air position he'd left it in. Her other arm was up in the air too. For a moment she was stretched out like a scarecrow. Dangling from the end of that one was the offending grey handbag, a scorched tattered smoking black hole through the middle of it. Like she was holding up a dead rat.

The old lady slid to the floor. Her eyes were shut. She was quiet at last. So was the man behind the counter, slack-jawed in disbelief. But Denny wasn't. Denny was shouting, Denny was ranting, Denny was raving at the still form of the old woman on the floor. Kelly couldn't tell what exactly. The noise of the gunshot had left his hearing shattered. Everything coming out of Denny's mouth was muffled like it was far away through thick city fog. He could just about make out something about it serving her right you stupid fuckin' old cow, etc. etc. It didn't take a genius to figure it out. Denny swung the gun back round to face the Postmaster. He mustn't be able to hear a fucking word Denny was saying to him either, but he seemed to be making a good guess. While the handover of the money played itself out before him like a telly programme with the sound turned down, Kelly crouched down and tried to check on the old lady. He was freaking now. The beautiful sunny countryside morning was turning into something resembling a bad acid trip, and he didn't know what the fuck he was looking for. Some sign of life. A pulse. Where do you feel for it? Fuck. She seemed to be breathing. He was sure she was breathing.

'Come on,' said Denny. It barely registered on Kelly's consciousness. Denny was looking down at Kelly with the gun still pointing at the Postmaster. If the obstruction of the counter hadn't been there, the old bastard might have been able to make a grab for it. But he didn't look like a brave man and he didn't look like a fool. No heroics from him. He just wanted to live another day. More than that, Kelly could tell that he was itching to see if the old woman was alive.

'*Come on!*' Denny screamed and Kelly got up and they were out of there and back in the car in a blur of action. 'Drive,' said Denny. Tyres squealed Hollywoodly.

Once they'd got the car going and were able to take their masks off, the world of sound began its slow return, tones of reality bleeding back into conscious awareness. Behind the wheel, Kelly slipped into automatic, driving from muscle memory, pure instinct. But instinct was overdoing it a little.

'Slow down,' said Denny. 'Remember I'm givin' the drivin' orders. Now slow down. Nobody's chasin' us. Not yet.'

'Yeah, but they'll get a look at the car, won't they?'

'Dun't matter. Slow down.'

Kelly lifted his foot off the gas and stroked the brake pedal, but kept it running in fifth for now.

'Take the Ripon road.'

'In't that where t'fuckin' coppers'll be comin' from? Must be t'nearest fuckin' cop shop, surely.'

'Trust me,' said Denny, and Kelly wished he hadn't heard that one.

'What we doin' with the car?' said Kelly, powering down into fourth and then third to take a bend in the road. These were country lanes, relatively speaking, and they still hadn't seen another car, but the turning back on to the main road was just up ahead and Kelly was getting ready for it. 'We're still gettin' rid of it, aren't we?'

'Yeah.'

'Where?'

'I'll let you know when it's time. No speedin' on t'main road, right? Take it steady, act like normal traffic an' get ready to turn off when I tell yer.'

'Turn off where?'

'I'll tell yer when we get there.'

'Tell me now. I'll be ready.'

'Soon. 'Bout three miles before Ripon. There's a dirt track comes off a t'road to t'left into some trees. That's where we're off. An' pray we don't hit heavy traffic afore we get there.'

'Or else what?'

'Or else the coppers comin' from Ripon'll have to pass us on t'other side. An' if anybody did see this car, they're gonna be watchin' out for it, aren't they?'

'Fuck,' said Kelly.

''S all right. Don't fuckin' panic. We've got time. We're nearly there. Look it's here, just a bit further on. Slow down... slow down... here... here... Get ready to turn. Sound.'

There wasn't even a sign or anything. If you didn't already know it was there, you probably wouldn't have noticed it at all. Kelly indicated without thinking and made the turn. In seconds, they were off the main road and obscured from it by trees.

'Don't stop. Keep goin'. Right down to t'end.'

Kelly let the car creep on in first.

'Where's it go?'

'A barn. Old barn. Nob'dy uses it any more. Surprised they 'an't tore it down.'

'Fuck – how do you know all this stuff?'

'Here,' said Denny. 'Just here. Park it inside.'

It was a ramshackle gaping old structure, but it was still standing, after a fashion. One mssing side where doors should have been allowed Kelly room to slide the car inside, and he switched off the engine.

'Right,' said Denny. 'Let's count it.'

Denny passed wads of notes out of the bag across to Kelly and they both totted it up.

'Four thousand seven hundred an' forty-two fuckin' quid. Yes! Fuckin' nice one. What's that? Two thousand three hundred an' seven-one quid apiece.'

'Er, no. Aren't we forgettin' our little arrangement with Hamed? Not to mention payin' off Jason—'

'Listen,' said Denny, holding up a hand.

The crazy *woo-woo* of police sirens had begun to distantly impinge on their still-recovering hearing faculties. It amplified to a peak that seemed alarmingly close, before trailing off into the distance. Sounded like two of them, maybe three.

130

'Right. Let's go. Now. Before they turn round an' come back.'

Kelly had to reverse out all the way back to the main road, but there was a long enough gap in the mid-morning traffic for him to back out unobtrusively on to the highway, to all appearances like some local squire backing out of his reclusive property and heading off into Ripon for a spot of shopping.

'That's exactly what we are gonna do,' Denny said.

The town was smaller even than Harrogate, so it was only a matter of a few minutes' driving to reach the central marketplace. However, Denny deliberately failed to inform Kelly that reaching the town centre entailed driving right past the police station on the way in. Bastard. Kelly got a cold sweat on.

'Keep yer fuckin' shirt on, we did it, didn't we?' said Denny. 'Right. Left here. Down by t'bus station. Round to the right. Yeah. That's it. Park up here.'

Kelly pulled up smoothly and brought the vehicle to rest. They were in Morrison's car park, tucked in the middle of one of several rows of hatchbacks, family saloons and 4WDs.

'Perfect,' said Denny.

'We gettin' the fuck out or what?'

'We certainly fuckin' are Kelly, me old mate, we certainly fuckin' are.'

Denny took the money, swinging it loosely, naturally, like shopping, in the plaggy bag. Morrison's. They were even outside the right supermarket. Kelly locked the car and pocketed the keys. He'd get rid of them in the canal later when they got back.

'How the fuck did you know about all that shit?' he asked Denny as they strolled across the tarmac towards the bus station and the number 36 back to Leeds.

'Me fuckin' gran,' said Denny at last. 'She used to live in Burton Leonard, didn't she? Visited her there loads a times as a kid. Used to stay with her in t'holidays.'

'Fuckinell,' said Kelly, impressed. 'She dun't still live there, does she?'

'Course she fuckin' dun't. D'yer think I'd rip off me own granny's pension? No, she died years ago. Tell you what though. I never did like that Mrs fuckin' Fiddis. 'Bout time some'dy took that snooty old fuckin' cow down a peg or two.'

20. Always Expect The Unexpected

FOUR THOUSAND seven hundred and forty-two quid. Four thousand seven hundred and forty-two fucking quid.

Of course, by the time they'd paid for their bus fare back from Ripon to Leeds and gone straight into the Templar pub at the other end to celebrate, not to mention a kebab over the road after to soak it all up, they'd spent the best part of forty quid between them. OK, so they're still walking around with four thousand seven hundred quid in the bag, and they're managing to keep it together, and it's about time they went to see Hamed before they took one more step towards one more pint. Where is the bag? You've still got it, haven't you? Yes, he'd still got it.

They got on a bus to Belle Isle. Kelly thought back to the day before, and how shit it had all been there. The rain. The mud. The shurrukens. And that stinking fucking pot leg. Responsible for *that* car journey with his leg in Hamed's lap, and so many other miseries. This afternoon it was different. He felt good again, like he had done this morning, embarking on their day out in the country. He was sure the old lady had been breathing. She didn't look bad. She'd be all right. If she wasn't, they'd hear something in the news, wouldn't they?

When they got to Hamed's he wasn't in but his wife was. Maha. That was it. Fucking well remembered from yesterday. Taz's sister.

'Do you want to come in an' wait for him? He won't be long.'

'Er...'

'Erm...'

'He's gone out runnin'. He should be back any minute.'

'Yeah, all right then,' said Kelly, making a decision.

'You lads been in t'boozer all afternoon?' said Maha as soon as the door was shut behind them.

'Fuckinell, is it that obvious?' said Kelly. 'I mean— Fuck— sorry I didn't mean to fuckin'— aw fuck— swear so much.'

'What's he fuckin' like?' said Denny to Maha. 'Can't hold his drink at all. Look, he's gonna start gigglin' in a minute.'

'Yeah, well tell him there's no standin' on ceremony in this house except when t'kids are around - an' they're out.' She looked out of the window and added, 'Oh, here's one of 'em coming back now. The *big* kid. I mean boy.'

They saw Hamed jogging up to the house with a pack on his back. It looked as huge and full as an army pack, and the bastard wasn't even sweating. How could he be a smoker and still do that?

'Hey boys,' he said, striding in when Maha opened the door. 'Your leg got better, eh?'

'Yeah,' said Kelly. 'Still can't run like that though. With that huge great pack on yer back. What's in it?'

'Oh, not much.' Hamed hoisted it off and down on to the floor before opening it and putting his hand in to drag out the contents. 'Just a rolled-up blanket,' he said, pulling out an enormous wad of bedding. He unrolled it on the floor in front of them and they stared at what was wrapped inside. 'And four house bricks.'

'How far did yer run?'

'Today? Not far. 'Bout five kilometers.'

'What's that?'

"Bout three mile,' said Maha. 'He's gettin' old.'

'Yes, but I did *four* miles this morning.' Hamed took in two huge lungfuls of air and thumped his chest like Tarzan, a picture of fitness and strength, if nothing else. Then his eyes went narrow as he looked askance at them. 'You boys been drinking, huh?'

Kelly actually swayed at that point, as if his body had been physically jolted by the mental expletive *Fuck.* He wondered how fundamental a Muslim Hamed was.

'Maybe you like to lift me up a little?'

Suddenly it had all gone haywire. What the hell was this guy talking about? Was it Hamed who'd just gone stark raving bonkers or was it him? Was Kelly hearing things or had Hamed just invited them to lift him up? Maybe this was something to do with the fitness thing. Maybe he wanted them to guess his weight. Or perhaps it was a challenge. Maybe he intended to wrestle them both into submission right here on the livingroom carpet to impress Taz's sister. You'd have thought they'd be beyond that stage.

'Eh?' both Kelly and Denny said together.

'You like a lift-me-up?'

'He means a pick-me-up,' said Maha.

'Oh.' Neither of them still much the wiser.

'A drink,' she said. 'A spirit. A short. A wee snifter.'

'Oh yeah, right. Yeah, brilliant.'

'Pick-me-up,' said Hamed.

'I'll get the whisky out, shall I?' said Maha.

Kelly and Denny were somewhat gobsmacked by this turn of events, but weren't ones to complain. As Lee Van Cleef used to like to say, 'Always expect the unexpected.' What was that old TV programme? Oh yeah. *The Ninja* – that was it. Probably one of Hamed's favourites, if they ever got it in Iraq.

Maha brought three shot glasses with the Scotch bottle and Hamed joined the two boys in firing one back. Kelly's admiration for the man was growing by the minute. Smokes, drinks and runs four miles twice a day. What couldn't he do? And would they find out about it before it was too late?

Up in Hamed's den, they handed over the cash.

'Five hundred now an' five hundred later after it's done,' Denny said, like a real pro.

'Or what?' Hamed said, like a real hard man.

'Come on,' Denny remonstrated, 'fair's fair, we need to see some results before we make the final payment.'

'What final payment? There's only one payment. One thousand pounds now before I do anything. For the rest, you got to trust me.'

Kelly said nothing, but he couldn't help wondering whether Denny had the bottle to tell this guy he didn't trust him. It could well have been significant then that Denny didn't say anything, just plucked another wad out of the carrier bag and placed it on the desk in front of Hamed. Maybe he did trust him, maybe he didn't, but he wasn't going to start arguing with this mad mullah. It was all the more then that Kelly surprised himself by putting his own hand down on the second wad.

'Hang on. What exactly is it that yer gonna do for this money?'

'The less you know about it, the better for you,' said Hamed. 'Take it from me – he won't die but it will do the trick. I'll get you what you want. I'll get him to leave you alone.'

'By doin' what? I mean, is it summat that's gonna point to us? Is it summat that we're gonna need alibis for?'

'Alibi is always good.'

'Yeah? So when? If we're gonna set up an alibi, then we need to know when we have to do it, don't we?'

'Tonight. If I find him. If not, tomorrow night. Or the next night. You keep an alibi every night till I tell you otherwise. That way you'll be covered.'

'We can't fuckin' ensure we've both got an alibi all night every night, that's barmy.'

'Tonight,' Hamed repeated.

'What if you don't find him? What then? Are we supposed to be left guessin' whether we need to be coverin' us arses or what?'

Hamed looked at Denny as if for support.

'I suppose he's got a point,' Denny said to Hamed. 'Yer know what I mean, 'Amed? I haven't got a clue what I might be doin' tomorrer night, never mind t'night after that. There's no guarantee we can... yer know...' His voice trailed off under Hamed's withering gaze.

Hamed allowed the wither factor to decline in intensity as he turned to look Kelly in the eye. 'I'm a man of honour,' he stated simply. 'Maybe I lead a violent life, but I'm a soldier. You understand? Huh? The two of you? You understand? A man has to live. A man has to look after his family. His sons. Leave them something behind when it is his time to go. But there is a wrong way and a right way. A soldier's way is a good way. And that's what I am. You understand? A soldier. You understand?'

'Yes,' said Denny, 'yes, sir.'

Kelly looked intensely at Hamed, as intensely as he was able to under the bleary effect of an afternoon's drinking.

'Hamed,' said Kelly. 'Don't let us down. All right? Just promise us that you won't let us down.'

'You have my word,' Hamed said. Then added: 'As an officer.'

Alone together, they spoke in Arabic.

'And what is it that those two have got you doing for them then? Come on, tell me.'

'I've told you before, Maha, not so many questions. All the time, the questions. A man's business is his own business...'

'... until he decides to make it his wife's business,' Maha said, completing the aphorism. 'I know. It's just that I worry about you.' She gestured up with her eyes towards the kids' bedroom. 'They need you. They need a good strong healthy father to look up to. You're their father. They need you.'

'I know. And you know I can take care of myself.'

She looked deep into his eyes – eyes that had always been hers since before she was old enough to remember, bound to her as hers to him in a long familial promise.

'I need you as well.'

He put one hand against the side of her face, caressing the soft down along her cheek, and smiled.

'Kiss the boys good night for me.'

That first time he'd met the lads and taken them down to the fields for some target practice – when Broken Leg still had his broken leg – he'd used Maha's beat-up old estate, but tonight he unlocked the garage and brought out the high proud 4WD with bullbars. That would be better for this job. In more ways than one. Where he was going, it'd probably blend in more than the antique his wife preferred. As he drove along the dual carriageway system – wide and swift and vehicle-friendly at night after the rush hour had died down – he enjoyed the lights of the city shining on the chromium bodywork fittings along its sides that he could see in the wing mirrors, while his mind ran over the options of what he was going to do to solve Denny and Broken Leg's problem with this Mr Barry Croft. This Big Baz.

Of course, there had been little or no chance of him finding this Big Baz with just the description that the lads had given him. Not without one or both of them coming with him and acting as his eyes to spot him and point him out – and that was one option that he had chosen not to take. Bettter for them, better for him, better for everyone. He'd gotten all he could out of them about Big Baz's habits and routines, where he lived, where his mother lived, where he was likely to be drinking, who he was likely to be visiting on his drug delivery rounds, his regular customers and where they lived. They'd given him as much as they could and as much as he could have wanted without an actual photograph, which was something they had not been able to provide him with.

But someone had.

Hamed had been proud to serve his motherland during the western imperialists' oil war against Saddam; there had been

136

nothing but honour and devotion at the heart of his personal involvement. But his side had tasted only humiliation and defeat at the end of it all, and he had seen little in the way of reward or security for the family he envisaged that he would raise there. Indeed, the war had served merely to compromise the plans he'd had to bring over his bride-to-be from the west. Ironic as it may seem, it was only the subsequent life of a mercenary – sometimes in the employ of those same western imperialists he'd previously been called upon to stand up to – that had brought him reward and security later on. It had also brought him a cosmopolitan collection of colleagues, many of whom were to go on to become firm friends, often through the necessity of interdependence in combat. And friendships forged in the heat of battle were the very strongest kind of friendships.

One such comrade, an Englishman known to his military mates as 'Chokie' Henderson, was now a sergeant in the Metropolitan Police Force. Chokie had gotten his nickname because of his speciality, a choke hold that squeezed like an iron vice, cutting off the blood supply to the brain and rendering the enemy unconscious in a matter of seconds. The technique itself was no secret from the initiated, they all knew how to do it, but Chokie Henderson had a particular fondness for the move and was quicker and better than any of them at manoeuvring an opponent into the necessary position of submission and succumbment. Chokie had taken more than his fair share of point duty on oppos where they had had to move in quietly, and so his particular skill would be a boon.

But the violent life was something that Chokie had wanted to get away from eventually, and a few years back he'd taken a job in the Met as a Duty Sergeant. With his background, they'd have had him in an armed response unit like a shot, but quoting the old *Lethal Weapon* cliché, Chokie claimed that he was getting too old for this shit, and plumped for a cushy desk job that would at least keep him in one piece for the sake of his wife and kids. Children, damn it, children! Besides, he was good at the job and he knew he was making a difference, even though it might not be quite as hands-on as he'd been used to. As to his comrades-in-arms from his former life... well, old loyalties died hard. And when one of them – one who'd saved his life in a very literal sense on at least one occasion he could recall as if it were yesterday – got in touch and asked him for a small favour... well, he didn't have too much of a problem with that. It may be unorthodox by the strictest of regulations, but it was hardly a serious breach of police conduct, surely. Chokie was able to access the West Yorkshire Police's digital database for records pertaining to Barry Croft, and he came up with plenty of previous. Once he'd got a patch on the mugshots from Croft's last arrest (four years ago for handling stolen goods) he used a way he'd already figured out to forward them to Hamed while making sure his own email tracks were sufficiently covered.

Hamed had the colour printouts with him now, laid out on the space above the dashboard. Two shots, one full-face, the other in profile. Scruffy moptop-length hair sitting on top of a hard man's face, a council estate face, a square-jawed chiselled and battle-scarred face, sub-civilised, Vinnie Jones with an overbite that should have looked goofy, but combined with the rest of it came across as sinister, threatening, ghoulish. That was the general impression most of the world got from Big Baz – someone you crossed the street to avoid walking past in case he took a dislike to the way you looked at him, or didn't look at him.

To Hamed, even though they'd never met, he was a familiar sight, and altogether somewhat comical, if not pathetic. He'd seen this kind of joker before. In Belle Isle where he lived now there was one on every street corner, and the local pubs were full of them on an evening, emptying their pint pots then turning them over on the table top as a challenge to anyone in the place who thought they were hard enough to come and have a go. Boys. That's all they were. Boys with fists for toys. Yes, they might be hard, yes, they might be capable of dishing out the damage, but they were hardly a sophisticated enemy, and that went for their fighting skills above all. They liked to fight as a pig likes to eat. Opportunistically. For the rest of it they were untrained, undsciplined and uncommitted. Pit them against real warriors and they were as inept and disorganised as the apes they resembled.

Maybe this one was different because he was a branch higher up in the tree: violence was part of his business, part of his livelihood, not just a pastime on the football terraces or a form of drunken self-expression on a Friday night. But Hamed could tell – he was no professional. What Denny and Broken Leg had told him would have been enough to confirm that anyway, but Hamed didn't need their testimony to know that this man was no pro. Looking at the photos, he had the testimony of his own eyes and the capacity of his own judgment, born of experience. It wasn't a boot-camp face. It was just a boxing-club face. A young tough, overgrown and ripe for another bashing.

The first call on Hamed's mental itinerary of locations to check was Big Baz's house. To be honest, it was the last place he expected him to be at this time of the evening, given his habits according to what the lads had told him, but it was on his way to other more likely spots so he might as well eliminate it first. Sure enough, as he swung by the first time, he could see that the lights were off and Baz's BMW was nowhere in sight, but a few streets further on he circled round and passed by again, just to be doubly sure. He pulled up, cut the engine, wound down the window and listened. Maybe he thought he heard something coming from the house. Maybe a voice. He listened again. Nothing.

After that, he carried on further across town and repeated the procedure at each possible vicinity on his list: locating an address in his *A-Z* and making two passes each time, looking for the BMW and checking the windows of those he knew to be on the ground floor, based on the information he had pumped out of Denny and Broken Leg. There was always the chance, however slim, that he would catch sight of his target in the light of a room with its curtains open.

In the end, 'slim' proved to be the operative word. 'Non-existent' would have been better. After an hour of driving around warren-like streets of back-to-backs in several neighbourhoods, Hamed had covered all the home addresses with the exception of one or two further afield that he was saving as last resorts. Next it was time to check the pubs.

There were five probables on the list he'd been given. Denny and Broken Leg had given him a brief rundown on them and had said that the Squinting Duck was the only one that was full of hodgefists. When he didn't know what that meant, they paraphrased it for him: it was the kind of pub where he might not fit in with the locals and could very well bump up against trouble-causers. The others around there were all OK; student pubs; no problem. The only other dodgy one was the Bullwhip, a pub in town where Baz might go boozing if he didn't have any business on in Leeds 6. That one Hamed was saving for the last resort of all.

He started with the Rising Sun, parked the Land-Rover in the patrons' car park and walked inside, slipping the pictures of Big Baz in the backside pocket of his jeans. The place was midweek mid-evening middling full. He didn't want to stay any longer than he had to. Instead of heading straight for the bar to order a drink, he strolled round and in and out of the rooms first of all, as if he was looking for a friend. Even if he stood out as a stranger, which seemed unlikely in such a big pub on the main road, it could be that he'd arranged to meet someone here and was looking to see if they were in yet. Or he might be someone who'd dropped in on the off chance of running into mates who lived locally and drank here regularly. The main thing was that nobody around here knew him or anything about him, and that was the most important thing. They could think what they liked as long as they didn't interfere. When his search turned up nothing, he decided it wasn't worth hanging around. He walked straight back out, got in the vehicle and drove on to the Royal Park.

This was the one that Broken Leg seemed to go in a lot. He knew a lot about the place and had told Hamed everything he could about the layout, the clientèle and exactly where Baz was likely to be found drinking inside, if he was in there at all. A quick snoop aorund the car park didn't reveal the BMW, but that didn't necessarily mean anything. This time Hamed went to the bar first. He ordered an orange juice and took it on a tour of the premises. It was bigger than the last place and pretty full – a barn of a pub, kitted out with all the student attractions: video-jukebox, games machines, air-hockey. He gravitated with his drink towards the pool tables. They were all busy, but no sign of Baz. The same went for the rest of the inside of the pub. That left one more place that Broken Leg had talked about: the beer garden. The weather hadn't been brilliant today, so he wasn't expecting anyone to be out there, but he was mistaken. There must have been a dozen drinkers of the hardier variety sitting at the wooden benches out back. Hamed spotted Baz almost immediately he set foot out the door and into the daylight.

Down the far end of the garden – that was him all right. At a table with two other men. Well, boys. He'd thought of Baz's face in his police mugshots as a boy earlier, but these two really were boys. Small, skinny, unhealthy looking when put next to Baz's frame. He hadn't got his nickname of 'Big' for nothing. But Hamed was bigger. And now Hamed was here. He had located his target. All that seemed to be required now was a little waiting before he would achieve his objective. He took a big chest-swelling gulp of the night air, stepped down into the garden area and picked an empty bench to sit at. Even out here in the open, occupying the same space as his quarry, he felt at ease and in control. He could rest easy in the knowledge that no one – including the target – knew who he was or what he was there for. Furthermore, nobody cared. It was perfect.

After twenty minutes sitting in the cool air and making sure Baz remained in view in the diminishing light of dusk, Hamed had finished his drink and had reached a minor quandary – whether to go to the bar for another, as custom would expect, and risk losing sight of his target, or stay put but maybe draw attention to himself sitting there alone with an empty glass in front of him. However, the moment of decision was made redundant by the will of God as Baz stood up and started to fasten the zip of his fleece, looking like he was ready to make a move.

The beer garden was completely enclosed by a wall and a fence so there was only one way out which was to go back through the pub. Bearing this in mind, Hamed made a point of standing up and moving back inside just ahead of Baz. He returned his empty glass to the bar and waited there a moment until Baz had walked past him. Once it became evident that he was making for the exit, Hamed followed him at a close distance. When he got outside he lingered another few seconds to see which way Baz was heading. Wherever he was going it seemed he was on foot. Seemed he'd thought on and not brought the car to the pub tonight, though where he'd left it was anybody's guess. Hamed hadn't spotted it at any of the places he'd trawled round earlier. It could be that Baz had parked it not far away and was heading for it now. That meant that now was the time for Hamed to make some fast choices. He climbed in behind the wheel of the Land Rover and reversed it out of the pub car park, reviewing the options in his head. Did he move in now while the target was on foot, in the open and vulnerable, or did he hang back and just follow for a while until he'd fully assessed the situation? It was a bit too public for his liking around here right now with punters still coming and going to and from the pub. But if he waited too long Baz might pick up his car and then Hamed would have to commit himself to a more complex and improvised operational strategy. One thing was for sure, he couldn't go on kerb-crawling behind Baz for much longer without tipping him on to the fact that something wasn't right. Hamed was about to gear-shift and overtake Baz when his fortune changed and the target turned a corner off the main road into a side street. Hamed indicated and turned as well. As soon as he got a view down the length of the street – not too brightly lit yet, the street lights only now at the pink stage as they warmed up, no sign of any traffic or pedestrians – he knew that the time to move was now.

The offroad vehicle took the climb up on to the pavement in its stride. A bit bouncy, but Hamed had strapped himself in for it. Baz was slow to look round – at one point Hamed thought he wasn't going to – it must have been all the beer he'd drunk. No idea about drinking in moderation, these Brits. No religion, no values, that was their problem. Hamed just needed to nudge him a little. The bullbars would do the rest. Through a combination of good timing and the will of God, he had taken the left side of the vehicle up on to the pavement at just the right point in the road to leave a good stretch of empty kerb between lamp-posts and avoid a catastrophe. As Hamed tibbed Baz with the end of the front bumper, the bullbars grabbed his trousers and took his right leg under the wheel.

When Hamed pulled up and glanced in the wing mirror, he saw immediately that his man was down. He released the seatbelt, left the engine running and got out. He could hear Baz groaning. Then he could hear Baz ranting.

'Me fuckin leg! Yer stupid fucker! You've broke me fuckin' leg!'

Hamed put a foot down on the leg in question and Baz screamed blue murder. Until a hand round his windpipe cut it off.

'Listen to me – Big Baz.' He pronounced the name like it was a joke – like 'Little John' but in reverse. 'You want Denny – and this other boy, the one with the broken leg.' Hamed looked down at Baz's twisted limb without comment. 'Well this time, you'll live. Leave them alone. Or the next time you won't.'

Baz howled in pain after Hamed's hand released its grip on his Adam's apple. Then his shoulders collapsed to the cold pavement and he just lay there gasping air in for a moment until the agony of his broken leg bore in on him again and he screamed. Who the fuck was he? Who the fuck was he, the Paki cunt?

'You're fuckin' dead,' he promised at the cunt's departing back. Then as near the top of his lungs as the pain would allow, he screamed for all the encroaching night to witness.

'YOU'RE FUCKIN' DEAD!'

But the car had already gone.

21. Smack Down

IT DIDN'T take them long to hear about what happened to Big Baz. First of all from Bea – or at least that's who they got their first inkling from. They were still keeping their heads down at Jason's at the time, partly providing that alibi on tap that Hamed had instructed them to have ready, partly playing with a big stack of drugs bought in with some of the Post Office money. Jason had sorted out the car for them for not much more than a song, and furnished them with an as-of-yet safe haven while Big Baz was on the rampage, so it was the least they could do to get him off his trolley for a couple of days free of charge. During a conversation on the phone, Bea happened to mention that Baz hadn't been turning up for his commercial appointments with his regular customers, which had become a matter of some concern to all those affected. Bea was still lying low herself with the young 'uns round at her sister's, but smoke signals disseminated quickly throughout the ever-growing community of mobile users, and it seemed there was a hefty backlog of people baying for their usual supplies of whizz, ganja, scag, Es, you name it, and all the other goodies besides that they were used to from Big Baz. Kids screaming for their candies. It was like the year had turned round full circle but Christmas hadn't come. Kelly and Denny, paranoid on hash, were freaking out over it for a while: *Where is he then? How come no one's seen him? Oh fuck, he's dead, isn't he? That mad fucking Arab's killed him.* But it wasn't long before Bea was back in touch with the lowdown again: Baz was in hospital apparently with a broken leg. (The irony was lost on them in the heat of the news.) Hit and run. Police had interviewed him but he hadn't seen anything, hadn't been able to give a description, had no idea who could have done it. Of course, they'd grilled him about it – Baz was known to them, and they were heavily sniffing around the likelihood that this had been no accident – but without witnesses or Baz's co-operation, they had fuck all to go on. Kelly said nothing to Bea about his part in it, of course. He got his own grilling from her but wouldn't commit. Not safe on the phone. Best keep schtum. Never know if somebody's ear-wigging. They'd be speaking soon enough face to face.

144

Jason, who hardly knew Big Baz, was probably the happiest to hear this news: it meant he didn't have to go on listening to these two wittering on about some potentially dead dude and plucking at their guilty consciences over it any longer. Nonetheless, Kelly and Denny spent a further day whizzing and smoking and drinking and dithering, generally getting their heads together, wondering where it left them now. Why didn't Hamed get in touch to confirm it? Why hadn't he let them know what had happened? Why didn't he let them know where they stood? Why wouldn't he do this? Why hadn't he done that? Jason got knobbed off again with their flapping in the end, told them to give him a ring if they were that bothered about it and ask the guy himself. Seemed to him they were more frightened of this Hamed dude than they were of the Big Bazzer. In the end, he virtually had to goad them into making the damn call. Denny got elected to do the honours, but even then, it took him the best part of an hour to make up his mind whether to snort a double line of whizz before dialling the number or just a single. (He did the double, of course: even Kelly hadn't understood the dilemma in the first place.)

'Hamed. What's happening?'

'Nothing.'

'Yeah, but' – with pantomime emphasis – '*what's happening?*'

'Nothing. What do you mean, what's happening? Should something be happening?'

'I mean what's goin' on?'

'Nothing is going on.'

'I mean— You know what I mean. Is it done, is it finished?'

'Our business? Yes, it's finished. How do you say? Our account is settled. That man will trouble you no longer.'

'But how do we know that? I mean, what happened exactly?'

'What happened? You would like me to spell it out for you on the telephone right now? I do not think this is such a good idea, do you?'

'Well... no, I s'pose not. It's just that we were wonderin' what's goin' on exactly? I mean, what happened with you-know-who.' (*You know who*. Kelly and Jason both winced and giggled together and Denny gave them the stiff middle digit.) 'Did yer say anythin' to him? Yer know. Did he definitely get the message?'

'He got the message.'

145

'But how do we know that? I mean... can you guarantee it?'

'My friend...' Hamed paused for a long time, until Denny wondered if he was still on the line. Shit, he bet he was gathering up a head of steam for that an-officer's-word-is-his-bond speech again. Just as he was about to chirp up, Hamed's voice resumed. 'There are few guarantees in this life. Men like you and I, Denny – we can guarantee very little. At the end, we must leave these matters to the will of God. You understand?'

Fuck, thought Denny, this was worse than the military code of honour. 'Hamed—'

'But I *can* guarantee for you that he got the message. That I *can* guarantee, because I delivered the message in person. Whether that man chooses to listen to that message or whether he chooses to ignore that message... well *insh'allah*. This I cannot guarantee. All I can say is that if that man refuses to listen to that message, then that man, he is a very foolish man.' He paused. 'But any – what's the word? Any... repercussions, of that man not listening to that message – that would be a separate matter between you and I. You understand?'

'Er... yeah, I guess so.'

'Good. Now you say hello to Broken Leg for me. The other Broken Leg. Haha. Hahaha.'

'OK, Hamed. OK. And thanks, yeah?'

Hamed was still laughing down the line at his own joke as Denny hung up.

*

When Kelly saw Bea's face, the black eye and the bruising on the cheek underneath it, he experienced the most redundant swell of emotion he'd ever felt in his life. He wanted to run out and batter the bastard who'd done it to her, batter him senseless and make *fucking* sure he put the cunt in hospital. But it was too late. Somebody had already done it for him. If he'd seen what Baz had done to Bea before, it would have made him feel so much better in the long run – driven him so much harder and more assuredly toward the action that Denny and he had precipitated anyway, and pre-emptively assuaged any traces of guilt he'd been feeling about it during the last day or so since they'd first heard that Baz was in the Infirmary. Now he felt angry because Baz was probably out

146

already by now, hobbling around on crutches (*for real* – the irony finallly sank in, but with a bitter fizz). Licking his wounds, no doubt. Well the cunt better be learning his lesson, that was all.

But the anger wouldn't stop; as though it had taken on a life and a grievance of its own, it couldn't just let it lie like that. Although he knew that the right time for anger was past, it continued to well up in him like a lava flue with nowhere to explode – except through the spike of a needle and into his arm. Not speed this time – he decided it was time to graduate to smack. It was what Bea had been using to get her through this. When you boiled this angrily and you needed to bleed it out of your system there was little point in becoming a 'whizzin' cunt', as Nev had put it: you had to chill out, chill out deep deep down inside, scoop all the useless negative emotions out of your soul and fill the void back up with pure heavenly bliss.

By the time Kelly and Bea returned home from their separate holiday hideaways (*like Posh and Becks*) of Jason's and Cheryl's, the house had been closed up for nigh on a week. Bea's stash of saleables had diminished way below its normal levels, and so had Kelly's. Business was slow to pick up at first. But there were always ways and means if you were prepared to seek them out, and within a day or two, like the wise men in the Bible story, there were visitors bearing gifts, the only difference being these gifts came with a price tag and were ear-marked for a bit of creative recycling.

Know anybody who's after any Es, Kel?

Bea – I hear yer might be interested in gettin' hold a some regular fast while Baz is out a commission.

Listen, got a right smart CD Walkman, if yer know anybody who might be interested. 'S not nicked. Well it is but...

Kelly, I've got this fuckin' engine block, right? I swear to God, I don't know where else I can take it. If I could stash it in your lass's cellar just for a couple a days... You don't mind, do yer Bea? I'll bung you a tenner.

Kelly, man, have yer still got them crutches? Cos I were thinkin' of having 'em off you if they're still kickin' around. It's just that I've started seein' this lass, right, an' she's fuckin' seriously into this fuckin' film right, yer know that fuckin' David Cronenberg film, Crash? You an't seen it, man? Oh, see it, it's fuckin' wicked.

But sick, yer know what I mean? But I were seriously thinkin' of offerin' yer some cash for them crutches, man. Some kelly for Kelly's crutches. She'd think that were fuckin' wicked.

Mind if I shoot this up round here, Bea? Honest, it's like a fuckin' madhouse back at ours. I wouldn't ask normally, but yer know what it's like. Well, course you do. You're welcome to a dig yerself, if yer fancy it.

Smack was becoming a friend, a healer, a soothsayer. They had both been through bad times recently, Kelly and Bea - unsettling times. OK, there were worse times behind them and quite probably there would be worse times ahead, but after the violence of Bea's conflict with Baz's fists and the tension of Kelly's participation in not one but two armed robberies, smack and the cash to pay for it proved to be the perfect stress-busting partnership. It was the nearest thing they were going to get to a holiday right now, what with the kids and school and Bea's community service – not that they could remember the last time they'd been away together anyway, kids or no kids – so make hay while the sun shines and all that.

Kelly had had to come clean to Bea about the petrol station job, of course. She'd known about the pretend broken leg before, but Kelly had always forestalled her from asking why with the warning that she didn't want to know and that it would be better if she didn't anyway. Better for whom was a question that she had asked herself subsequently on several occasions, not least when Baz had been trying to punch Kelly's and Denny's whereabouts out of her. She'd been too distressed at the time to be shocked at the revelation that Kelly would have anything to do with guns. If anything, she'd been loath to believe it on the strength of Baz's revenge fantasy alone. Later, hiding out at her sister's and waiting to get word from Kelly himself, she'd pondered it more seriously. Theft yes. But guns? That wasn't Kelly. She wasn't sure if it was Denny or not – he could be a hothead for certain, and if he got his hands on one he might wave it around a bit and show off with it. But she hadn't believed that even Denny would ever be capable of using one on a real living person. Now that Kelly was back at home though and life was returning to a semblance of normality, he owed her a full explanation; and though she wouldn't have put it past Kelly to come up with some sweet-sounding bullshit to avoid compromising himself in her eyes, what he confessed did seem to square with everything that she already knew of what had happened thanks to the past couple of weeks: Baz's suspicion and rage, Poz's beating and humiliation, Stan's flight south and Kelly and Denny going to ground. There was just one thing Bea still didn't understand.

'So how come it's all right to come out of hidin' now all of a sudden?'

'Well... he's in hospital, isn't he?'

'Was. They don't keep you in that long with a broken leg. He'll be out an' about by now.'

'Yeah, but he's not gonna come after us with a broken leg, is he? What's he gonna do, hit us with his crutches? He'd fall over.'

'If Baz still wanted to make you an' Denny suffer, I'm sure there's plenty a people he could get to do it for him. So why hasn't he sent anyone?'

'You sound like you wish he had.'

'Nooo, I'm just sayin – he could've easily arranged it.'

'Bea, calm down.'

'What d'yer mean, calm down? I'm just curious, that's all.'

'Well....' Kelly continued to procrastinate uselessly, trying to stave off the inevitable, but Bea soon had him like a fish flapping on a line. Finally there was no wriggling out of it. 'OK, look. Me an' Denny got someone to put frighteners on him.'

'Yer did what?'

'We paid some'dy to have a go at him an' make him back off of us. Me an' Denny. We sent some'dy to scare him so that he'd leave us alone.'

'I can't believe I'm hearin' this. You *paid* somebody to scare Big Baz off?'

'Yeah.'

'Who?'

'Does it matter? Somebody bigger than him.'

'Hang on. Is that what Baz's broken leg's all about? Was it this hit-n-run driver? Is that who yer paid?'

'Bea – it dun't matter who it were or how they did it. What matters is that we got him off us backs. If we hadn'ta done, he'd still be after us now, wouldn't he? An' that means that me an' Denny'd still be in hidin' somewhere, lookin' over us shoulders. Is that what you'd want? Eh? Is that what you'd really want? Can't yer just be thankful that we're back to normal?'

'But we're not back to normal, are we? I've lost my regular supplier through all this bleedin' commotion. I know he wan't exactly what you'd call a friend as it turned out, but he were me regular supplier. An' he's gonna go on bein' a regular supplier, but not to me, not after this. Didn't yer for once ever stop to think about that?'

'Will yer talk sense, woman? How the fuck were we supposed to know that the kid behind the cash register were Baz's nephew? Anyway, *I* didn't wanna fuckin' hurt the kid. It's Denny yer should be havin' a go at, not me.'

'Oh, and one other thing. So you an' Denny paid some'dy to run Baz down an' break his leg, right?'

'We didn't—'

'So how much did yer pay 'em? An' where did yer get the money from? Yer mighta robbed a garage, but when you did a runner cos Baz were after yer, yer didn't have a penny to yer name.'

'That's not true—'

'You can't've had because what you did have – from that petrol station, presumably – you gave to me to look after.'

'Fuck, that four hundred quid – yer din't give it to Baz, did yer?'

'No, don't worry. I've still got it. I don't know why I hung on to it. I were gonna buy some speed off him with it like you suggested. I'm just glad I didn't give him it in advance.'

'Aw, that's brilliant.'

'I suppose you'll be wanting it back now.'

'No. You keep hold of it for us. In fact, don't even tell us where you've put it.'

'So where did it come from then?' Bea continued undistracted. 'This money that you used to pay for yer little contract. An' what about all this money that you've been splashin' about since you've resurfaced? Where's all that come from, eh?'

'When have you ever bothered about where money comes from? As long as it's there, what does it matter?'

'*Don't start tellin' me* not to ask awkward questions again Kelly, cos *I'm not 'avin' it, do you hear?*'

'Keep yer fuckin' voice down—'

'I won't. It's my house. An' I'm not havin' it. Not after last time.'

'All right, all right, we've heard yer. Now will yer fuckin' give it a rest?'

'Fuckin' guns an' shit,' Bea muttered. 'I'm not havin' it. I'm not havin' Denny round here either, so if he comes round, yer can tell him straight.'

'Just fuckin' leave it, will yer?' said Kelly disconsolately. 'Yer givin' me a fuckin' headache.' He flicked a finger at the barrel he was loading to get rid of the bubbles, then squirted out a little jet of the brownish liquid. 'You havin' some a this or what?'

Bea took the needle off him without a please or thank you.

22. Cast About

BLADES OF SUNLIGHT cut through the haze of thick green-smelling ganja smoke from way in the back somewhere of the otherwise low-lit afternoon bar in the Hayfield. It was a large room and the floor was wooden, and the tick of metal crutches was noticeable even above the slap of dominoes, and caught everybody's attention. When they saw it was a big evil-looking white sonofabitch with his leg all plastered up in a big white cast prodding them things at the floorboards, some of them paused in the middle of their game and slowly twisted in their chairs to watch his progress. When they saw him prop himself up at the bar right next to Delroy Parks, they knew it was gonna be either trouble for the white man or none of their business. And when, after a few seconds, the white man was still standing, they turned back to their game. That Delroy Parks had been a bad boy ever since he arrived over from Jamaica. That big ugly white sonofabitch looked like a bad boy too. It was none of their business.

'What you come here fer?' was how Delroy greeted Big Baz. 'Hope it not be no more trouble fer me.'

'That's very nice of ya,' said Baz. 'I'll have a tin a Red Stripe.'

After a moody pause, Delroy turned to the girl behind the bar. 'Debra, give 'im a Red Stripe.' The girl put the tin on the bar and Delroy grumpily pushed it towards Baz. 'After that, ya go. Don't do me reputation no good to be seen tarkin' wi' the likes a you.'

Baz cracked open the Red Stripe and guzzled from the tin.

'Yer find dem boys?' said Delroy.

Baz belched and sighed as the beer went down. 'Yeah.'

'Whatcha do to 'em?'

'Nothin'. Yet. I 'an't decided. But don't worry. I know where they are. They're not goin' anywhere.'

'So why ya come see me? You want Langston to do yer dirty work fer you again, is dat it?'

'No. It's nowt to do with them two. It's summat else altogether.'

'I told yer last time an' I'll tell you again – yer sort out yer own problems from now on.'

'But what if it's a problem for you an' all?'

152

'Only time it become a problem fer me, it seem, is when you bring it to me.'

'D'yer mean yer don't want me business?' said Baz. 'How much am I shiftin' each week for you, by the way?'

Delroy slapped the bar top hard; the sound banged off the walls. 'Don't get cheeky wit' me, man. I know where you stand with the Posse. Jus' state yer trouble and be on yer way.' He took a tetchy sip of his lager and scowled down at Baz's leg. 'What happen to you, anyway? What happen to your leg?'

'Fucker ran us down on purpose.'

'Which fucker yer tarkin' about?'

'I dunno, do I? That's why I've come to you. See if you might know him. Or help us find him.'

'Now why should I help you wit' that? It got nothin' to do with me or mine.'

'Well I think it does. This guy's dangerous. He were inteferin' in my business. In our business. He's obviously up for anythin' as long as somedy's payin' him. An' he's no fuckin' pushover. You wouldn't want to see anybody send him up against you.'

'Who gonna send him up against me, uh? Who is this guy? Ya think he got the *balls* to get mixed up in a Posse war? What is he, is he black or white?'

'I dunno.'

'Whatcha mean, ya don't know? Did ya see the man?'

'He looked like a Paki, but he didn't sound like one. He mighta been a camel jockey.'

'An Arabian? What make yer say that?'

'I dunno. Just what I thought afterwards. Yer know, thinkin' about it.'

'So ya think somebody send him to punish you. Fer what?'

'No, it wan't a punishment. It were a warnin'.'

'Who sent him?'

'Oh, don't worry. I know who sent him. But I'll deal with them in me own way.'

'Why yer tellin' me all this shit, man? Is it about me drugs? If this be anything like that last time... What was that kid's name?'

'Who? Oh, Moz.'

'Langston didn't like it, man. He's a sensitive soul. And he don't like killin' fer whitey. Haha.'

153

'All fuckin' right,' said Baz threateningly, instantly regretting it. Cool down. Just let the black bastard have his little laugh. 'Listen,' he continued in a conciliatory tone, 'it *was* about drugs – these bastards had 'em off me, but I've got 'em back now.' It was a lie, of course, but who cared, if it drew Delroy into the fray on his side? All he wanted was to get that Arab cunt off his back and out of the way permanently. Then he'd be free to square things with Denny and Kelly. That was the next step. The other two, Michael and Simon, could wait on the back burner. 'That's not the problem,' he went on. 'Thing is, now they've got this Arab nutter involved, he could be after gettin' hold a the drugs himself. I mean... he knows about 'em. He's already had a go. Guy like that, workin' as a pro, as a fuckin' rogue agent...'

Watchin' too much whitey shit on TV, Delroy thought.

'... they're out to plunder whatever bounty they can lay their hands on along the way, aren't they? Who knows what his connections are? Russian mafia? Arab mafia? Fuck knows.'

'Arab mafia! What ya tarkin' 'bout, man? Ain't no such thing as fuckin' Arab mafia. Hyeh hyeh.'

'I don't know that. Do you know that?'

'Too right, I fuckin' know that. Arab mafia...'

If he'da been white, thought Baz, he'da said 'Arab mafia, my arse'.

'So you're prepared to risk it all, are yer? Yer cars an' yer women an' yer big mansion back in Kingston. Cos I'm tellin' yer, this bloke's a player if ever I saw one.' Using the term 'player', kidnapping it from Delroy's lingo, was a gamble. He watched Delroy think, watched it sinking in. After a long shrewd silence, the so-called Man leaned back his head and spoke.

'All right. I'll help ya wit' yer little problem. But only cos it *might* involve me commodity. An' it better be the last time. What you want me to do?'

'Just find him. He needs takin' out. Like I said, he's a loose cannon. A wild card. If you find him first, just let me know where he is an' I'll do t'rest.'

Delroy looked at the big white man from stoned eyes pitted deep in their sockets. It was a gaze in which Baz could read nothing. Who cared what he was thinking, as long as he helped him sort out this fucking mess?

'You take care a your people,' he said at last, 'an' you let my people take care a this... Arabian man.'

'Nice one,' said Big Baz, raising his tin.

Delroy reached over and took a fistful of Baz's shirt front. The stoned eyes widened and focused like yellow headlights on a country road at night.

'But ya owe me.'

'No problem,' Baz said, looking down at the black fist. When it let him go, he leaned back on his crutches and backed away a step. Then he drained the tin of Red Stripe and put it down on the bar.

'We'll be tarkin',' said Delroy.

As Baz left, the clicking of the crutches drew all the black gazes again. He couldn't care less. He just stared them back with a look in his eyes that acknowledged them as the shit they were.

23. Combat Ready

HAMED WAS in training for real this time.

Of course, technically speaking, he was never out of training. He ran twice a day, swam about ten kilometers a week on average, and normally worked out at the gym three times a week for two hours each session. Sometimes a neighbour might see him down at the pool, and there were even one or two he'd overtaken jogging along his running route, but few knew enough about his physical fitness regimen to ask the questions 'Where does he find the time for all this exercise?' or 'How does he manage to fit it all in around his family life and his work?' The fact of the matter was that nobody on the estate knew what Hamed's work really was, or that he even had any. Let's face it, he wouldn't be the only man in Belle Isle to not have a job, though if he *was* unemployed, where did he get the money to be able to afford to drive round in a big fuck-off four wheel drive? That was another of the types of question that rarely got asked directly of anyone round here. If people had a bit of money, it was best not to be too nosy about it. At least to their faces. Where it came from was their business. It might make a good topic of speculation with your mates in the boozer but, at the end of the day, you respected people's privacy and you left them to it – unless it was a case of some lowlife shitting on their own doorstep and making themselves too much of an obvious nuisance to the community. That was something they weren't having any of round here. But Hamed wasn't that sort. Hamed was OK. Granted, he might be an Arab, which wasn't your run-of-the-mill resident in these parts, but pretty soon after he'd moved on to the estate, any potential unwelcome visitors learnt to leave him and his family alone. There'd been a couple of squaddies who hadn't liked finding him on their turf when they'd come home on leave; he remembered an ugly fight outside a pub one night with one who'd been in the Paras and had got wind of the fact that Hamed wasn't just an Arab, he was an Iraqi. By the time the Para's old school mates had finished asking how he could be both – was he from Iraq or Arabia? – he'd decided to have a go at Hamed single-handedly. But he was a boy, that was all. Only a few years of service behind him. It was unfortunate that Hamed had to dislocate both his arms to stop him from making a complete

156

fool of himself; on the other hand, he had the good grace not to involve the police, and he and his friends on the estate learnt the lesson of the incident to good advantage. Now they left him alone. Some of them had even become friends of a sort.

Right now, Hamed was doing more than his customary number of kilometers, laps and calisthenic repetitions because he'd had word from the agency that a job was coming up, if he was ready for it. They had put out no official details about it yet, but he had spoken with some of the lads and found out they were all invited to the party as well. Speculation, as ever among them, was rife, and the word going round was that it was probably going to be in Southeast Asia – the Philippines was being touted as the best bet, maybe another kidnapping – but no one had a slant on how long for. Could be a week, could be a month; unlikely to be any longer, God willing. A month in hell was long enough out of anyone's life. But if it was going to be as long as that, the remuneration would see him and his family all right for anything up to a year or two.

Beside nearly doubling his regular exercise schedule, Hamed was spending several hours a week following his own personal programme of fighting and weapons drills. It was rare that he got the chance for any one-on-one sparring; there should be anything from three days to a week of intensive brushing up of combat skills at the private boot camp down in Hertfordshire that the agency always sent them to before a mission. In the meantime, there was a local aikido instructor – black belt, third dan – whose services he was occasionally able to obtain for practising close manoeuvres, which they went through on the mats up in Hamed's attic den at home. Sometimes he allowed the boys to watch, but for him, it was just a matter of keeping his hand in and occasionally teaching the instructor a new trick into the bargain. Also, when the opportunity arose to use a location that was not too conspicuous – like the other evening on the rec at twilight with Denny and Broken Leg – he would work out with the blades, sticks and shurrukens. The only thing that was altogether impossible to stay up to scratch with was firearms, which he never kept at home because of the boys and because, for a man in his profession, the less he was known to the police, the better. That part of his retraining would take place at the boot camp. He anticipated that the last few days before they flew out would be spent practising intensively on the range under all-but-live-ammo battlefield conditions.

It had been easier setting up the target board, on the stretch of wasteland (for some, pastureland) that bordered the estate before edging on to the dual carriageway that skirted Belle Isle, with Denny and Broken Leg to help him, but Hamed was in peak physical condition, and manhandling it out of the 4X4 by himself didn't prove too hard. As he walked back to the car to take out the shurruken belt and a range of throwing-knives, he noticed a BMW signal and pull off the road to stop on the fringe of the rec. Three black men got out of the car while one stayed behind the wheel. The three out of the vehicle began walking towards him across the short grass. Hamed could see in the fading light of the day's end that two of them wore their skulls close-cropped, while the third had baby dreadlocks. He did not know any of them. But whoever they were, it would appear that their business was with him. They were definitely coming his way.

'Yo,' one of them called ahead at Hamed while he waited for them beside the open passenger-side door of the car. 'What's up?' They thought they were Americans. What were they? Not Africans. He knew Africans. 'Yo, man, this your car here?'

'What? You think I steal it from you?' said Hamed.

The trio laughed and grinned at each other as they planted themselves at a distance of about five meters away. While their attention was focused on his little humourism, Hamed reached into the car and slipped one of the metal death-stars up the sleeve next to his right wrist. Good. The move went well. The positioning just right. He allowed himself to be momentarily pleased with himself. Then casually, he lifted out the whole belt, carefully folded inward so as not to reveal its contents, balancing it on his two hands, handling it unselfconsciously, almost as if he might toss it across to them if they asked him what it was. Here, take a look for yourselves.

'Just answer the question, man. Is this your car?' He pointed vaguely in the direction of the bullbars.

'Of course it is my car.'

'Ya ain't from aroun' here, are ya? Where ya from? Ya from one a them there Arabic countries?'

'Where are you from my friend? You not from Africa.'

'Of *course* I'm from Africa, man. *All* black men from Africa.'

'But you were not born in Africa.'

'Mi born in Jamaica. Anyway what's it to you? I is the one that's askin' the questions.'

'Why you ask these questions?'

'Ya know a man name Baz? Him a big white motherfucker. Ya know him, right?'

'No. I know nobody by that name.'

'Yes ya do,' said the black man indignantly. 'We know ya know him. We bin askin' aroun'.'

'Y—'

Just as Hamed was about to say 'You got the wrong person' was when it all kicked off. The black man who'd been doing all the talking interrupted him with the sentence, 'Baz send you a message,' and reached into his inside coat pocket and started pulling something out into what remained of the meagre twilight. Hamed decided there was no real hurry. He may as well see what this man pulled out first just to make perfectly sure it was the gun that he expected it to be. Sure enough, he saw enough of the dully gleaming barrel to confirm it before the hand doing the pulling froze in a crooked claw-like posture in front of the black man's chest. Hamed even took a nano-moment to appreciate the expression on his face as he looked down in bewilderment at the sharp metal octangle embedded in the bunch of tendons connecting his thumb to his wrist.

As the gun dropped from the black man's disabled hand, so Hamed also dropped to the relatively soft springy earth, moving forward towards the second cropped-head, whose hand had reached into the interior of his own jacket in a shadow motion of his leader's. Forward-rolling and twisting into the disarming manoeuvre, Hamed came up just in front of him but facing away from him, gripped the gun hand and pulled it through the crook of his elbow from behind to snap the forearm over the back of his raised knee. At the moment that the man's hand relinquished its hold on the pistol, Hamed caught it in his own fist and aimed it squarely at the chest of the third member of the group.

'Don't,' he said – but to no avail. Baby Dreadlocks obviously hadn't been going to – had obviously intended to be nothing more than an onlooker in the killing of the Arab man – but seeing the demise of his brothers, he started going for his own piece as some kind of emergency response. Hamed had him covered and shouted his warning at him long before Baby Dreads had brought the weapon out into the open, but it failed to stop him in time. Hamed didn't have any time left to hesitate and squeezed the handgun's trigger. The man's upper body suddenly teetered forward, and his feet rocked back on to their heels. It was like a mime act as the bullet tore clean through his chest with such speed and ferocity that he was left a spasm-frozen sculpture in space. Winston Parks, Delroy Parks's nephew, his sweet sister Marie's little boy, died in that instant. Hamed just saw him drop out of his death pose to the ground in a heap from the corner of his eye as he pivoted and drove his free elbow up into the teeth of the man behind him, whose broken arm he still had pinioned. The man crumpled to the grass. In the meantime, he had re-aimed the handgun at the group leader, still clutching his useless hand pierced by the shurruken.

'Go now,' Hamed said. The black man's eyes – hooded with pain, but still questing for advantage – slid to his own gun on the ground, but Hamed told him, 'No.' The black man started to move away. Hamed became aware of the one behind him stirring too. He moved himself round so that he had both of them covered as they started limping back towards the edge of the dual carriageway and their friend waiting with the BMW. Funny. He hadn't even touched their legs. So what was this limping business all about?

But that wasn't important. There were other problems to be addressed – and quickly. If these men sent to kill him were connected with that job he had done for Denny and Broken Leg, then they might come again. It was unlikely that they would give up altogether this easily. It was more than likely that it wasn't just these four involved anyway. They would send more. And if they learned anything at all from this first encounter, then they would come better prepared next time. Not that it frightened him particularly. He had just proved one thing to himself, without it having been a stated intention, but now put beyond all doubt in his own mind at least: he was combat ready. No, he would be all right. But it was his family he was worried for.

And as he crouched over the stretched-out form of the man he had been forced to take out, he knew there was another reason he must move them to a new home, and move them now. Because for the first time in what passed for his normal everyday civilian life, they had just become the family of a murderer.

24. Touch Wood

'GOT ANY spare food for some change?'

The homeless guy in the woolly hat and fingerless mitts squatting in the shop doorway had repeated his spiritless chant so often to the stream of passersby that he'd failed to notice his own reversal of the key words 'food' and 'change', while his dog on a string was curled up next to him half asleep, seemingly without a care in the world. Not that it mattered much anyway, since no one really noticed: either they would drop money into his polystyrene cup or they wouldn't. Only Kelly noticed (or so he believed) as the fractured sentence floated across the pavement out of his smack euphoria like a mischievous ghost, making him smile in bemused terror at the otherworldly intimation of it all. At a conscious level, his brain responded with its most habitual response: *You're asking the wrong person mate.* A block further along, he turned to Bea, walking beside him, and said, 'Can we get the fuck out of here? It's doin' me head in.'

'We're not finished yet. We've just got to get our Casey's school blazer.'

'Where from?'

'Dunn's.'

'Then are we done?'

'Ha ha.'

'I'm not tryin' to be funny.'

'Yeah, after Dunn's, then we're done.'

'How we gettin' home?'

'I know what you're gonna say.' She engaged her Kelly-mimicking voice. 'Can we get a taxi?'

'Damn right,' said Kelly.

'We can get a stretch limo, as long as you're payin' for it.'

'Sound. Let's get it over with.'

Kelly hated shopping at the best of times – he didn't even like coming into the city centre for whatever reason, really – so why was he here? He could have got out of it if he'd wanted to, as he had done many times before. It wasn't like Bea would have minded normally, anyway. He knew that. She'd told him as much on many occasions, her general philosophy being, *I'd rather go on me own than have you dragging your heels round after me.* And

162

after all, it was her kids they were shopping for, so why weren't they here? It wasn't Christmas or birthday presents. No big surprise. It was all stuff they needed for school.

But that was all beside the point. He was here because he needed to be with Bea. It was a need he'd analysed again and again, cutting and re-cutting the scenario into a welter of interconnected images and emotions. Guilt was a part of it. At having got Bea involved. No, that wasn't it. She'd already been involved. The real guilt was for the violence that she'd had to take from Baz. For him. That was eating at him still. There were lesser guilts too. The guilt at having kept her in the dark about the petrol station robbery – not to mention the Post Office robbery, which she still didn't know about. The fact that she didn't want to know made him feel a little better, and he hadn't been tight-fisted with the money either. But the guilt was still there to be dealt with. He refused to feel guilty about Bea losing her business connection with Baz. The start of all this trouble with Baz had been a pure fluke. How could they have known it was Baz's nephew working there? Anyway, she'd found a new supply with no bother and, besides, they were best shut of Baz all round.

Except, were they shut of him? And that was another major part of the picture. Nobody knew what Baz might still do. They only had Hamed's word, after all, that he had sufficiently put the wind up Baz to stop him from coming after them again. But Baz was a nutter, and just that knowledge alone meant that Kelly was always looking over his own shoulder – and Bea's. That was its name, this need to be with her: protectiveness. He couldn't bear to let anything else happen to her. She didn't deserve it, she'd had enough knocks in life already, and at her age, he wasn't being funny, she didn't need any more. He was determined above everything else to see that she didn't get any. That was why he was here.

That. And smack.

It wasn't like they were doing it all the time. Obviously, they'd have a dig when they got up, or not as the case may be. Bea used to get up to get the kids ready for school, but they were old enough to do it for themselves now anyway, so she'd been catching up recently on some well deserved lie-ins. OK, she'd missed a couple of her community services, but it was nearly coming to an end anyway. No shit had gone down yet, touch wood. So they'd usually have the alarm set for just after the young 'uns had gone out, which was when they'd spike up a vein each before settling back into bed. So that first dig gave them a chance to chill out and get their heads together for the rest of the day, because let's face it, by the time it gets round to night time again, the last thing you can expect is to be able to chill out with a house full of drunken nutters all stoned out their heads or speeding and fighting over who controlled the loud music. It was a good job there was sound insulation in the floor beneath the kids' bedrooms. Since all that business with Baz and Denny and Hamed, Kelly and Bea had been doing more together, though. Not doing much at all really, apart from the other not doing much at all with a bunch of other people as well. But always, the two of them together. And he was getting to like it. Shit, what was happening to him in his old age?

And you know what else? Since he'd started doing smack, he hadn't thought about Teresa Corchran one damn time. Not one damn time.

He'd thought a lot about Clint though. And the way Clint died. He wasn't there when it happened, but he knew those who had been. They were all doing it. Heroin. A regular dose, but way purer than any of them knew. It was only Clint who OD'd. He went first. The one after him, the ambulance crew saved. The others left off it, realising by then that something was wrong with Clint. Stupid thing was, Clint hardly ever did heroin. It was maybe his second dig in three years. Thinking back across the years about Clint, Kelly raised his gaze in the back of the taxi to Bea's profile, looking ahead through the windscreen, and a feeling familiar from what seemed like long ago came over him of being in a comfortable place.

By the time they pulled up at the house, Damien was home from school and out in the street already, playing footie with his mates. The front door was standing wide open, and The Damned were blasting out from the record player in the kitchen at the back of the house.

'Who's inside?' Bea asked Damien.

'Two a your mates.'

'Who?'

'I dunno, do I? Two a Kelly's mates. Him wit' tattoos.'

164

'Yer mean Nev?' said Kelly.

'Yeah.'

'Well why don't yer say Nev? You know his name.'

'Yeah, well, you know who I mean.'

'Who else?'

'Somebody else wi' tattoos.'

Shit. Kelly had a bad feeling, even though it could have been almost any of the blokes they knew. And most of the women as well.

'Aw, let's go see,' said Bea, 'we're gettin' nowt out of him. Don't go far, cos I'll be makin' tea soon.'

'Yeah,' said Damien, 'as if.'

'Don't talk to yer mam like that.'

'Kelly – stay out of it.'

Nev was crouching at the kitchen gas fire pulling a hot knife for someone who had their back to them, but even with his sweatshirt hood up, Kelly recognised Denny straight away – and it didn't take Bea long either. The speakers were pumping out 'Smash It Up', not the most tactful song to be playing under the circumstances of coming home and finding uninvited guests in your kitchen. In Denny's case, with all the bridge-building he had to do with Bea, perhaps 'New Rose' would have been a more appropriate gesture, unless there was a Damned song he hadn't heard about olive branches.

'I thought I told you not to come round here,' said Bea to Denny, who was just rising from the knives and blowing out smoke. 'Will yer turn that off, please, Kelly?'

'Bea, listen.' Denny spoke into the void left by the killed music. 'I'm sorry for what happened, really.'

'That's not good enough—'

'I know, but listen, I had to come round. I've got a bit a news that might be important.'

'Why? What's happened?' Kelly said.

'Havin' an 'ottie, Kel? Bea?' said Nev.

'Nev,' said Bea, still looking at Denny, 'you know I don't do hot knives.'

'I'll have one,' said Kelly. 'So what's happened?'

Denny looked at Bea expectantly, and Bea exploded.

'I am not leavin' the fuckin' room, if that's what you're thinkin', so you can say yer piece an' then fuck – off.'

'Come on, Bea, don't be like that,' said Kelly, taking the bottle.

'I'm staying where I am.'

'I didn't mean that. Yer can at least be civil, even if you want him out.'

'I wanna hear what's so important that he couldn't tell you over the phone. Not that I even want him phonin' the place.'

'Denny,' Kelly said, bending to the knives, 'what's it all about?'

'Can I sit down?' Denny said to Bea. Bea pulled a chair out for him. 'Thanks, Bea.'

'Denny,' said Kelly, his voice audibly reverberating in the bottle neck as he spoke while blowing smoke out of the corner of his mouth and simultaneously sucking in more, employing the kind of circular breathing required of didgeridoo players. 'Spit it out.'

'Oh yeah. It were about Hamed.'

'What about him?'

'He's done a runner.'

'What d'yer mean, he's done a runner?' Kelly stood up, puffing out the last residues of smoke from his lungs.

'Well, not a runner exactly. I think he's gone off on a job. At least, that's what Taz thinks.'

Kelly took one of the other chairs round the kitchen table. 'So? We knew he were goin' some time, didn't we? He wasn't doin' all that trainin' for nowt, I hope.'

'Yeah, actually, it's not just Hamed. It's Maha as well.'

'Maha?' said Bea.

'Taz's sister,' said Kelly, knowing Bea would be none the wiser.

'Yeah, and the kids. Obviously. I mean, she's not gonna leave the kids behind, is she?'

'What you on about? Are you tellin' me that Hamed's gone off on some soldierin' job an' he's taken his family with him?'

'No. I don't think so. Aw, fuckinell, I don't know, do I? All I know is what Taz told me. Hamed's gone abroad on some business, but he's moved Taz's sister an' t'kids away somewhere. Apparently, said it weren't safe for 'em round here any more.'

'Well what's that got to do with you two?' said Bea.

'I'm just puttin' two an' two together,' said Denny, 'but it looks to me like I'm comin' up with four. I mean, think about it. Puttin'

166

t'frighteners on Baz were t'last job he did round here before they all went to ground. Don't yer think that tells us something?'

'Hang on,' said Kelly, 'we don't know that that were the last job he did.'

'Aw, come on. When has he had time to pull summat else like that? An' besides, we'd've heard about it.'

'Bollocks. How would we have heard about it? He coulda been up to flamin' Scotland an' back on a job in the meantime, for all we know. It's been what? Two weeks.'

'I just know it, Kel. It dun't feel right.'

'Even if you are right, what can you do about it? An' besides, have *you* seen owt a Baz recently?' As soon as he'd said it, Kelly experienced an emotion with all the clarity of a mental sign that read BEA'S SAFETY, and he felt himself reaching out to touch the wood of the underside of the table for luck.

'I know he's about. He were round at Football Terry's the other day.'

'An' did he say owt about us?'

'Terry didn't say owt if he did.'

'Well, there you are then. Look, I'm not sayin' that means everything's hunky dory, but yer can't walk around livin' in fear all day every day either, can yer?'

'Oh an' I suppose it dun't worry you at all, then.'

'Course it does. But short a movin', what can yer do about it? All we can do is wait an' see what happens. An' it's my guess it'll all blow over eventually. If we lie low an' avoid Baz, he's gonna lose interest. He'll forget about us. He's got bigger fish to fry.'

Denny stood up.

'I can't believe that *you* accused *me* of not knowin' what Baz were like. In fact, I can't even fuckin' believe I'm hearin' this. He's a fuckin' nutter. Yer *know* that. What yer fuckin' givin' it all of a sudden?' Denny was shouting. It was a good job they'd shut the front door.

'I'm just askin', what can we do? What do you suggest we do? Got any more Hameds up yer sleeve? No. Didn't think so. So we're just gonna have to wait an' see what happens, aren't we? Like I said in the first place. Now if you'll excuse me, I'm gonna go upstairs for a dig.'

With that, Kelly pushed back his chair, stood up and left the room.

'Maybe he's right,' said Bea, after a moment. 'Maybe you're over-reactin'.'

Denny looked Bea in the eye, and could faintly make out the tiny broken blood vessels that were the last vestiges of the bruising around it.

'You don't believe that. And I don't know why he does. Oh yeah, I do. Smack.' Denny looked down at Nev, still crouching beside the fire, with something like disgust. Fortunately, Nev didn't notice, but it wasn't wasted on Bea.

Bea looked Denny back in the eye and spoke in a high tone of conciliation. 'Oh, come on, Denny, that's rubbish. He's got that under control, anyway, we both have. How do yer think I'd be able to run a house with four kids if I didn't have?'

'Two of 'em are never here. Have you ever thought why? Anyway, I'm not talkin' about you, I'm talking about Kelly. He wants to watch himself, that's all.'

'What? By carryin' guns around down t'waistband of his trousers? Don't think I hadn't noticed, Denny, I'm not stupid.'

'Baz is a nutter. The piece makes me feel that little bit safer, that's all.'

'Aw, will yer listen to yerself? Yer can't even bring yerself to call it what it is. A gun.'

'I know what it is,' said Denny, 'an' I know where it's stayin'. With me. An' yer can tell Kelly, if he ever wants one, I can sort it out for him.'

'I think you'd better get out.'

'I'm only sayin'—'

'Out! Now! Nev, will yer give me hand gettin' him out of here?'

Before he knew it, Denny had been propelled out of the kitchen, down the hall and out into the front garden. He didn't exactly land on his ass, but there was a good deal of stumbling involved to prevent it from happening. As he turned back round to face the doorway, he was actually thanking his lucky stars that Nev hadn't thumped him into the bargain. Funny. All that time he'd wasted underestimating Big Baz, believing something about him, in him, some dark honour, beating beneath the exterior of aggression and, let's face it, sheer fucking madness – some ultimate sense of fair play. But no. And yet, in all these years, he would never have dreamed of underestimating Nev's capability for extreme and irrational blind fury at the drop of a hat. Now was not the time to take him on. Never was the time to take Nev on. Oh, he had the gun, yes. But he wasn't about to waste that on Nev. He was saving that for the day he ran into Baz.

'Just be careful, Bea. That's all I'm sayin'. Please be careful.'

Bea, putting an arm on Nev's shoulder and drawing him in, looked at Denny long and hard as she slowly shut the door.

Oddly enough, Bea had probably read it and thought nothing of it. Hadn't made a connection. And, under other circumstances that previously had constituted the normal, Kelly would have been unlikely to read it himself. But spending more time monging at home, drifting in and out of the warm cloud of the feel of the smack, meant he was more prone to picking up a newspaper if one was lying round just to give his eyes something new to look at besides daytime TV. And once the headline had swum into focus, Kelly realised this was something maybe even he ought to read.

BELLE ISLE BODY IDENTIFIED AS 'YARDIE'
By Neil Reucroft

West Yorkshire Police have released the identity of a man shot dead in Belle Isle, Leeds, as Jamaican Winston Parks, 22. The shooting is believed to have taken place some time last Monday night at the spot where the body was discovered by local children on a stretch of waste-ground next to the A61 Wakefield Road. A police spokesman said today that the incident may have been a gang shootout gone wrong. Although no other bullets have been found at the scene, police say there are traces of blood other than the victim's.

> Parks, of Harrogate Road, Chapeltown,
> was known to the police as a suspected
> member of a Yardie gang believed to be
> linked to drugs and prostitution in Leeds,
> London and Jamaica. West Yorkshire
> CID have been working with officers
> from the Met's Operation Trident...

That was as far as he read. It was enough to cast his mind adrift. The waste ground in Belle Isle. The place where Hamed practised with his Chinese death-stars. The Yardies. He'd fucking *told* Denny that Baz'd be able to rely on his Yardie chums, hadn't he? Well, that didn't matter now. Denny knew the score now. Pity it was too late to do anything about it. He just wanted to hide in bed and forget all about it. Let Denny run around with his gun and find himself coming face to face with the Yardies. That was Denny's business. Bea was right: they should have nothing more to do with him. It was fucking Denny who'd talked him into all this shit in the first place. All he wanted to do was just ignore it, forget about it, let it all float away. He let his mind wander down the blind alleys of useless thought before turning back on itself and flowing out into the enormous flooded plaza of warm oblivion where conscious thought was not banned but diluted, liquefied, and ultimately melted away.

A picture of the fight as it might have happened coalesced on the screen of his mind's eye, and a soundtrack in the speaker of his mind's ear. Hamed flicking the ornately shaped eight-pointed wheels of steel at the roughly assembled rampart of builder's planks. The satisfying sound of the objects impacting and burying themselves in the wood. Hamed watching the approach of four black men as their sinister hands fluttered into their jackets and came out tooled up. The first speeding star unzipping the air in its flight path, the roar and smoke of gunplay, the slow-mo tumble of figures to the ground, the first to fall in the heat of battle. Was Hamed one of them?

The images excited and stirred the rational conscious part of his brain, and it began to take over. It couldn't have been like that though, could it? Only one body with one bullet wound in it left behind. And it wasn't Hamed. But why no more bullets or cartridge shells? Maybe the other blood the police found was Hamed's. And if it was Hamed's blood, did that mean he was now languishing in a hospital somewhere? In which case, the *Yorkshire Post* report would have mentioned it, surely. And Denny seemed pretty categorical at least about what Taz had told him. It sounded like Hamed had specifically gone to the trouble of relocating his family personally – hardly likely, or even possible, if he'd been shot and hospitalised for the past week. Everything seemed to support Denny's theory after all. Baz must have got his Yardie contacts to turn the tables. Hamed must have known what was good for him and his family.

In a way, none of it surprised Kelly. Yes, deep down, of course, he'd known that Denny was probably right. But he'd told Denny that anyway. The other point still hung in the air: what realistically could they do about it but wait?

And hope that it was Baz who came after them and not the Yardies.

In the meantime, life had to go on. There was some money left from the Post Office job still, but it was hardly enough for them to run off to Acapulco. Money wasn't a problem for now, but it would run out soon. And there was still the four hundred quid that Bea had squirreled away for him – at least, in theory: he hoped she hadn't spent it on smack. But after that ran out, then what? Back to the old days, he supposed, getting by doing whatever you have to do to do it. But no more robberies and no more guns. Even if it meant giving up the smack. Well. He'd cross that bridge when they came to it. And they wouldn't come to it. Bea was doing OK. She was still dealing speed and hash. She could keep the smack coming, no problem. So where was the worry? In fact, it was time to stop worrying and start living a little. Get back to the old days. Go out and enjoy themselves instead of festering in this dump all day and all night. Not that it *was* a dump. Well, Bea kept downstairs clean for the kids, and they all chipped in and did their bit from time to time. But his and Bea's bedroom was a complete pit. A nest of objects and paraphernalia had built up on the floor around the mattress that served for a bed: brimming ashtrays, empty or dreg-laden lager tins, unwashed coffee cups, needles, tablespoons, candles, matches, lighters, papers (of both the Rizla and the news-bearing variety), an assortment of cassette tapes and their boxes (separated), partly consumed bars of chocolate and dirty plates and cutlery. Things they wanted close by, things they couldn't be bothered to clear away and deal with. The rest of the room was like a bomb site – discarded clothes, mainly. But the kids never came in here anyway except to pop their heads round the door ocasionally, and besides, their bedrooms were no better, except for the drugs paraphernalia, which he didn't think Bea would tolerate. As far as Kelly was concerned, they had managed to maintain a clear line of sight to the little portable colour telly on a chair under the window with its indoor aerial pointing sonewhere roughly in the direction of Emley Moor, and that was just about all they gave a fuck about right now.

'Who were that?' Kelly asked as Bea came back up and slumped on to the mattress next to him.

'You know that lad Darren? I think he's a student. Welsh Terry brought him round last time. I sorted him out with a couple a wraps an' an eighth a blow.'

'Nice one.' Kelly looked down at the headline in the paper still in his hand and decided he should go for it. 'Have yer seen this?' He pointed out the story.

'What about it?'

'I think it's connected to what Denny were on about the other day.'

Bea listened while he explained the signs that he'd read between the lines of the article. 'What d'yer think we should do about it?' she said.

'What can we do about it?'

'Well not what Denny suggested, that's for sure.'

'No, course not.'

'Maybe we *should* think about goin' away somewhere.'

'Whaddaya mean?'

'I don't know. Oh I'm bein' stupid, it's not possible. What about the kids? The house?'

'Come on, Bea, love. Don't get down. It might all just blow over. Yer still never know.'

'Yer don't really think that though, do yer?'

'I don't know what I think. I mean, it's like you've just said. We can't just take

172

off. Even if we could afford it. We can't just pull Casey an' Damien out a school, can we? It must be comin' up to t'crucial time for exams for Damien, innit? Fuckin' GCSEs or whatever. We can't just pick up sticks an' fuck off. Therefore, whatever happens is gonna happen. We've just got to stay an' face it. But if we lay low like we are doin', it might just stay quiet long enough for it to blow over.'

'Kelly, I wish I had your optimism, I really do. But I've seen what he's like, haven't I?'

Kelly swallowed and looked aside. 'Well what do you think we should do?'

'I don't know. Maybe you should talk it out with Denny.'

'What, after we slung him out last time with a fuckin' flea in his ear?'

'Well I'm just thinkin' that he's had longer to think about it, hasn't he? He mighta thought a summat that we haven't. I mean, it was him that came up with this Hamed bloke. He might have summat else up his sleeve.'

'Bea, I think yer givin' Denny more credit than where credit's due there. Hamed were his trump card. His *only* trump card. An' yer know what his plan is, anyway. An' *I* know *you* don't like it.'

Bea said nothing.

Kelly got sucked into the space where words should have been, but had nothing to say himself. His next line required a cue and it wasn't forthcoming.

Bea looked neutrally around the room and lit a cigarette.

Kelly wondered what Bea was thinking. His mind focused on the first deep drag she took on that cigarette, maybe her first of the day. The feel of the smoke shocking the inner senses, converting that wakeup chemical kick of the residue of all the nicotine hits you've ever had and setting you up for all those yet to come. He pondered the effect it was having on her consciousness. Not so much pondered as tried to feel his way into it. What was all this dumb-show about? Was he supposed to think that she was coming round to Denny's way of thinking? The way of the gun? Well, he wasn't buying it. It was too obvious. She was testing him. Either she was testing him or there was something that he was badly missing out on here. But then again, that wouldn't be a first.

'Kelly.' Eventually she spoke. 'Talk to Denny.'

'Are you sure you want me to do that? That's if he hasn't fucked off out a Leeds, if he's got any sense. He's got nothin' to tie him down.'

Bea chose to overlook the implicit insult.

'I think you should.'

Maybe safety in numbers was what Bea was thinking about. Still, there was something fighting against the tide. But whatever it was, it was pulling him along in its wake. 'OK,' he sighed. 'I'll talk to him.'

25. The Way Of The Gun

ONE GOOD THING about dub was that Baz wasn't into it. Now if it had been hardcore techno, it might've been a different matter. But Kelly knew for a fact that Baz and reggae didn't get along. Which meant it extremely unlikely that he'd be at Minstrel's dub disco in the basement of the Royal Park tonight. Which was why that was where they'd arranged to meet Denny. Both of them, him and Bea together. It had the added advantage that there'd be tons of people down there – dub nights always pulled in the punters. So – safety in numbers, safety in a crowd.

'All right, man,' Kelly said to Minstrel as they walked into the pub. Even at the bar upstairs, and over the sound of the jukebox, they could hear the bass from the sound system down in the basement pumping up through the solidly built pub floor.

Minstrel turned round at the bar and gave him a big grin. 'All right, Kelly. Haven't seen you down here for a while. You got rid a your pot leg, then.'

'Yeah, it's a long story. I'll have to tell you it some time.'

'Yer comin' downstairs?'

'Yeah, just sort some drinks out, we'll see yer down there.'

'All right, Bea?' Minstrel said as he passed with his pint towards the basement steps.

'Baz in't gonna be here is he?' said Bea to Kelly, but really to herself.

'I told yer, he doesn't like dub.'

'Yeah, but it's not dub up here, is it? He could come in this bit.'

'Well, let's get served an' then get downstairs.'

As they descended into the dimness of the basement room, the volume rose until the bass was shaking their innards. Slowly, they became aware of the press of people in this small space – no more than the size of two or three average living rooms put together. The coloured lights, barely set higher than the dancers' heads in the low cavern-like ceiling, winked at them through the twisting mass, casting evanescent halos around the mostly dreadlocked hair of the girls and boys. It was packed all right but, miraculously, Denny, who was already in there, had bagged a corner table that would just fit the three of them nicely.

Kelly nodded at Denny and they sat down. Denny said something, but Kelly couldn't hear for the music.

'What?' he shouted.

'I said, you're here then.'

'Yeah.'

Denny said something else but Kelly wasn't leaning in close enough. He mimed that he couldn't hear a fucking word. How the fuck hadn't it dawned on them before now that a dub disco was the last place they'd be able to hold a conversation? Bea sat by looking puzzled as they persevered for a while, but it was hopeless. Finally, Denny pointed his thumb at the ceiling, a signal to suggest they go upstairs. It meant they'd lose their table, but they needed to talk. Denny stood up with his pint and led the way.

Free seats were few and far between upstairs as well, so they gravitated towards the pool tables, the three of them standing in a huddle in a corner with a drinks ledge. Kelly swigged some of his lager then rested his glass up on the ledge.

'Any more news about Hamed?'

'No. But it's been in t'paper.'

'Yeah. We've seen it.'

'Oh. So yer believe me now, do yer?'

'I believed yer to start with. Point is, what we gonna do about it? What *is* there that we can do about it? That's what we came here to talk about.' Pause. 'Any suggestions?'

'Not now that Hamed's gone. I mean, basically, if he's not here we're gonna have to sort it ourselves.'

'Well, that's what I were gonna suggest an' all,' said Kelly.

'What?' said Bea.

'We're gonna have to talk to him. Explain what happened. Apologise.'

Denny laughed. He didn't make a drama or a mockery out of it. He just laughed. 'You are jokin', aren't yer?' But Kelly wasn't laughing, and Bea looked gobsmacked.

'No. I'm not jokin'. It's gone far enough. We've got to clear the air, an' I can't think how else we're gonna do it. I mean, how the fuck were we to know that it were Baz's nephew in that petrol station? Surely he can understand that. He's still a human being, isn't he?'

Bea and Denny looked united at last, in their scepticism.

'It's him you've got to convince,' said Denny, 'not me.' While Bea was thinking something similar.

'It's not like it were personal. So why did he have to go an' make it so fuckin' personal? Thing is, it's gone on long enough, an' I reckon he'll think that it has as well. If we just explain that the reason we were doin' the fuckin' robbery in the first place were to pay off us debts to him...'

'An' what about his broken leg? How yer gonna apologise for that?'

'Maybe there's some way we can make it up to him. I dunno. Offer to do some work for him or summat.'

'I think you've gone soft in the head, that's what I think,' said Denny. 'When I say sort it out with him, I mean sort it out. OK, go in there an' try an' reason with him, yeah, all right, but when that dun't work, then shoot the cunt.'

'No,' Bea cut in. 'An' will yer keep yer voice down?'

Groups of students shot pool around them, hopefully oblivious to the other world in their midst.

'I'm tellin' yer, Kel, I think you'll be wastin' yer time tryin' to reason with him. By all means, have a go, but we've got to go in there ready for a fight. An' do *you* wanna fight Baz without a gun? Because I don't.'

'Hold on,' said Kelly, putting his hand up to stop Bea from jumping back in. 'Slow down, slow down. Denny, yer talkin' about murder.'

'I'm no-o-ot,' he said, screwing his face up at the very idea. 'I'm talkin' about shootin' him. Not killin' him.'

'But wouldn't that be just prolonging the inevitable? And makin' it a fuck of a sight worse for when he does get us back. I mean, Denny, it doesn't make sense.'

'Well what are you sayin'? Kill him?'

'*No*. No. I'm sayin' what I've already said. Let's just try an' square things with him by whatever means it takes to do that.'

Denny paused to finish his pint. He put the empty glass down. 'This is a waste a time. There's no way any amount of apologisin' is gonna cut it with Baz. Tell you what. You try an' do it your way an' I'll do it mine. Good luck. I'm out of 'ere.'

'Denny, hang on—' But he was walking quickly towards the exit. Kelly started wolfing his drink.

177

'Just leave it, Kelly.'

'I think I should go after him.'

'He's not gonna go for it. Why bother?'

'Cos if we are gonna apologise to Baz, it'll be a lot better comin' from him as well. An' besides, I can't just let him go off plannin' to shoot some'dy.'

Teresa Corchran: suddenly, there she was, even for Big Baz. Or was it for Denny?

'He'll get himself either fuckin' arrested or fuckin' killed, I know he will.'

'Well hang on then, I'm comin' with yer.'

But by the time they'd finished their drinks and got themselves together, what they didn't know was that almost the second Denny walked out of the door of the pub, the world went all skew-whiff for him at the very same instant that a comet struck him just above the left eyebrow. The next thing he knew, he was on his back on the floor, watching the world through a red mist, as Baz leant over him, pot leg and all, he would swear to Christ till his dying day, and hoisted him back up to his feet by the scruff of his jacket. Well, not just the jacket, everything beneath it as well, really, with some ripping noises involved. Not that Denny was worried about that. They could call it quits now any time Baz liked.

'Hello, Denny,' Baz said. 'Just happened to pop me head in and Minstrel mentioned you were in tonight. Dopey cunt dun't know when to keep his mouth shut.'

The first punch, right on the bottom edge of his rib cage, told Denny the calling-it-quits part just wasn't going to happen. He felt sick, but he hadn't drunk enough to be sick. What was going on? Oh yeah. Pain. He'd forgotten what it was like, the way you always did between bouts of it. He vaguely hoped that Baz's knuckles were feeling it too but, less vaguely, he doubted it somehow. When the same fist went in for a second jab, that doubt was resolved unhappily.

Denny gazed unsteadily at the face above him.

'Baz.'

Then Baz's mouth opened wide and the Blackpool donkey teeth were coming down on his face like in some childhood nightmare not yet had.

'Yeah, I know,' Kelly was saying as they were walking out the door, 'but he mighta gone headin' round to Jason's gaff.' He glanced up to take the step and then looked around, and his next thought was, *What the fuck?*

'Baz! Stop it!'

It was Bea who responded first, Bea who leapt straight on to Baz's back, trying to stop the pummelling that he was giving Denny against the wall of the pub, and pulling his gorilla-like jaw away from biting Denny's face. Kelly even paused to look around. Who else was here? No one. Fucking typical. He looked back in time to see Baz shake Bea off like a bulldog shaking off a squirrel. Funny, that. When had he last seen a squirrel? What he wasn't sure about afterwards, though, was whether he saw exactly how Bea grabbed Denny before she hit the ground. Certainly they both tumbled to the ground together, and Kelly may have heard the clatter of metal on stone as Baz turned his attentions in his direction, first with a blow from the companion crutch to the one he'd first battered Denny across the skull with. It caught Kelly on the jaw, and it wasn't pleasant *at* all. For a second, the world went black – not just black, the world went *away* – and he had a job on keeping himself upright, even though all his instincts were screaming at him that *this was something important.* Then he was wondering why it *was* so important, since Baz was pounding him anyway.

It was like a production line. First Denny, and now Kelly, was up against exactly the same bit of wall, taking the same kind of punishment. Oh, he might raise his arms and try and crouch away from it, but being in the arms of Baz, when he was about this kind of work, was like being in the arms of a particularly cruel and sadistic lover who had you bound to the bed-post. The only difference was that the consent was all one way. Somewhere deep inside the pain, behind the test-drive range of sickening blows that made a brief strobe in his head, Kelly thought he heard something, and he thought it sounded like Bea saying:

'BAZ! STOP IT! NOW! OR YER FUCKIN' DEAD!'

Baz must have taken time out to look round at that point, because the lightning bolts stopped slamming through Kelly's face and body. It took a second or two for the cessation to sink in. Then slowly, gratefully, eighty-quid leather jacket being ripped to fuck on his back, but what the fuck, at least his back was against the wall, he sank to the ground of the car park. And opened his eyes and looked up.

Denny was in a bad state. Lying on the ground, his nose streaming blood. Didn't look unconscious, though. That's good, he thought. Hopefully not an ambulance job. Not like poor Clint. For whom it was too late anyway. Too late. Always too late. Then he looked at Bea. Who was holding Denny's gun. Not just holding it. Pointing it at Baz. Who, with the aid of the one crutch he still had hold of, was gradually edging his way forward towards her.

'I'm warnin' yer, Baz. I'll fuckin' pull this fuckin' trigger, I swear to fuckin' Christ I will.'

She should have been screaming it. She should have been screaming it at the top of her lungs. That was what Kelly would have been doing if he'd had any wind left. Attract some attention. Get Trevor, the landlord, out here; he's always sitting on the door. But no – Bea was cool about it. Bea was trying to act firm. But how far was she prepared to take it? Even in his beat-up haze, Kelly really believed afterwards that, for a second or two, focusing on the end of the gun barrel trembling only ever so slightly in her two-handed grip and the concentration in the way she met Baz's manic drug-and-power-muddled gaze, he saw for a swift second exactly how far she was prepared to take it.

'Yo, white boy.'

Baz turned round, half away from Bea, seemingly to a voice he recognised, and the new voice – somewhere distant from outside the pub car park, but booming like the bass from the dub inside, carrying even in the open night air – continued. To be honest, Kelly couldn't tell exactly what it said, but him and Bea pieced it together afterwards to their mutual satisfaction.

Baz, on the other hand, recognised Delroy's voice straight away as that of the guy leaning out of the van window, pulling up next to the car park frontage of the pub. So what was the balaclava mask for? Then he noticed the eyes behind the mask of the guy in the driving seat. He'd seen those eyes before. The whites of them in the woods after they'd done Moz together. The wilfully blind stare – or had there really been a nod? – above the clicking finger bones in Delroy's smoke-strangled office. Fucking Langston. What was he doing here? What were they doing here?

180

'Ya got mi nephew killed,' said Delroy. 'Yer gonna pay fer that.'
They were the last things that Baz noticed. He never saw
Delroy's hand rising, or what was in it.

Kelly didn't think he'd heard it, just seen it. And even seeing it,
at first he honestly thought, *Fuck, a bird's shat on him – at a time
like this, a fuckin' bird's shat on him.* He expected to hear a splat.
Because that's what it looked like, a little splat of bird shit landing
on the middle of Baz's chest. But it was a bit dark for bird shit,
wasn't it? And by the time the van had driven off and Baz had
slumped to the ground like a sack of shit with a pot leg stitched on
to it, only then did Kelly's conscious mind register the loud crack
that had preceded it all and made him temporarily deaf for the
third time in about as many weeks.

Bea was still pointing Denny's gun at the spot where Baz had
been standing. She looked as though she'd seen a ghost. Maybe
she was doing. Somewhere not too far off, a pack of dogs was
barking. Or was it the Rottweilers up on the roof?

'Bea. Give me the gun.' It was Denny. He'd managed to raise
himself up off the ground and was holding out his hand, wiping the
blood off his face with the other.

Bea still stood frozen in shock as Denny gently took the pistol
out of her outstretched wedge-shaped fists.

Fuck! Kelly was thinking. *Oh no, Bea. No.*

'It's all right, Bea. It's all right. It weren't you, it's all right.'
Denny was holding it together. He put an arm in the crook of
Kelly's armpit and helped him to his feet. 'Come on, we've gotta
get out of here. Fast.'

Kelly was groggy, didn't know what was happening, God, he
could do with a fix right now. He *hated* being on his feet.

'It's all right,' Denny was repeating to Bea, 'it weren't you. It
were some'dy else, it weren't you.' He was dusting off the back of
Kelly's jacket with one palm, like an attentive butler. 'I'll wipe
Bea's prints off, right? Just get out of here. Now.'

Kelly tried to take a good look at Denny, holding his friend
unsteadily at arm's length.

'We need to get you to a hospital,' he said.

Denny pulled Kelly towards him and hugged him tight.

'I'm OK, man. I swear. I'm OK now.'

Kelly didn't know what was happening. All he could hear was Bea saying from somewhere behind him, 'Come on, Kelly love, come on.' Urging him on somewhere.

For a while it was like he was hanging in space. Not drifting – hanging, like a fake astronaut in a cheap movie, dangling in front of a backdrop on a wire. But he could feel his feet moving and he could sense himself running enough to make him want to try to propel his body forward even more, even though he could barely see anything. But he had hold of Bea's hand, and they were running away. Him and Bea, her hand clasped tightly round his. They were running away through the streets, towards home. For once, at last, just the two of them were running away together into the comfort of the night.

26. The Final Testament

IT WAS the final testament to Baz's brutality. The last marker that his violent soul – or the physically and psychotically embodied absence of one, if you believed in such things – had once walked the earth. Even after he'd gone, despatched by the Yardies to a place beyond any further acts of retribution, the evidence of his true nature lived on. Well, not lived exactly.

It transpired that the neighbours on either side of Baz's house had heard a continual succession of unusual noises for a week or so. Actually, they said unusual, but not much usual ever happened at Baz's house. Both sets of neighbours – an elderly married couple on one side, children long since grown up and flown the coop, and on the other side, a single mum of two in her late thirties on welfare, studying part-time and playing mother to her itinerant boyfriend when she wasn't busy bringing up her own daughters – had lived next door to Baz for many years and had learnt not to interfere in his business. They knew what he was like – someone you didn't mess with. All right to say hello to from time to time, but by, there were always some right goings on at his house. You wouldn't believe some of the stuff they'd heard coming through the walls. Blazing rows. Hollering death threats. Furniture being thrown around. Occasionally, a woman's screams. Course, most of the time he wasn't in, and they were thankful for that. But everybody round here knew not to mess with Baz or go near his property. Besides, what could you do? You didn't want to go grassing anybody up to the police. Not round here. It was a rough area around Burley Lodge Road. Always had been. 'The most burgled streets in Europe', that's what all the leaflets from security firms said. They made a good living round here, fitting security gates and window grilles. Most houses round here had them. The few that didn't probably contained nothing worth nicking. It was mostly kids. They were always hanging round on the streets, causing trouble, abandoning cars, breaking the pavement slabs out of boredom, running down alleys with their hoods up and their arms laden with stolen hi-fi or computer equipment. Rioting, for God's sake. They burnt down the Newlands. And there were always a few dodgy adults behind it all, supplying them with drugs, fencing the goods they nicked. That was Baz. So, no –

hearing the odd faint voice, possibly shouting, possibly emanating from somewhere in the bowels of Baz's house, (possibly the same one Hamed thought he'd heard but dismissed as an illusion the night he'd driven by looking for Baz) was not unusual. After about a week, it stopped. In fact, neither neighbour had really even thought about it having stopped, until now.

When the police went round to Baz's house after he'd been found shot dead outside the Royal Park, what they found was not what they were looking for. It was the flies that gave it away. Not many, six or seven, hovering around the the thick oak door down to the cellar, the one that someone had gone to the trouble of not just triple-locking but also barricading up with a Welsh dresser. The key was on a hook in the kitchen, but even as they began to slide back the heavy bolts, they could hear the buzzing frenzy of the much greater numbers of flies inside that these misplaced comrades outside were desperate to join, and they knew it was time to call in a specialist team.

The eventual conclusions from the inspection of the crime scene, plus subsequent investigations, suggested that the young men, Michael Chapman and Simon Hollister, two second-year students at the Metropolitan University, had been down there for about three weeks, and had probably died after two. The police would never be certain of how Barry Croft had got them there, but the forensic evidence was consistent with the theory that he'd worked alone. From samples of the victims' blood and signs of a struggle found during a search of their flat at Kensington Terrace, it appeared Croft may have used violence to subdue them there before driving them back to his house and locking them in the cellar. Evidence from his car also attested to that scenario.

Through dozens of hours of interviews with other students who'd known the victims, they traced the motive back to drugs the victims may have stolen or swindled from Croft. Through interviews with various snouts and subsequent leads who knew Croft, they were working up a case that could tie Croft to another death, one Maurice Szczotarska, seventeen years old; his father was Edward Szczotarska, currently in Armley doing a two-year stretch for credit card theft and fraud. The boy, judging from the results of the postmortem examination just recently in, could have been deliberately thrown or pushed under the bus that killed him:

there were signs of bruising and injuries to the wrists, legs, groin, face and ribs, sustained immediately prior to the physical trauma caused by the wheels, the undercarriage and the road surface. If Croft had been physically strong enough to manhandle two young men from their house to his on his own, he would certainly have had the strength to handle a young, frightened teenage boy alone. But the possibility of someone helping him couldn't be ruled out at this early stage. Something else would come out in the wash of all this. Arrests would be made down the line, the police were certain of that. Just too bad Croft had escaped punishment.

What they couldn't establish in the final analysis was whether he'd intended the boys in the cellar to die. When they put the pieces together, they believed that Croft might have inadvertently abandoned them to a slow death down there when he was put in hospital with a broken leg by an unidentified hit-and-run driver. The time scale fit. At the scene, there were signs that until then, he'd gone to some trouble to accommodate them, at least keep them alive. For the first few days they would both have been sore from the beatings they'd taken, but the reports indicateded no life-threatening injuries. Nothing was broken, except for Simon's nose. Baz left them some food and water. They had access to the light switch. There was even a working toilet down there in a tiny room off to the side, not an uncommon feature in a house like that. Croft probably returned and unlocked the cellar door and threw stuff down to them from time to time – bottles of water, tins of beans, a tin opener, bars of chocolate, cigarettes. There was evidence of all that. There were even roaches, and empty bags on the floor containing residues of skunk. Croft may have deliberately not come back after the hospital, he may have intended to kill them all along, but he'd had the good grace to leave them their ganja.

But the ganja ran out. And it was cold and damp and stark down there, just the stone floor and the white plaster walls for comfort. Walls so thick that neither one of them had been able to squeeze far enough into the narrow space to the coal chute door to reach it. Not that it mattered. The metal plate had been welded shut years ago, against burglars.

Nobody in their right mind would want to try to imagine the panic, misery, frustration, exhaustion, recrimination, hunger, fear, desperation and despair they went through down there. But the funny thing was, when the first officers on the scene searched their pockets, they were found between them to be in possession of five grammes of heroin. In the long run, it became one more thing that didn't make sense. They were found to be heroin users, so why didn't they use it? They were only ever snorters anyway, it wasn't like they needed a needle. So why didn't they snort it? Maybe, when they were facing death, they didn't want to die that way. Maybe they wanted a normal death, like the normal life they would've had if they hadn't been quite so stupid. As the first officer who searched the bodies remarked to his colleague, it looked like they'd learnt their lesson, but too late to save themselves.

The End

Lightning Source UK Ltd.
Milton Keynes UK
UKOW042155260613

212875UK00002B/404/P